The Last Homily

Michael Carlon

ISBN:0-9979839-3-0
ISBN-13:978-0-9979839-3-7

Also by Michael Carlon

All the F*cks I Cannot Give

Winning Streak

Uncorking a Murder

Return to Casa Grande

Praise for
Uncorking a Murder

"It is a real page turner murder mystery with so many interesting plot twists. The best part of the book is how the mystery gets solved - it brings a whole new level of excitement to the storyline. Michael is a fun and creative writer." - Tracy, 5 Star Review on Amazon.com

"Whoever likes Patterson, Harlan Coben or Patricia Cornwell, you need to check out Michael Carlon's book Uncorking a Murder! Just finished reading it and I love it. Can't wait for more! Michael Carlon, you better hurry up with your next book!" - Monkia, 5 Star review on Amazon.com

"Uncorking a Murder had interesting characters, plot twists and of course a good old mystery to keep you guessing. Kept my interest and found it hard to put down. Can't wait to read the next book in the series and see how the characters develop." - Susan, 5 Star review on Amazon.com

"Wow, I had fun reading this book and can't wait for the next one! I looked forward to turning the page as I enjoyed picking up on all of the clues and finding the humorous references." - Laurie, 5 Star review on Amazon.com

For my siblings Greg, Mia, and Jim, — funny how your
names always wind up in my books.

CHAPTER ONE

The Death of Fr. Gregory Hart

Father Gregory Hart looked at the congregation assembled in front of him and mentally separated his flock into three different categories: those who liked him, those who hated him, and those who were still making up their minds. He was a reformer in every sense of the word, and the homily he was about to preach would certainly underscore that.

Six months ago Fr. Hart was assigned to Our Lady of Healing Church in the resort community of Chatham, Massachusetts, by the bishop of the Diocese of Fall River, Robert Hurley. Though in Fr. Hart's mind, he was more banished than assigned — even if he clearly understood why the bishop sent him to the Cape.

Chatham is located on the elbow of Cape Cod; it wasn't exactly where an idealistic priest wanted to go in order to set the world on fire with his preaching. While between Memorial Day and Labor Day the town was flooded with families looking to take a break from the stresses of daily life, during the other nine months of the year, the town was, for lack of a better term, dead — not the place for a priest looking to change the face of Catholicism in the United States.

Fr. Hart had been a thorn in the side of Church hierarchy ever since the sexual abuse scandal broke fifteen years ago. He publicly advocated for the excommunication of any priest who was convicted of abusing a child, but his vitriol didn't end there. He was also outspoken in his steadfast belief that higher ups in the Church should have their feet held to the fire for their role in covering up abuse — a fight he took to both press and pulpit.

These days, with the sexual abuse scandal farther in the rearview mirror, the impresario priest had taken to speaking out on his beliefs that homosexual couples should be welcomed into full union with the Church, clergy should be able to marry, and women should be allowed ordination into the priesthood.

Bishop Hurley was pressured by his peers and superiors to do something about the controversial priest in his diocese, and therefore had him assigned to a series of positions at parishes in Fall River that most clergy would deem undesirable, either due to their size or aging population, but this did nothing to put out the fire that was ablaze inside his problem priest. When the need for a new pastor for a small church in the town of Chatham came up, Fr. Hart's name was on top of Bishop Hurley's list. The bishop knew he couldn't completely silence his problem child, but placing him in a small church on the outskirts of Massachusetts would surely help to police his reach.

However, the plan wasn't working. While the fiery Fr.

Hart was speaking to a much smaller population in the small town of Chatham, he had taken to recording his homilies and distributing them as free podcasts that could be downloaded from the Internet. He had tens of thousands of followers on social media and was a frequent contributor to blogs that welcomed a voice of reform in the Church.

Fr. Hart left the ambo where he had just finished reading the Gospel and walked to the center aisle of the church where he preferred to preach his homilies. Before starting to speak, he reached under his clerical robes to turn on both his wireless microphone and the digital audio recorder he used to capture each of his homilies. He looked up and smiled at the congregation assembled that Sunday morning. He was about to preach a homily reflecting on the story of the Prodigal Son — a parable Jesus used to teach his followers about the nature of forgiveness.

"Who here identifies with the prodigal son we heard about in today's Gospel reading?" Fr. Hart's confident voice boomed throughout the small church. He typically started his homilies off with a question as a way of making them more interactive. He saw a few people smiling and nodding their heads and then continued, "Some of you may have a hard time believing this, but when I was younger, I was a bit of a rebel. I lived lavishly and spent money as soon as quickly as I earned it."

Before becoming a priest, Greg Hart had worked in the financial services industry and lived the unrestrained lifestyle of a young investment banker in Boston. He was a handsome man, and the women of the parish remarked how he resembled to Jared Leto. One in particular gave him the nickname "Father What-a-Waste," referring to the Church's requirement that its priests be celibate.

"So in my younger years, I absolutely identified with the prodigal son. But depending on what I have going on in my life when I reflect on this passage, I find that I relate to other characters more so than I do with the son. Who are some of the other characters in the story?"

"The father," shouted out a parishioner.

"Excellent!" Fr. Hart exclaimed. "There would be no story without him, would there? He's the one with the money the prodigal son asks for. Imagine the pain and disappointment he must have felt when his son left home with his early inheritance; in some ways the prodigal son asking for his inheritance early could have been a way of wishing a premature death upon his father. Ouch!"

This led to a few laughs from the assembled congregation.

"Imagine the sadness the father must have felt when he learned his son was poor and destitute. And this, of course, is counterbalanced by the joy he felt upon his son's return home. He's a very important character, but he's not the one I relate to more today. Name another character," Fr. Hart challenged his congregation.

"The pigs," a young boy shouted out. This caused others in the congregation to laugh, including Fr. Hart.

"I've been a priest for over fifteen years, and this is the first time I have heard someone mention the pigs in the story. But you do have a point; we have to remember that the Jewish crowds Jesus was preaching to at the time would find it abhorrent that the prodigal son would have been working with animals that our Jewish brothers and sisters then, as now, considered unclean. The presence of pigs is important to the parable because the thought of working with swine conveyed how down and out the prodigal son really was. But it's not the pigs who I relate to today." Fr. Hart walked toward the kid who answered his question and gave him a high five. "Okay, one last chance — name another character in the story."

"The brother," answered Emily Rose, a fifty-two-year-old single woman who was sitting in the front row of the church because she was serving the Mass as a Eucharistic Minister that day. She was dressed conservatively in a blue skirt and matching jacket and wore a veil over her head to signify her humility, submissiveness, and obedience to the Church. It was a practice that went out with the reforms of the second Vatican Council in the late 1960s, but one she did not shed.

"Yes, the brother!" exclaimed Fr. Hart. "The man who does not feel the excitement of his father upon his own brother's return but rather is filled with anger and jealousy. Today, I relate more toward the brother than the other characters. Here's a guy who has done everything right his entire life, yet his brother not only gets an early inheritance, but then he gets a party thrown for him after he comes back having spent it on women and wine. Who wouldn't be upset by that?"

Fr. Hart was conscious that this particular homily did not yet include one of his trademark jabs at the Catholic establishment, and he didn't want to disappoint any of the fans who would be downloading his homily later on. "As much as we want to place ourselves in the shoes of the welcoming father, the fact of the matter is most of us will have a very hard time doing so – just look within your own families for proof. Certainly some of you have been wronged by your parents. Have you forgiven them for any harm they may have caused you? Or maybe you have a brother or sister who hurt you at some point — have you offered them forgiveness even if it has not been asked for? Maybe you have a son or daughter that hurt you in ways that only your children can. Was forgiveness granted to them?"

Fr. Hart let these words sink in and then drove the point home. "And more often than not, the Church assumes the role of the forgiving father in the story when, in reality, it behaves more like the jealous brother. There are people that our Church has historically turned away and continues to turn away — homosexuals and the divorced, just to name a few. Oftentimes, the Church feels as if these marginalized groups are the prodigal son who should be seeking forgiveness, but the fact of the matter is that we as a Church have to humble ourselves and ask for compassion from those whom we have historically oppressed."

Father Hart paused to look over the faces of his congregation and saw some who were smiling, some who were clearly irritated, and some who wore no expression whatsoever. To signify that he had finished preaching, he said, "Let us now stand to profess our faith," and the congregation rose and recited the Profession of Faith.

Farrah Graham, the creator and host of the Uncorking a Murder podcast, was in the congregation that morning. Many vacationers in the town of Chatham mistook her for Gwyneth Paltrow, and she had been hit on by just about every single guy in town. These gentlemen, however, were shocked to find that Farrah was in a committed relationship with another woman, Melody Note, who was sitting beside her in the pew that morning.

The two were vacationing in Chatham after having spent a year researching, recording, and producing Uncorking a Murder's second season, which focused on a case in South Florida involving Sonny Michaels, a man who was wrongly convicted for the death of his wife. Farrah's investigation into that case led to Sonny's release from a Florida prison, and she had just spent the past six weeks on a national media tour to promote the podcast. In short, she was burned out and had promised Melody she would take the summer off and spend it at their beach house on Cape Cod.

Melody was skeptical that Farrah would follow through with this plan; Farrah was a workaholic who once worked eighty-hour weeks at a prestigious law firm in Manhattan. When Melody gave her an ultimatum of "the job or me," Farrah resigned her partnership in the law firm, and the two moved out of the city into the town of Stamford, Connecticut.

Things were going great until Farrah read a book about Brandon Nash, a famous football player and actor who was convicted of murdering his wife. Farrah could not help but believe that she could have done a better job than the book's author at investigating the case, and she decided to start her own investigation as a hobby. Since Melody was a radio producer, the two hatched the idea that Farrah's findings could be distributed as a podcast.

Farrah had a knack for storytelling, evidenced in the first season of Uncorking a Murder, which had been described by one reviewer as a "delicious throwback to an old-fashioned radio drama." The contradiction wasn't lost on Farrah; in a sense she had produced something that would have been popular in the 1930s but required someone to listen to it on devices made in the twenty-first century.

The podcast was an instant success, and the millions of downloads led to a significant amount of advertising revenue, but along with ad dollars came pressure to repeat its success. Last year, Farrah's intern Jimmy Rella, (nicknamed Jimmy Doubts due to his nervous tendencies) took a call from Rodney Peters, a retired detective from Ft. Lauderdale, who asked Farrah to look into a case he had been involved with years prior.

Curious to hear why a retired detective would want a conviction overturned, Farrah and Jimmy went down to visit Rodney, and the three unraveled a conspiracy involving a greedy and narcissistic CEO of a pharmaceutical company, a corrupt United States senator, and a wrongly imprisoned man. It was a dangerous investigation, however. Melody, who did not join Farrah in Florida due to her own personal boycott of the Sunshine State, had almost been kidnapped and killed, and the couple's relationship had been on rocky ground ever since.

"I guess when they say 'all are welcome,' this church really means it." Melody quipped to Farrah as the two stood after the homily. The fact that Farrah was a cradle Catholic was another bone of contention for Melody, who had been raised without religion. Melody had a disdain for any religious establishment and went to Mass begrudgingly.

"My brother took a homiletics class with this priest at

Catholic University in D.C. They definitely have similar styles," Farrah whispered to Melody.

Farrah's brother, Michael, was a Catholic priest in the well-to-do town of Greenwich, Connecticut. His parish was located near a small airport, and Farrah and Melody had dropped by to say hello to him on their way to the Cape. The airport offered a flight to Hyannis, Massachusetts – not far from Chatham - and flying was a great way to beat the weekend traffic that crawled up north like an army of marching ants. This time of year it might take someone over five hours to drive to Massachusetts' most desirable summer destination; conversely, flying took all of forty-five minutes.

Like Fr. Hart, Farrah's brother was a more liberal priest but much less outspoken lest the more conservative congregants of his Greenwich parish reduce their weekly donations. Farrah's brother had encouraged her to visit his old friend at his parish in Chatham, and it was this request that led Farrah and Melody to attend Mass that Sunday morning at Our Lady of Healing Church.

The liturgy continued, and Farrah watched as the priest said the blessing over the bread and wine. After consecrating the bread and wine, the priest broke off a piece of the bread and put it in his mouth. He then put the chalice to his lips and appeared to take a small sip. Farrah couldn't help but notice that the priest had made a strange face afterward — though at the time she chalked it up to sipping wine that had turned sour.

Melody remained in the pew as Farrah stood and got in line to receive Communion. As Farrah approached Fr.

Hart, she noticed that he was breathing quite rapidly, which seemed odd to her since the priest looked to be in good shape. As she approached, she bowed her head and replied, "Amen," when he said, "Body of Christ."

Farrah and Melody were seated in the middle of the church, so it was still some time before all congregants received Communion. Farrah knew she should be praying, but she couldn't take her eyes off the priest, who seemed to be struggling to take in enough air.

After the last congregant received Communion, Fr. Hart and Emily Rose, who had been helping to distribute Communion, returned to the altar. The priest placed the leftover consecrated hosts into the Tabernacle where they would be stored until they were needed for the next Mass and then walked back to the altar to consume the rest of the wine in the chalice, a practice required by church law.

The altar server, a boy of twelve, approached the altar with a cruet of water, which Fr. Hart poured into his chalice. After swishing it around for a brief moment, he brought the chalice to his lips again and appeared to finish the wine. Farrah could not help but notice that, once again, the priest grimaced as if he were drinking, or smelling, something unpleasant.

Picking up a chasuble to clean out the chalice, Fr. Hart looked out at his congregation and began to gasp for air as if he were choking. He tried to speak into the microphone, but no words came out. He started to breathe in an increasingly rapid manner and appeared to be lightheaded, as evidenced by his swaying back and forth. The altar server, sensing that something was amiss, cried into the microphone, "There's something wrong with Fr. Hart!"

The congregation began to buzz with people wondering what was happening. Emotions went from confusion to fear quickly as those assembled saw Fr. Hart clutch his throat, fall to his knees, and then onto his stomach. His body started to convulse.

Fortunately, that Sunday morning the town's medical examiner was attending Mass, and he rushed over to take the priest's vital signs. He was amazed to find that Fr. Hart was no longer breathing but his pulse was still racing. He screamed for someone to call for an ambulance and immediately started prepping to give the priest CPR, but his efforts would be in vain: Fr. Gregory Hart, a forty-nine-year-old priest in perfect health, was pronounced dead by the medical examiner just minutes later. The million-dollar question was *why*?

CHAPTER TWO

The Investigation Begins

The town of Chatham had little need for a police department; in the off-season it is basically a quiet fishing village where the most exciting thing that happens is a new release coming to the town's small movie house, the Chatham Orpheum. In the tourist season, however, police officers have a little more to do — namely pull people over for driving while intoxicated or break up fights over the all too few parking spots in town. A murder was certainly out of the question, which is why Detective William Nickerson, known simply as Nick by those in the community, was confused as he stood in the coroner's office Monday morning, the day after the priest died.

Nick was an imposing six feet, three inches tall and had hands the size of baseball mitts. He was only forty-five years old, but his mane of all-white hair gave him the appearance of someone much older. He wore his hair cropped closely over his ears and longer on top so it flipped from one side to the other; it was as if he had a hard time coming to terms with the fact that the nineties were over.

A lifelong Chatham resident, the detective could recount only one murder in his tenure as a cop, that of a heroin addict whose lifeless body washed up on the shores of Lighthouse Beach just a few years after Nick left the police academy. That case was technically still open, but it was colder than the body of Fr. Gregory Hart, which Detective Nickerson was about to lay eyes on for the first time.

"At first I thought it was probably just a heart attack," said the coroner, Dr. Charles Stemper, better known as Charlie. He had been in the Barnstable County coroner's office for the past twenty years. This was only his second murder since leaving the city of Boston two decades ago. "But this man was poisoned, no doubt about it."

"Poisoned?" questioned Nick. "In Chatham?"

"I know it's hard to believe, but take a look at this," Charlie lifted up the sheet covering the priest's body; he was careful to do so from the feet rather than the head — perhaps out of respect for the dead. Nick expected the skin to be bluish in color, given the amount of time that had passed since the priest died, but it still appeared pink.

"Shouldn't he be a different color, doc?"

"Bingo! Should be as blue as the tie you are wearing — but that's not the only funny thing." Charlie paused for dramatic effect.

Nick raised one eyebrow as if to say, "Get on with it."

"Right. Take a look at this." Charlie went to his cabinet and handed Nick what appeared to be a test tube containing a cherry-red liquid.

"What am I looking at here, doc?"

"That's a sample of the priest's blood. Notice anything

strange about it?"

As a diabetic, Nick had seen more than his fair share of blood, and he knew that, when drawn, the color was crimson-like. What he was looking at here, though, was more like the color of an Italian sports car. "Why is the color off?"

"That was the second clue that led me to believe that the priest was poisoned. There is one poison in particular that turns a person's blood bright red."

"Don't leave me hanging, doc."

"Hold your horses, sonny. I had to be sure before determining the cause of death, so I had to give his blood the old sniff test."

"Sniff test?" Nick was becoming impatient with the coroner; if the priest were really poisoned as the coroner believed, he was eager to get started on finding out who did it, and why.

"Open the top of that vile and see, I mean smell, for yourself."

Nick raised his eyebrow again, thinking the coroner might be slightly off his rocker. Nevertheless, he complied with the coroner's request and put the vile up to his nose.

"It smells like almonds — sour almonds."

"Well, winner winner, chicken dinner, detective. I didn't know if you would be able to actually smell that since it's a recessive genetic trait to be able to do so."

"Can you please cut to the chase and tell me what this means?" Nick said, exasperation evident in his tone of voice.

"The color of the priest's skin, the redness of his blood, and the scent of sour almonds lead me to believe that this man was poisoned by cyanide."

"Cyanide?"

"It all makes sense. Eyewitnesses in the church yesterday stated that the priest appeared to be having a hard time breathing as they approached him for Communion. Those closer to the altar at the end of Mass saw him gasping for air and then start convulsing after he lost consciousness. These are all classic signs of cyanide poisoning. Once the drug is in the body, it prevents red blood cells from absorbing oxygen, and therefore the body dies by internal asphyxia."

"How does someone get their hands on cyanide?"

"Anyone with an advanced knowledge of chemistry can actually create it from apricot pits."

"Well, that might certainly narrow my list of suspects, but who would want to kill a priest?"

"That's well above my pay grade, detective."

Nick left the coroner's office and made a call to the parish office; he wanted to start interviewing people who knew the priest best and thought it wise to start with the parish staff. He made an appointment to meet Betty Conyers, the church secretary, in ten minutes — although he soon realized he should have said twenty. A light rain was falling, and when Chatham's tourists couldn't make it to the beach, they flock to the art galleries and clothing boutiques lining Main Street as if shopping were a sport and the winner was the person who spent the most.

As the detective waited at the traffic circle located at the intersection of Main Street and Old Harbor Road, he observed the number of women adorned in Lily Pulitzer dresses and Lulu Lemon yoga pants — the unofficial uniforms of the upper-class female vacationer in Chatham. He and his colleagues referred to these women as the LuLu Lillies and often remarked how it was them, not their husbands, that caused the police the most trouble during evenings in season. Apparently a cocktail of Xanax and wine doesn't mix well and leads to unpredictable — and regrettable — behavior.

Once on Old Harbor Road, Nick made a right onto Highland Street and pulled into the parking lot for Our Lady of Healing Church. He exited his car and rang the doorbell of the rectory.

Betty Conyers was a seventy-two-year-old woman who worked part-time at the rectory to handle Fr. Hart's calendar as well as take care of the parish's bookkeeping. She was devastated by the death of her boss as evidenced by the redness in her eyes Nick spotted immediately after she opened the door.

"I am Detective William Nickerson. We just spoke on the phone a few minutes ago. Is now still a good time for me to come in?"

"Yes, detective, come on in."

"Feel free to call me Nick," the detective said.

"But your name is William — why would I want to call you Nick?"

"My last name is Nickerson, so most people just call me Nick."

"Well, my name is Betty, and you can call me Betty." The detective followed her to the office in the back of the house, noticing that the rectory was decorated very modestly. He had only been inside this house once before at the request of the former pastor, Fr. Paul Hewson, who had it decorated in a much more ostentatious manner. Fr. Paul's retirement prompted the opening filled by Fr. Hart. The former pastor moved back to his native Ireland and was enjoying retirement.

"Fr. Hart was a minimalist, it seems."

"He didn't want to spend any money decorating this place. In fact, most of the furniture you see here was donated by parishioners. Fr. Hart was adamant that any money received by the church in the form of donations strictly be used for the operation of the church or donated to those in need."

"He sounds like a true man of the cloth."

Betty began to tear up again, "I can't believe he's gone. I was just starting to like him."

Nick was not a Catholic, nor had he been a close adherent to the Episcopal church in which he was raised. He didn't travel in religious circles and had no knowledge of Fr. Hart's polarity in the community. "Why do you say that?"

"Well, it's just that he was a different kind of priest. More outspoken on social issues than ones we've had previously."

"Outspoken in what way?"

"He would often preach about how we should be more welcoming of homosexual couples entering the church, how priests should be able to get married, and how it was criminal that church leaders got away with covering up sexual abuse for so long. Things like that."

"Would you say that Fr. Hart had any enemies in the community?" Nick removed a pen and small notepad from the inner pocket of his blue suit jacket and began to take notes on what Betty was saying.

"I wouldn't call anyone an enemy, but we have received some e-mail from parishioners asking that Fr. Hart not harp on sex so much during his homilies. Apparently many have had to have the sex talk with their children earlier than anticipated."

"Does anyone come to mind as someone who was particularly upset at Fr. Hart?"

Betty paused to think for a moment. "No one in the parish, but I can tell you that the bishop wasn't happy with him at all. His Excellence called the rectory multiple times a week, and Fr. Hart avoided those calls like the plague."

As Nick wrote a note to contact the bishop's office, the doorbell rang, and Betty excused herself to answer the door. She came back with Emily Rose in tow. When the two women entered the office, the detective stood up, the way his mother taught him to do when a woman entered a room.

"Emily just stopped by to purchase a Mass card to send to Fr. Hart's family. I hope you don't mind the interruption, detective."

"Not at all."

While Betty looked through her desk for a Mass card, Nick engaged Emily in conversation.

"Did you know Fr. Hart well?"

"Oh yes," Emily replied. "I have been a Eucharistic Minister in this parish for a long time and have had close relationships with all the pastors."

"Do you know anyone who may have had an issue with Fr. Hart? Someone who may have wanted to harm him?"

Emily had a look of concern on her face. "Why do you ask, detective? Do you think someone wanted to hurt Fr. Hart?"

Nick knew that the minute he said anything about the priest being murdered, word would spread like wildfire throughout the town of Chatham, but there was no use hiding the fact. It would come out sooner or later and divulging it now might help to get some leads. "We have reason to believe he was poisoned."

"Poisoned!" Betty exclaimed. "Who would want to poison Fr. Hart?"

"I was hoping you could tell me."

Betty replied, "He said some things that not everyone agreed with, but I don't think anyone would have wanted to hurt him."

"What about you, Ms. Rose? Can you think of anyone who would have wanted to hurt Fr. Hart?"

Emily thought for a minute before responding. Looking at her, Nick could tell that her wheels were turning.

"There is one man who argued with Fr. Hart quite frequently. His name is Christopher Mitchell, and he's a pharmacist here in town."

Nick's ears perked up upon hearing the word pharmacist. He remembered the coroner saying that anyone with an advanced knowledge of chemistry could create cyanide, and a pharmacist would certainly fit that bill. He wrote down the name in his notebook with a question mark next to it.

"What do you know about Mr. Mitchell?"

Emily replied, "He runs the local SNAP chapter here on the cape."

"SNAP?" Nick questioned.

"It stands for 'Survivors Network for Those Abused by Priests.' It's a support group for men who were abused by priests as children."

Nick wrote this down in his notebook next to Mitchell's name.

While Nick and Emily were talking, Betty had opened her computer and pulled up Fr. Hart's schedule for the past six months. "Wow!" she exclaimed.

"What?" Nick asked.

"I just pulled up Fr. Hart's calendar, and he had six meetings with a C. Mitchell since coming to the parish."

"Don't you manage Fr. Hart's calendar? Why didn't his name ring a bell to you before?" Nick asked, sounding a bit accusatory.

"I only work part time, detective — Tuesdays and Thursdays. Every single one of these meetings occurred on either a Monday, Wednesday, or Friday."

"Clearly he didn't want anyone around when they met," Emily introjected.

"Clearly," Nick agreed. "Ms. Rose, how did you know about the arguments Fr. Hart would have with Mitchell?"

"I've been in this parish my entire life and active in many of its ministries. There's not much that goes on here that I don't know about."

Nick wrote down her name in his notebook. "Ms. Rose, can I have your phone number? I'm thinking you may be very helpful in this investigation in the event the Mitchell lead winds up being a dead end."

"I am happy to help in any way I can, detective." Emily gave Nick her number as well as her home address.

"One more question Ms. Rose, do you know what pharmacy Mitchell works at?"

"As a matter of fact, I do. He runs the Chatham Apothecary right down the street on Main Street next to the Yellow Umbrella Bookstore."

"I know the place," Nick said. "Thank you both very much for your time." The detective left the rectory and placed a call back to the station. He wanted to find someone to do some research on Christopher Mitchell before paying him a visit.

"Chatham Police Department, how can I direct your call?" It was Arlene Mazzone, the department's administrative assistant. She was in her late fifties, had salt-and-pepper hair, and acted more like the station's mother than its secretary. As such, she was treated with the utmost respect by anyone who walked through the station's doors. At the time of Nick's call, she was sitting at her desk holding her rosary beads; she made a habit of saying the Rosary every day around lunchtime.

"Arlene, it's Nick. I assume your son is home for college, right?" It was the end of June, and the Fourth of July was a few days away. Nick was hoping to use Arlene's son Robert as a research assistant.

"Yes, Bobby's been home for a while now. Why do you ask?"

"He's a journalism major, isn't he?"

"Don't remind me. I wanted him to be a doctor, but he seems hell-bent on working in the newspaper business. Talk about a job that will be obsolete in ten years."

"If he wouldn't mind making a little extra money, I could use his help with something."

"Aside from working concessions at the home games for the Chatham As, he's got nothing going on." The Chatham As were the town's Cape League baseball team, part of an old Cape tradition that attracted the best of the best collegiate ball players to play in its summer league.

"Can you ask him to find any news stories that mention the name Christopher Mitchell? He's a local pharmacist here in Chatham."

"Does this have anything to do with the death of Fr. Hart?"

"It might. I'm just following up on a lead some ladies at the church just gave me."

"I'll call him, but he may not be up yet."

Nick looked at his watch, an old wind-up Seiko given to him by his grandfather. "It's 12:30 in the afternoon!"

"I know you don't have any children, detective, but should you be so blessed, you will learn that when they are college age, waking up any time before noon is considered waking up early."

"I appreciate the assist, Arlene."

"I'll call him now. Oh, and Nick . . ."

"What's that, Arlene?"

"Remember to eat lunch today. You sometimes forget to eat when you start working a case, and it sounds like you're going to need your strength."

"Thank you, Arlene."

Nick hung up the phone and drove down Main Street to the corner of Main and Barn Hill Road where the Shop Ahoy shopping center was located. He parked his car and entered his favorite diner, Larry's PX, to have some lunch; Arlene's guilt had set in.

CHAPTER THREE

The Bishop's Office

The news of Fr. Gregory Hart's death was reported to the bishop's office by the Chatham Police Department on Sunday afternoon. Fr. Peter Cossa, Chancellor of the Diocese of Fall River, took the call in the bishop's absence; Bishop Robert Hurley was administering Last Rights to a parishioner who was under hospice care and had remained at her side until she passed after midnight on Monday morning. Once he heard the news, Bishop Hurley called an emergency meeting with Fr. Cossa to discuss what had happened. While losing a priest required the bishop to find someone to cover the deceased priest's duties in Chatham, given the circumstances around Fr. Hart's death, the bishop also would have to do damage control with the press — most of whom were highly critical of him to begin with.

Fr. Cossa was appointed chancellor by the bishop as a reward for his steadfast loyalty; historically Bishop Hurley could always trust Fr. Cossa to back his decisions and carry out the unpleasant actions that were sometimes necessary in a diocese. As chancellor, Fr. Cossa was the bishop's confidential secretary, and it was also his job to draw up and curate all documents and records for the diocese, including those concerning the movement of priests between parishes as well as those involving succession upon the bishop's retirement or death.

Fr. Cossa was dressed in an ankle-length black cassock; while many priests wore black suits, he wore his clerics as a testament to his conservatism. Along those lines, he was the founder of a secret society, the ultra-conservative Order of John XXIII, an organization that attracted men who believed the Church was wrong in its reforms of the Second Vatican Council. They felt the Church should go back to the old ways before the 1960s when the liturgy was in Latin and priests celebrated Mass with their backs to the congregation. The Church seemed to have more authority back then, and authority led to order and respect. Fr. Cossa and his group of like-minded men longed for those days.

Referred to simply as The Order by its members, the society was named after antipope John XXIII who, while presiding over the Church during the western schism, rose to and held onto power by any means necessary including violence, corruption, and even murder. After the Western Schism ended, his reign was declared in opposition to the true papacy, and he was given the title antipope.

A reformer named Angelo Giuseppe Roncalli would take the name of John XXIII on October 28, 1958, upon his election to the papacy by the College of Cardinals; he would later go on to convene the Second Vatican Council which led to a number of progressive reforms in the Catholic Church. He was canonized by Pope Francis in

2014 and is now known as Pope Saint John the XXIII. The irony of this was not lost on the members of The Order, who disdained these reforms.

Membership in the society was secret because ultraconservatism was the exception, no longer the rule, in the modern Catholic church — though priests like Fr. Cossa wished to change that. It was other priests, such as the recently deceased Fr. Greg Hart, who were getting in the way.

Bishop Hurley turned to his confidant and asked, "What did you learn after talking to the coroner's office?"

He wasn't nearly as conservative as the chancellor, but certainly not as liberal as Fr. Hart. While he sympathized with some of Fr. Hart's positions, the bishop had a responsibility to tow the company line, and that meant not rocking the boat when it came to traditional doctrine.

Father Cossa's cold eyes looked directly into those of the bishop. "I spoke with the police as well as to Dr. Charles Stemper this morning. Dr. Stemper has concluded that Fr. Hart did not die of natural causes."

"Fr. Hart was a bit of a wild child — could drugs have been involved?"

"The medical examiner determined that Fr. Hart was poisoned and told as much to the detective who called when you were at hospice."

The bishop looked distressed. To say he had a tumultuous relationship with the dead priest would be putting it mildly; still, he didn't want it to end this way.

"Does the detective have a name, Peter?" Bishop Hurley was becoming agitated; he was clearly anxious about the events that had unfolded in Chatham.

"William Nickerson, but apparently everyone calls him

Nick.”

“Is he a Catholic?”

“If he is, he is not registered with the parish in Chatham. You sound nervous, Robert.” Fr. Cossa was the only person besides the bishop‘s ninety-five-year-old mother who could speak to him so informally.

“It‘s no secret that Fr. Hart and I didn‘t see eye to eye. Hell, I sent him to Chatham to get him out of my hair, only to find that doing so had the opposite effect. This diocese has gone through enough trouble in the past decade and a half; we don‘t need any more unwanted attention. Can you keep the wolves at bay?”

“Have I ever failed you, Your Excellency?”

Bishop Hurley smiled at his chancellor’s confident and formal tone.

“Of course not, Peter — that‘s why you are my chancellor.”

While it is true that Peter appeared to be loyal, Bishop Hurley believed in the old adage, “Keep your friends close, but your enemies closer.” Over the years he came to suspect that Fr. Cossa was power hungry and wanted him close by so he could keep an eye on him.

“Are you going to go to Chatham to celebrate the funeral?”

It was tradition for the bishop to celebrate the funeral of any priest who passed away in his diocese.

“No,” Bishop Hurley said dismissively.

“I didn‘t take you for someone to shirk tradition,” Fr. Cossa replied, snickering.

“Not I, but we are going to Chatham to concelebrate the funeral. I thought you might like a trip to the Cape; it‘s lovely this time of year.”

"What do you want to do about Fr. Hart's temporary replacement? We don't have many to choose from."

Before he could reply, there was a knock on the door.

"Come in," the bishop said.

Fr. Jim Watts, the bishop's personal assistant, came into the office. "I am sorry to interrupt you, Bishop Hurly, but there's a call for you on line two."

"Who is it?" the bishop asked.

"A priest from the Diocese of Bridgeport. His name is Fr. Michael Graham. He's apparently a friend of Fr. Hart and would like to come and concelebrate his funeral."

Bishop Hurley turned to Fr. Cossa. "I believe you now have the answer to your question."

"The Lord works in mysterious ways," the chancellor replied.

CHAPTER FOUR

Melody Leaves

While Nick was eating lunch at Larry's PX and Bishop Hurley was meeting with his chancellor, Farrah and Melody were sitting on the second-floor deck of Farrah's house on Harding's Beach. Farrah had grown up vacationing on Cape Cod and, due to the success of Uncorking a Murder, was able to purchase the summer house of her dreams.

The home was located on a private street at the end of Harding's Beach Road and offered a magnificent view of Nantucket Sound. All the houses on her street had names, and Farrah struggled over what to name hers, as she had a tendency to both overthink things and second-guess just about everything. Melody finally suggested The Golden Note, combining Golden, Farrah's childhood nickname, and Note, Melody's last name.

The two were waiting for Farrah's brother, Michael, to arrive; he had been devastated to hear the news that his friend Fr. Hart had died and wanted to come up to Chatham to pay his respects and hopefully concelebrate the funeral with the bishop. While looking out on Nantucket Sound from the second-story patio, Farrah was curious why her partner was acting so distant toward her.

"Is everything okay with you?" Farrah asked. "You've barely said a word all morning."

The past twelve months had been a true test of their relationship. The previous year while Farrah was in Florida doing research on the Sonny Michaels case, a former IRA assassin had broken into their Connecticut home intending to kidnap Melody as a means of intimidating Farrah. Fortunately Melody was able to catch him by surprise and wound up sending him to the hospital; her dedication to training in the martial arts may have saved her life. The fact that Farrah decided to remain in Florida to finish her research instead of going home immediately was still a bone of contention between them.

"I've got a bad feeling about this priest's death, that's all. Something inside me suggests that you are going to get involved somehow and our summer vacation will come to a halt."

Farrah took a sip of tea and thought carefully about her next words. "It was probably just a heart attack. Who would want to kill a priest?"

"I don't know, but I'm just sayin' I've got a bad feeling about it, that's all. When is your brother supposed to get here?"

As if on cue, the doorbell rang, and Mulder started barking. Farrah was a big X-Files fan and had named her dog Mulder after the male lead on the show. She also had a cat named Scully, but the feline showed absolutely no interest when anyone came to visit.

"Speak of the devil, and the devil appears." Farrah got

up from her chaise lounge and went inside the house to answer the door.

Fr. Michael Graham was not dressed in his clerical robes; instead he was wearing a button-down shirt that was a little too tight around his belly and a pair of pleated Bermuda shorts. Capping off his look were a pair of black dress socks and topsider shoes.

Farrah opened the door and couldn't help throwing a verbal jab at her brother. "Hey Melody," she yelled upstairs, "I thought Mikey was coming over, but my dad is here instead."

"Real funny, sis," Michael said. "And please don't call me Mikey — you know how much I hate it when you call me Mikey. Plus I'm not in the mood for jokes. Lovely place by the way; the podcasting business must be good." While Farrah had shared pictures of the beach house with her brother, this was the first time he had actually visited.

"I was thinking that you should do a podcast – wait, we could call it a Godcast. Maybe you could earn a little extra dough for retirement. I'm guessing the diocese doesn't have a great 401K."

Her brother tried hard not to laugh, but he couldn't help it. Seeing his sister always lifted his spirits. "Where is Melody?"

"She's still upstairs. We were sitting out on the deck when you arrived."

"Wouldn't the deck be downstairs?"

"We have patio downstairs and a deck upstairs; it gives us a better view of the water. Come up and I'll show you."

Farrah led her brother upstairs where Melody was waiting for them on the deck. Farrah was a little upset when her partner didn't get up to greet Michael at the door, but she knew she had to pick her battles carefully with Melody. Farrah was still in the penalty box for the events of last year.

"Hello, Melody,"

"Hey Mike," Melody replied. She wasn't a religious person and refused to call Farrah's brother Father on the grounds that she had only one father, and it wasn't him.

"Did I come at a bad time?" Fr. Michael asked, sensing the tension between his sister and her partner.

"I was just going to go for a run so you two could catch up."

"Please, stay for just a minute," Fr. Michael said. "There is something that I want to talk to both of you about, given what you do for a living."

Farrah looked over at Melody and saw the blood immediately drain from her face.

"I think we'd better sit down," Fr. Michael suggested.

"What's the matter, Mike?" Farrah asked.

"I called the bishop's office this morning on my way up here to request that I concelebrate the funeral on Wednesday, and I spoke to the bishop personally. Do you know what he told me?"

Farrah looked over at Melody, who shook her head from side to side.

"What?" Farrah asked.

"My friend Fr. Hart was murdered, and I need your help to find out why."

Upon hearing this, Melody got up from where she was sitting and stormed back into the house. Fr. Michael looked over at his sister and shrugged his shoulders as if to say, "Was it something I said?"

"Stay here for a second; let me see what is going on."

Farrah followed her partner's path into the house. "Melody," she called out. No response. "Melody, where are you?"

"In the bedroom."

Farrah walked down the hall to the master bedroom. It had floor-to-ceiling windows, and the view overlooked the water; Farrah considered it a piece of paradise, but at the moment it felt like anything but. She saw a suitcase on the bed, and Melody was busy throwing clothes into it.

"What are you doing?" Farrah asked.

"I know how this story ends. You're going to get involved in this investigation, and I may as well be alone up here. Well, I'd rather be alone at home, wherever that is."

"What's that supposed to mean?" Farrah tried unsuccessfully to hide the anger in her voice.

"Don't you dare get short with me, Farrah Graham! For a while now I have been wondering where this relationship is going, and I've been landing on one answer: Nowhere. I thought when you quit your job as a lawyer we could live a normal life, but then you started that damn podcast, and I can't help but feel as if I take a back seat to that."

"That podcast funds our lifestyle. Look around you — without the podcast, we don't have all of this!"

"I never wanted any of this; I just wanted you."

"Well, I'm sorry, but I'm not cut out to be a housewife."

"I am not asking you to be a goddamn housewife – we're not even fucking married. I just want you to be there for me when I need you, and you haven't been."

Farrah knew Melody had a point. She had worked night and day on launching the second season of

Uncorking a Murder and then had been gone for the past six weeks on a worldwide media tour to promote the show. She was a workaholic, and at some point Farrah knew she had to address those tendencies.

"I promised you I would take the entire summer off, and here we are."

"Yeah, here we are – with Mikey asking for your help in a murder investigation." Melody stopped throwing clothes into her suitcase and stared at Farrah.

"It's decision time, Farrah Graham. It's him or me. What's it gonna be?"

"Farrah, he's my brother, and he needs my help."

"Him or me?" Melody repeated indignantly.

"It will only be for a couple of days at the most . . ."

Before Farrah could even finish her reply, Melody slammed her suitcase shut. Farrah tried to block the doorway, but the intense look she saw in Melody's eyes convinced her to step aside.

Melody left the room and headed downstairs, her bag banging loudly on each step as she descended. Farrah didn't bother running after her because she knew Melody's mind was made up; she would give her time to be alone and then call her in a couple of days to try and patch things up. This wasn't the first time Melody had walked out, and Farrah knew from experience that her partner needed a cooling-off period.

Melody didn't even turn around to look at Farrah before she walked out of the door, slamming it hard behind her. Maybe three days, Farrah thought to herself.

Her brother heard the commotion and came inside. "What happened?" he asked.

"Let's just say I am not high up on her list right now. I

need a beer — would you like a beer?"

"I'd love one."

Farrah went downstairs and got two cold beers out of the refrigerator and brought them up. She handed one to her brother and asked, "What do you need me for? Shouldn't the police handle this?"

"I am sure the Chatham police department is fine," Fr. Michael said after a long pull on his beer, "but there is one matter which requires some discretion."

"Funny business regarding a priest?"

"Kind of, but not what you think. Fr. Hart had a girlfriend."

Farrah's mouth dropped wide open. "Girlfriend! I knew he was progressive, but I had no idea he was that progressive. That's pretty much against the rules as you can get, right?"

"Look, sis, while this may come as a surprise to you, celibacy is somewhat of a myth in the Catholic church. Priests slip up all the time."

"Even you?"

Farrah's brother was a good-looking guy and had enjoyed a host of girlfriends in high school and college. Everyone was shocked when he decided to enter the seminary upon graduating from Boston College.

"I'm not going to answer that question."

"So if it's not all that common to have a girlfriend, why do you need me?"

"Because after I talked to him last week, he told me that his conscience was bothering him and he broke up with her. Not only that, but rumors had started to fly; rumors that made their way up to the bishop's office in Fall River."

"How did the girl take it?"

"Apparently not very well. According to him, she lost her mind."

"Do you know where she lives?"

"Yeah, she's a waitress at a restaurant up in Wellfleet called Pal's Captain's Table. Her name is Amanda Brooks."

"Wellfleet is thirty minutes from here; couldn't he find a girlfriend closer to home?"

"He wanted to reduce the chances of being seen with her in public."

"Makes sense, I guess. With Melody gone, I'm going to need someone to help me with this investigation. Do you mind if I call someone to help?"

"Do you have someone in mind?"

"Yep."

"There's one more thing you should know," Farrah's brother said and paused for dramatic effect. "Amanda Brooks has a kid."

CHAPTER FIVE

Jimmy Checks is Privilege

Jimmy Rella returned to his cubicle at Manhattan-based Kriz, Post, and Piniciaro LLP after having an extended lunch with the founding partner, Albert Pinciaro. Jimmy was between his first and second year of law school and knew that exceeding expectations in this first internship at such a prestigious firm would set him up for a full-time job after graduation. The problem was, he was only one week into his internship at KPP and he hated every minute of it.

The source of his frustration was Ella Franklin, the crimson-haired director of human resources who was responsible for the summer internship program. She was known internally as the Red Storm, and most people, even the three founding partners, tried to steer clear of her, particularly when she was having a bad today. Unfortunately for Jimmy, today was a bad day.

After getting through the e-mails that had come in while he was at lunch, Jimmy planned to turn his attention to the brief he had been asked to proofread when he saw the red message light blinking on his phone. As he listened to the message, the blood drained from his face.

"James, this is Ella Franklin. I'm just calling to remind you that you are given sixty minutes for lunch every day and are expected to take that at your desk. Please come down to my office when you get back so we can discuss this further."

He hung up the phone and let out a sigh loud enough for Kayla Nichols to hear. Kayla was also interning at KPP for the summer, and unlike Jimmy, she seemed to be the perfect intern: in the office before everyone else, sociable with all the right people, and never left her desk — leading Jimmy to question whether she was hooked up to a discreet catheter.

"Ella was looking for you," Kayla said, peeking over the gray cloth wall that separated their cubicles. Jimmy noticed that Kayla had died her hair red over the weekend.

"I heard. I'm heading to her office now."

"Don't worry about it, Doubts, you still have two more strikes to go before you get put on probation."

Jimmy hated the fact that Kayla knew the nickname his former bosses, Farrah and Melody, had bestowed up on him. During his final year as a communications major at Fairfield University, Jimmy interned with Uncorking a Murder. While he was inquisitive by nature, sometimes the way he asked questions led others to believe he was a pessimist, and this led Melody to call him Jimmy Doubts . . . and the nickname stuck. Kayla, who was an expert at trolling people on social media, came across a picture of Jimmy on the Facebook page for Uncorking a Murder where the nickname had been included in a photo caption.

"I'll keep that in mind, and please don't call me Doubts."

"Whatever you say . . . Doubts." Kayla let out a giggle as Jimmy left his cubicle and walked down the hall toward Ella's office.

While walking toward Ella's office, Jimmy thought of the advice that Albert Pinciaro, one of the founding partners, had given him over lunch. "Being a great lawyer is the price of entry into this firm, but in order to succeed, you have to be adept at politics."

"I am learning that quickly, sir." Jimmy was raised to be polite and respectful to people in authority and used the term sincerely.

"I'm afraid you're not learning quickly enough. Last week one of the senior associates was selling candy bars for his daughter's softball team and you didn't purchase any."

Jimmy remembered seeing a dozen candy bars on Kayla's desk last Friday. He had wondered what she could possibly want with all that chocolate since she was as thin as a rail and a self-proclaimed health freak.

"I have a nut allergy, sir, and one of those bars would have put me in the hospital."

"That, dear boy, is immaterial," Albert chortled while eating his salad. "And then there's the fact that you did not attend the intern happy hour last Friday."

Most happy hours start at 5:00 p.m.; the one in question actually started at 10:00 p.m. — interns were not expected to clock out before 9:30.

Jimmy couldn't believe that he was getting scolded for not drinking with the staff. "It was my uncle's fiftieth birthday, and my mother threw him a surprise party back home in Norwalk."

"Your uncle will have more birthdays son; you only get one chance at an internship with KPP."

Jimmy neglected to mention the fact that he worked until 11:00 p.m. that evening and missed the party anyway. If this was what being a lawyer at a prestigious firm was like, he was second-guessing his decision to pursue law as a profession.

Just before he knocked on Ella's closed door, Jimmy felt his phone vibrate. He checked the caller ID and noticed it was Farrah Graham calling. He was tempted to send the call to voicemail, but wanting to hear a friendly voice before going into the Red Storm's office, he answered.

"Hi, this is Jimmy," he said whispering into the phone.

"Doubts!" Farrah said gleefully. "Good to hear your voice. Why are you whispering?"

"I'm at my internship at KPP; it's kind of a bad time."

Farrah had spent fifteen years as a lawyer in Manhattan and knew the firm well. "It's always going to be a bad time there. What would I have to pay you to ditch your internship and help me out on the Cape for a week or so?"

Jimmy paused for a second, imagining spending time on the Cape versus being chained to his desk. He also reasoned that Farrah must have an interesting opportunity for her podcast if she required his help.

"I thought you were taking time off this summer and delaying research on your third season until the fall."

Farrah gave him a quick overview of what had happened in Chatham the previous day and the information her brother had shared with her that morning.

"That sounds so much better than being forced to buy candy bars."

"What?" Farrah asked.

"Never mind. Listen, I'm going into a meeting now — can I call you back later?"

"Sure. And Doubts, don't forget who advised you not to go into the legal profession. You are too nice and too smart to be a lawyer."

"I'll keep that in mind." Jimmy terminated the call, returned his phone to his pocket, and knocked on Ella Franklin's door.

"Come in," he heard a stern voice say from behind the giant oak door that separated them. As he crossed through the doorway, the temperature change was dramatic; Jimmy thought it was cool enough to store a cadaver in Ella's office.

"Were you taking a personal call outside my office just now, James?"

"I'm sorry if I was too loud, ma'am; I was trying to be discreet."

"Section two, page five of the employee handbook states that you shall keep any personal phone calls to a minimum. Was that not clear?"

Jimmy didn't know how the firm defined the word minimum, but in his mind it seemed to suggest that personal calls weren't off limits all together; that said, his instincts told him not to argue.

"Thank you for the reminder. I won't let it happen again, Ms. Franklin."

Ella looked at him disapprovingly. She didn't know what to make of the young man in front of her and assumed he was just another privileged white male whose life was made easy through silver spoons and personal connections. She had a natural disdain for people like that and made it her mission to humble them.

Nothing could have been further from Jimmy's reality, though. Jimmy was raised by a single mother who worked two jobs to make ends meet for their family. He personally had been working since the age of eleven when he got a job picking up golf balls at the driving range near his home. A paper route, now a thing of the past, soon followed. Later he worked at an ice-cream store, and once he turned eighteen, he worked as a letter carrier in the summertime for the post office. While Jimmy never struggled, his life was far from charmed.

"I stopped by your desk at 12:30, and you weren't there. Can you tell me where you were?"

Jimmy knew that, while it was expected he would eat lunch at his desk, there was no formal rule that could be cited chapter and verse dictating he could not leave the office. "I was invited to lunch by Mr. Pinciaro."

Ella's mouth fell open. "A founding partner invited you to lunch?" The tone of her voice suggested that she did not believe it.

Jimmy nodded his head.

"Why didn't you tell me?"

"I didn't know that I needed to."

Ella sighed indignantly. "You can't just waltz in here as another privileged white male and not know that a founding partner inviting an intern to lunch is anything but out of the ordinary. Then again, I suppose guys like you are used to being wined and dined every day."

"Pardon me, ma'am?" Jimmy was honestly confused

about Ella's accusation.

"And that's another thing. Stop patronizing me with your Mayberry bullshit. It won't endear yourself to me or anyone else in this firm."

Jimmy was stunned. Was she chastising him for being polite?

"So you would have recommended that I turn down the invitation to have lunch with a founding partner?"

"I would have recommended that you check your privilege!"

"I'm sorry, ma'am, but I'm not familiar with that term."

"Of course you aren't. You are just like any of the other rich white males we bring in here every summer. Well, the world doesn't revolve around you and your country club friends!"

Jimmy was starting to get hot under the collar. He took a deep breath, desperately wanting to keep his emotions in check. "Just to be clear, I should have said no to lunch."

"No, that would have been suicide."

"I'm sorry, ma'am, but I'm confused."

"Let me spell it out for you, James. Your mistake wasn't accepting Mr. Pinciaro's invitation to lunch; your mistake was not telling me about it. What if he caught me in the hallway and told me about your lunch together, and I looked foolish because I didn't know anything about it. How do you think that makes me look in the eyes of our leadership team?"

So that's it, Jimmy thought. Ella wasn't upset that he went to lunch, she was upset that she didn't know about it and feared that she might look bad as a result. He knew it was ridiculous, but then he remembered what Albert said to him at lunch about being able to navigate the politics in the firm.

"I will be sure to let you know the next time a partner invites me to lunch."

"I am afraid that the time for apologies is past. What you need to do is a penance for this infraction."

Penance? Suddenly Jimmy felt as if he were back in Catholic school.

"Excuse me?"

"I'm having a party for some of my old classmates from Choate, and we need a bartender."

Having grown up in Connecticut, Jimmy was familiar with the exclusive boarding school. He also had seen on her wall a diploma from Middlebury, a small but exclusive liberal arts college in Vermont, as well as pictures of Ella at various political fund raisers for left-leaning politicians. It seemed as if her life was a hell of a lot more charmed than his.

"I don't know anything about bartending."

"That's all right — you'll look good in the outfit." Ella reached into her drawer, removed a black object, and tossed it to Jimmy. He looked down into his hands and saw that it was a black bow tie. "No experience required as long as you can pull off wearing this without a shirt."

Jimmy was stunned. He was being sexually harassed by the director of human resources a major New York City law firm, and there was nothing he could do about it. Just then, the phone in his pocket started to vibrate.

"What was that noise?" Ella asked.

"My phone," Jimmy replied as he reached into his pocket. He glanced at his phone, not caring that doing so would cause Ella's face to turn the color of her hair, and saw a text message from Farrah who had sent him a picture of her current view of Harding's Beach. It was a beautiful summer day in Chatham.

"And that, dear boy, is the second biggest mistake you've made all day."

Jimmy returned the phone to his pocket and stood up to leave.

"Where are you going? I have not dismissed you yet!"

Jimmy turned around and flung the bowtie at Ella; it hit her squarely in the nose, causing her face to turn an even brighter shade of red. He said, "Check your privilege," and walked out the door. He returned to his cubicle, grabbed his briefcase, and left the law offices of KPP, fully aware that his future legal career might fail to launch.

CHAPTER SIX

The Arrest of Christopher Mitchell

Detective William Nickerson asked his waitress, Alice, for the check. He was eager to find out what information Arlene's son Robert may have uncovered about Christopher Mitchell, the pharmacist Emily Rose suggested might be involved in the murder of Fr. Greg Hart. Alice was never the quickest waitress at Larry's, but today she seemed off her game completely.

"What's the matter, Alice? You seem to be moving at half-speed today."

"I'm sorry, Nick — I'm just devastated over this Fr. Hart business; he was a good priest and he just dropped dead! If a guy like that can go at any minute, what might happen to an old, out-of-shape lady like me?"

Nick tried to reassure her. "You're being too hard on yourself, Alice." While it was true that Alice could stand to shed a few pounds, her weight wasn't dangerously high. "But I do need my check as I have to get back to the station."

"Working on anything interesting?"

"Even if I were, I couldn't talk about it."

Nick was cautious not to mention anything about the investigation into Fr. Hart's murder. He knew word would spread quickly about the murder now that the two women at the church knew, but he didn't want to fan the flames — and telling Alice, who was dubbed the mouth of Chatham, would definitely fan the flames. Plus, he preferred not to say anything until they had a suspect in custody to limit the hysteria that would be sure to follow once it was announced there was a murderer in town.

Alice handed him the check and saw that it was blank. "We're running a special today: Detectives eat free."

"That's very kind of you Alice," Nick said, leaving a ten-dollar tip on the table. "Will you be at the Bleeding Seal Wednesday night for comedy night?"

The Bleeding Seal was Chatham's favorite watering hole. Located on the east end of Main Street, it was a landmark where locals and tourists came together to eat, drink, and make merry. The name of the bar was a reference to Chatham's shark problem; seals are common in the waters off Chatham and are a natural source of prey for sharks. Much like tourists, Great Whites have been flocking to Chatham for years and have left more than one seal bleeding on the shores of Lighthouse Beach. The owner of the bar, Topher Roberts, wanted to capitalize on the shark frenzy that enveloped the town of Chatham in recent years and opened the Bleeding Seal to much fanfare.

"Will Brett be there?"

Brett Dwyer was a New York City comedian who grew up in nearby Dennis, just south of Chatham. While he worked the New York clubs Thursday through Saturday, it was common for him to come back home and do some shows for tourists on the Cape.

"I hope so," Nick replied. "Funniest guy I've ever seen."

Alice thought for a minute and then said, "Yeah, I'll probably go. I could use a laugh after last weekend."

Nick's phone started to buzz. He pulled the phone out of his pocket and noticed it was Arlene calling from the station. "Sorry, Alice, I have to take this."

"No problem, Nick. See you around."

Nick left the diner and put the phone to his ear. "Hi, Arlene. If you are calling to make sure I had lunch, I'll have you know that I am just leaving Larry's PX."

"I think you better get down here now."

"Was Robert able to find anything about this Christopher Mitchell guy?"

"Some news articles, but there's been a development."

"What kind of development?"

"Like the kind of development where Mr. Mitchell just walked in here five minutes ago and asked to speak with you."

"Well ain't that something!" Nick said while opening the door to his car. "I'll be there in five minutes. Where do you guys have him?"

"We set him up in the interview room where he's currently enjoying a cup of coffee. There's definitely something off about him, Nick."

"What do you mean?"

"He just kind of stares blankly at you, as if he is looking through you and not at you. He made me feel uncomfortable when he came in."

"Alright, let him know I will be there shortly, but I'm going to want to look at what Robert found first. Let him know I'll be back in twenty minutes."

"Will do."

After starting his car and backing out of his space, Nick made a right onto Main Street and followed that for about a mile until he came to Crowell Road. After making a left onto Crowell, he made an immediate right onto Depot Road and pulled into his designated spot in front of the station.

The police station was located to the right of the firehouse and had a great view of Veteran's Field, home of the Chatham As. While in some municipalities there was a rivalry between the police department and the fire department, the relationship between the two in Chatham was quite cordial, likely because many cops volunteered at the fire department in their off-hours.

Nick entered the building and greeted Arlene at the front desk.

"He's really fidgety," Arlene said, pointing to the closed door of the station's only interview room. "Bobby's research is on your chair. He just left, and he suggested you owe him lunch for making him wake up so early."

Nick looked at his old Seiko and said, "It's almost 2:00 p.m. — the day is half over. Tell him I'll get him a shaved ice at Chillers later this week."

Chillers was the brainchild of Nicole Miller, a single mom who took all the money she had to erect a small, cash-only roadside stand selling homemade snow cones for five dollars each. The venture was so successful that she franchised the concept and became one of Chatham's biggest success stories.

"I'm sure he'd be fine with that," Arlene replied.

Nick walked down the hall and entered the main room

of the station. It was an open design with six desks in the center of the room, one private office belonging to the captain, and a large conference room designated for staff meetings (but used more frequently as communal lunchroom).

Nick went directly to his desk, which was littered with paper. Arlene constantly gave him hell about the perpetual mess, but Nick argued that he knew were everything was and warned her not to mess with his unique filing system. He picked up the folder Robert left on his chair, flipped through the papers, and read through the headlines:

"SNAP Organizes Rally in Boston: Mitchell Arrested"

"Mitchell Points Finger at Bishop Hurley"

"Another DUI for SNAP's Mitchell"

"SNAP's Mitchell Arrested after Threatening Bishop"

This last headline caught Nick's attention. He read the article and learned that Christopher Mitchell had been arrested after sending several threatening letters to the bishop's office, the contents of which were never released to the press. Nick read through each of the other articles, noting that the most recent one had been written three years earlier. Satisfied that he knew enough about Mitchell to conducted a successful interview, he grabbed the folder and walked toward the interview room.

Nick entered the room and saw a very frail man in his fifties seated inside. When Christopher Mitchell stood to shake Nick's hand, the detective estimated he could not have been more than five feet, seven inches tall; and as Arlene did, Nick observed that the man had a difficult time making eye contact.

"Have a seat, Mr. Mitchell," Nick said.

"Thank you," Christopher replied in a soft voice,

similar to that of a young woman's.

Nick sat down and placed the folder of articles he had been carrying on the table in front of them. The suspect glanced down at the folder, and a look of concern came over his face.

"What brings you here today?" Nick asked.

"I wanted to talk with someone about Fr. Hart," Christopher replied.

Nick was familiar with an odd dynamic against guilty people; they often offered to help in investigations. Mitchell's offer to volunteer his thoughts about Fr. Hart was a source of concern. While the two women at the church knew that Fr. Hart did not die from natural causes, news of that fact had yet to travel through town. This made Nick very suspicious of the man in front of him.

Nick took an audio recorder out of his pocket, placed it on the table, and hit record. "You don't mind if I record our conversation, do you?"

The suspect squirmed uncomfortably in his chair and crossed his arms to prevent them from fidgeting. "I guess not," he replied in his soft-spoken way.

"What did you want to tell me about Fr. Hart?" Nick asked.

"I think somebody may have killed him."

"What makes you say that?"

"He had received a death threat a few days before he died and told me about it."

"What exactly was your relationship to Fr. Hart?" Nick's tone was very direct, with no room for pleasantries.

The suspect uncrossed his arms and tried his best to look the detective in the eyes. "I had been meeting with Fr. Hart regularly; he was trying to get me to come back into the Church."

Nick opened the folder in front of him, turned over one of the articles quickly so that the frail man sitting in front of him could not see the headline, and started to take notes on the back of the page.

"Is that so?"

"Do you know what SNAP is, detective?"

"Some kind of support group for abuse victims, right?"

"Yes, it stands for Survivors Network for Those Abused by Priests," Mitchell avoided the detective's eyes as he continued to speak. "When I was ten years old, I was an altar boy at St. Paul's Catholic Church in Fall River. Our pastor, Fr. John Carrier, sexually abused me over a three-year period. It led to a lot of anger within me and took years of therapy to get my life back together. I'm only telling you this because I'm the president of our local SNAP chapter."

"How many people belong to SNAP in this area?"

Mitchell folded his arms, leaned in, and looked at Nick right in the eyes. "Our last count was 120, but our local support meetings only attract a fraction of them."

Nick was stunned. He knew the abuse scandal was big, but he had no idea that so many people in the little part of Massachusetts known as Cape Cod were impacted.

"If that number sounds high to you detective, let me remind you that the Archdiocese of Boston itself has said that 7 percent of its priests were accused of abusing minors between 1950 and 2003. Do you know how many priests that equates to?"

The detective shook his head.

"A total of 162," Mitchell said emphatically. "The abuse was more widespread than most realize."

"When did you first come into contact with Fr. Hart?"

"He was assigned to the parish in Chatham about six months ago, and as president of our SNAP chapter, I got wind of it. I thought something was wrong because parishes on the Cape typically get priests on the verge of either death or retirement, so I had my suspicions that history was repeating itself and the new priest may have been a bad guy."

"So what did you do?"

"I made some calls to people back in Fall River where Fr. Hart came from, and I learned he was a bit of a radical as far as the Catholic Church goes."

"What do you mean by radical?" Nick questioned.

"Friends of mine in Fall River told me that Fr. Hart often condemned the Church for the way it handled the sexual abuse crisis. He felt it did not go far enough to punish either the priests or those in charge of them."

"That doesn't sound too radical to me — that just sounds fair."

"I agree with you, detective, but change in the Church happens over centuries, not years. That Fr. Hart was so outspoken about the abuse crisis put him at odds with the bishop's office."

"I see. When did you first meet him?"

"Not long after he arrived. I contacted him directly and introduced myself. He immediately freed his calendar up for me and agreed to meet me at my apartment."

"And what did you two talk about?"

"I could tell when I met him that Fr. Hart was not like any other priest I had ever known. His presence was very comforting, and I opened up to him about the abuse I experienced as a child and the problems I faced as a result. He listened to my story and cried with me, and afterward he apologized on behalf of the Church for what had happened to me. No priest had ever done that before."

"So after that first meeting six months ago, did you keep meeting with him?" Although Nick already knew the answer to that question, he needed to get Nick to admit to it on the recording.

"Yes, Fr. Hart and I met at least once a month."

"Why so frequently?" Nick wondered how close their relationship actually was.

"While I had put my troubles behind me, Fr. Hart knew that I was still in a lot of pain. He was aware that wounds like mine don't necessarily heal altogether. He was trying to get me to consider coming back into the Catholic Church. Fr. Hart was passionate that the Church had to be more welcoming to those it had traditionally pushed away. He said as much in his last homily yesterday."

Nick wrote a note on the piece of paper in front of him and then turned his attention back toward Mitchell.

"So you were at the church yesterday when Fr. Hart died?"

"Yes. It was actually my first Mass in over twenty years. Fr. Hart was beaming when I saw him in the vestibule before Mass."

"I'm not a Catholic, Mr. Mitchell, so please excuse my ignorance. Where is the vestibule?"

"It's the area between the doors of the church that lead outside and the doors that lead into the church. Oftentimes priests greet parishioners in the vestibule before and after Mass."

"Were you alone with Fr. Hart yesterday?"

"Not in the vestibule because there were other people coming into the church at the time, but he took me into the sacristy where we could have a moment alone."

The detective looked at Mitchell with a raised eyebrow.

"The sacristy is where the priest puts on his vestments before celebrating Mass."

"And you two were alone in the sacristy just before the service began?"

"That's right, but only for a minute."

Nick made a note of this on the paper in front of him. "Tell me about the threat Fr. Hart received."

"I met with Fr. Hart just last Friday, and he seemed distraught. When I asked him why, he said he had received a death threat the day before; somebody had called him threatening to kill him unless he abandoned the crusades he was on."

"Why do you suppose he came to you instead of going to the police?"

"He trusted me, I guess."

Nick shifted in his chair, deciding it was time to turn up the heat on the conversation. He leaned forward and opened the folder in front of him. "It seems as if you are no stranger to making threats, are you?"

Nick slid the article Bobby found about Christopher's arrest three years ago across the table. Mitchell looked down at the paper and became uncomfortable.

"What's the matter?"

Christopher was so stunned, he could barely speak. When he could finally get the words out, he said in his timid voice, "Why do you have that?"

"Just doing a little research. You were arrested for making threats to the bishop, were you not?"

"That was years ago, and I'm a different person now," he said defensively.

"And that wasn't the first time you were arrested, was it? I see you have some DUIs under your belt."

"When I was younger, before I got help, I developed a bad drinking problem. Unfortunately, most of us in SNAP had turned to self-medication to cope with the trauma of being sexually abused by someone we trusted. But I'm clean now. I've been sober for two years and four days."

"You are a pharmacist — is that right?"

"Yes. What does that have to do with anything?"

"Did you have to study chemistry in pharmacy school?"

Looking confused about where this was going, Christopher replied, "Yes, of course."

"So, for the sake of argument, could someone with your knowledge of chemistry create cyanide?"

Mitchell was taken aback by the mention of the poison.

"Of course, but what does that have to do with Fr. Hart's death?"

Just then there was a knock at the door. Christopher looked grateful for the interruption.

"Come in," Nick stated.

Arlene opened the door and stood in the doorway. "Pardon the interruption, detective, but there's a call for you."

"Who is it?"

"Fr. Peter Cossa from the bishop's office. He said it was quite urgent."

Nick turned around and looked at Christopher Mitchell threateningly. "I advise you not to go anywhere while I'm gone."

Mitchell looked at him and started to shake visibly. Nick

took this as a good sign and hoped that his one and only suspect was close to breaking. A full-out confession would save him a lot of time – and the taxpayers a lot of money — if the case did not go to trial.

Nick closed the door behind him, and Christopher heard a dead bolt engage; he was now locked in. He stood up and started pacing nervously, asking himself how things could have turned so quickly. All he wanted to do was tip off the police that Fr. Hart may have been murdered, and now he was locked in an interview room at the police station, feeling like a suspect himself.

He was only alone in the interview room for five minutes, but it felt like five hours. The silence in the room was deafening, only broken by the dead bolt on the door disengaging. Detective William "Nick" Nickerson walked back in along with two uniformed officers.

"What's this all about?" Christopher asked weakly, clearly on the brink of tears.

Nick walked into the room, motioned for Christopher to turn around, and asked him to place his hands on his head. He then began to read him his Miranda rights: "Christopher Mitchell, you have the right to remain silent. Anything you say can, and will, be used against you in a court of law . . ."

CHAPTER SEVEN

Doubts Arrives

Jimmy couldn't believe what he had done earlier in the day — rocking the boat was out of character for him. After leaving the law firm, he went straight to Grand Central Terminal and caught a New Haven Line train back to his mother's home in Norwalk, Connecticut. His mother didn't expect him home so early, and he startled her when he entered the house that afternoon. After explaining what happened at the firm, she congratulated him for "finally growing a pair of balls."

"You're not disappointed in me?" he asked.

"I was disappointed when you decided to go to law school. You've been working since you were ten years old; it's time for you to live a little," she replied.

After packing a bag, Jimmy explained that he was going to meet his old boss on the Cape to help her with a project.

"How are you going to get there? I need my car this week," his mother asked.

It's true that Jimmy didn't own a car, but he did own

something better: a single engine Cessna bequeathed to him by Rodney Peters, the detective who called him almost two years ago to help in Farrah Graham's search. He kept the plane tied down at a small airfield in Danbury, Connecticut.

"Can you give me a ride to Danbury?"

"You're going to fly there?" His mother sounded surprised.

The notion that Jimmy would get inside a small airplane would have been downright laughable just two years ago; up until that point, he was scared to death of small planes. However, Rodney Peters had helped him get over his fear of flying and then left his plane to Jimmy in his will. Over the twenty months Jimmy had owned the plane, which he named Murder One, he took flying lessons and earned his pilot's license. He had yet to take a passenger other than his instructor up in the plane; it wasn't for lack of trying, though. None of his friends, including his former employer Farrah Graham, wanted to get in a small aircraft with a pilot whose nickname was Doubts.

"Well, I can't take a train, and we only have one car. Plus they have a small airstrip right in Chatham, and flying will save time."

"Let me get my keys."

On their way to the airstrip, Jimmy called Farrah and told him he would be there by early evening. She told him she'd pick him up from the airstrip, which wasn't far from her home on Harding's Beach.

Kissing his mother on the cheek, Jimmy went into the small office and filed a flight plan to Chatham. The weather was good, and he had plenty of daylight left to make it before nightfall. After taking care of all the necessary paperwork in the office, Jimmy went outside to do a visual inspection of the plane and check fuel levels. The first thing Rodney had told him was that instruments don't always tell the truth and pilots should always check fuel levels manually. Satisfied that his plane was ready to fly, Jimmy stored his bag in the small cargo compartment and hopped into the plane.

He put on his seat belt, started the engine, and connected his microphone's headset to the plane's radio system. When he was given clearance to taxi to the runway, he used the pedals at his feet to make three right turns. Upon takeoff, Jimmy opened up the throttle, and the plane started its roll down the runway. Thirty seconds later Jimmy was airborne. After climbing a bit, he banked to the left until he met the coastline and then banked the plane to head north. He landed in Chatham an hour later.

After tying down his plane at an empty spot in the field near the runway, Jimmy went to the office to take care of the paperwork and pay the parking fee. After everything was in order, he walked outside to the parking lot, where Farrah was waiting for him in her Silver Audi SUV.

"Made it in one piece, Doubts — I'm impressed."

While he hated the nickname, he didn't mind it when Farrah called him Doubts. They had been through a lot together, and he felt as if she were the older sister he'd never had, albeit one he secretly lusted after.

"One day I'm going to get you to fly with me," Jimmy said.

"Only if there's a life on the line!" Farrah retorted.

"Where's Melody?" Jimmy asked, getting into her car.

Farrah told him what had transpired earlier.

"How many days till she cools off?"

"Probably a good four or five," Farrah responded, having increased her estimate from the one she gave her brother in the morning. "She was pretty pissed."

"So why am I here?"

"How hungry are you, Doubts?"

He hadn't eaten anything since his lunch with the law firm partner earlier that day, and he suddenly realized he was starving.

"Very."

"Good! Let's talk over dinner. Steak okay?"

"Perfect."

Farrah drove a mile down the road to Pates Steakhouse, which reminded Jimmy of the Regal Beagle, the singles bar on the 1980s sitcom *Three's Company*. Red leather booths with dark wooden tables adorned the dining room, and Jimmy was sure he stepped through a time warp upon walking through the restaurant's doors.

"I know it's a bit out-dated," Farrah admitted after reading the look on Jimmy's face, "but the steaks are amazing."

"I'll take your word for it."

After being shown to their table, the two placed a drink order and made small talk until their drinks arrived.

Farrah transitioned the conversation back to business. "Here's what I know. Yesterday a priest dropped dead at the end of Mass, and I have reason to believe he was murdered."

"Why do you think that?"

"Remember my brother, Mikey?"

"Fr. Mike — how could I forget! We met him before heading down to Ft. Lauderdale for the Sonny Michaels case. What does he have to do with it?"

"Mikey and the dead priest were friends. Someone in the bishop's office told him that the police in Chatham were opening up a murder investigation into the priest's death."

"Does your brother have any idea who would want to kill his friend?"

Farrah told Jimmy about the late Fr. Hart's girlfriend, as well as his tenuous relationship with the Diocese of Fall River. "So, jilted lover or angry employer? Season three just kind of fell into your lap, huh?"

"I've never been one to look a gift horse in the mouth."

Their conversation was interrupted by a platinum blond waitress named Molly. She reviewed the specials, which may as well have been standard menu items as they hadn't changed in over twenty-five years. After studying their menus, Farrah and Jimmy resumed their conversation.

"What do you need from me?" Jimmy asked.

"I could use your help doing some research into Fr. Hart's relationship with this mystery woman up in Wellfleet while I poke around the bishop's office."

"Or we could just let the police do their job," Jimmy said sarcastically.

Farrah frowned. She knew there was some truth to what Jimmy said, but her gut told her that the cops in Chatham might not do a thorough investigation into the case. It would behoove them to solve it quickly while the tourist season was in its infancy; a resort town with a murderer on the loose would be at risk for a decline in visitors.

"You ever see the movie Jaws, Doubts?"

"Who hasn't?"

"Do you remember why the mayor didn't want to close

the beaches even though there was a killer shark on the loose?"

"Other than the fact that the movie would have been really short if he did?"

"Seriously, Doubts. Do you remember or not?"

"Calm down," Jimmy said. "Yes, he knew that hysteria over a killer shark would mean a loss of revenue for all the local businesses. And no one would ever reelect him."

"Bingo! This could be a case of life imitating art, and you and I might be Brody and Hooper."

"Wait, I'm Brody and you're Hooper? I thought you'd be Brody because he was the leader."

Farrah replied, "Brody was the one with the nervous tendencies who sometimes doubted the decisions that were being made around him. Sound like anyone you know?"

"Point taken."

Molly came back to take their dinner order. She thought Farrah looked familiar, and it was eating her up inside not to be able to place a name with a face.

"Excuse me . . . I recognize you from somewhere, but I can't put my finger on it."

Jimmy chuckled and said, "Have you ever seen Shakespeare in Love?" Referring to Farrah constantly being mistaken for Gwyneth Paltrow, he never missed an opportunity to suggest it whenever the opportunity presented itself. Farrah kicked him under the table.

"Shut up, Doubts!" she said. Turning to Molly, she said, "My name is Farrah. Farrah Graham."

"That's it! You host that podcast. I binged on season two with all my roommates. You're like our hero!"

Farrah was getting used to her celebrity slowly. A year

ago she would have been annoyed by this interruption, but now deep inside she was starting to enjoy the attention.

"Thank you — that means a lot."

Jimmy sat there in silence. Apparently the waitress was not interested in meeting the almost-famous Jimmy Doubts.

"Did you hear about the priest who was murdered in town yesterday?" Molly asked.

The question caught Farrah off-guard. She wasn't aware it was public knowledge that Fr. Hart had been murdered.

"I heard that a priest had died, but I didn't know he was murdered." Farrah tried to play it cool to see if the waitress would provide any more information.

"Well, I really shouldn't be saying anything, but my boyfriend's mom works at the police station, and she asked him to do some Internet research on a local pharmacist who had ties to the priest. They wound up arresting him earlier today."

Having come over after Robert's mother went to work, Molly was in bed next to him when his mother called with the request to do some research on Christopher Mitchell. She and Bobby did the research together.

"Do you know the pharmacist's name?"

"Christopher Mitchell," Molly replied and went on to tell Farrah some highlights of what she and Bobby found.

"Any idea where is he now?" Farrah wanted to know if Mitchell was still being held in Chatham, or if he had been moved to another facility for booking.

"I can find out from my boyfriend. I'll text him after I put your orders in."

Molly left the table and went to a kiosk in the corner to

place Farrah and Jimmy's dinner orders. She came back a few minutes later.

"My boyfriend said he's still here in Chatham; they're keeping him overnight and plan to move him to the Barnstable County Correctional Facility in Bourne tomorrow morning. He's scheduled to be arraigned tomorrow morning at the courthouse in Barnstable."

"Thanks for looking into that for us, Molly."

Molly left the table again, and Jimmy looked at Farrah suspiciously. "What are you thinking?"

"I am thinking that this Christopher Mitchell character may need a lawyer."

"You aren't a lawyer anymore."

"If anyone at the station asks around, and I doubt they will, they'll find that I was admitted into the bar in Massachusetts."

"We're going to the police station after dinner, aren't we?"

"You're a lot smarter than you look, Doubts."

"So I've been told."

CHAPTER EIGHT

Farrah Meets Christopher

Christopher Mitchell sat in his cell, rocking back and forth, staring at the wall, and focusing on how his life had changed in the past forty-eight hours. He went from being a lapsed Catholic to accepting an invitation to come back to the Church from a priest who seemed like one of the good guys to being the chief suspect in that priest's murder. All he had wanted to do was let the police know that his friend Fr. Hart may have been murdered, and now he seemed to be the only suspect in the priest's death. As if being the victim of sexual abuse wasn't enough, he was now sitting in a jail cell for a crime he didn't commit.

After being arrested for the priest's murder, he was offered the opportunity to call a lawyer to see to his defense. Unfortunately, he had few friends in the legal community due to two unfortunate facts: His past behavior as a troublemaker gave him the reputation as a client with poor chances of victory, and — perhaps more importantly — he didn't have the means to pay a top-notch attorney. For these reasons he accepted a public defender to take on his case, and for those same reasons, he would be flabbergasted at what was about to happen.

His rocking back and forth was interrupted by the sound of a door opening down the hall and the sound of footsteps coming toward his cell. Mealtime had just ended, so Christopher figured it was someone coming to collect his meal tray. He got the shock of his life when he found out that he indeed had a visitor — one claiming to be a lawyer seeking to represent him.

"Me?" Christopher asked the guard staring at him through the cold bars of his cell.

"I personally don't know anyone who would agree to defend a priest killer," the guard, whose name was Mason, replied, "but nevertheless, there's a woman lawyer here who wants to speak with you."

Puzzled, Christopher Mitchell stood up in his cell and place his hands behind his back as he was instructed. Mason then unlocked his cell, cuffed Christopher's hands, and escorted the prisoner down the hall to a conference room, where Farrah Graham was seated and waiting for him. Once the chain securing Christopher's wrists were secured to the desk by Mason, the guard left the room, allowing Christopher and his mystery attorney to have a private conversation.

Christopher studied Farrah suspiciously. He thought she looked familiar but couldn't place her face.

"Who are you?"

Farrah stared at him intently. "My name is Farrah Graham, and I am interested in your case," she replied, attempting to sound reserved. She was simply on a fact-finding mission and didn't want to come across as overly eager to take on his case.

After hearing her name, Christopher became visibly upset.

"I've heard your name. You're that podcaster who looks into the wrongly accused; if I came across your radar screen, I must be in pretty bad shape."

Farrah thought for a minute before responding; she observed how upset and fragile Christopher was and didn't want to do anything to upset him even more. She decided to be completely transparent with him.

"I happened to be vacationing up here and saw the priest die on the altar. I also know that the police in this town are going to want to bring closure to this case quickly. When I heard of your arrest, I wanted to meet you myself to determine whether or not you might be someone worth defending."

"I had nothing to do with Fr. Hart's death. He was one of my only friends; in fact, he came to me a few days ago claiming that someone had sent him death threats."

"Why would he come to you?" Farrah asked.

Christopher then relayed his experiences with the Church over the years, including his abuse at the hands of his parish priest over two decades ago and Fr. Hart's attempt to bring him back into the flock. "I guess it was his way of opening up to me, to help me earn his trust."

Farrah was very intuitive when it came to people, and over the course of their brief time together, she concluded that Christopher Mitchell most likely had nothing to do with Fr. Hart's death. It was true that he seemed slightly off emotionally, but Farrah had to remind herself that he was the victim of child sexual abuse, and after experiencing trauma like that it was understandable someone would be outside the range of normal, whatever normal was. Yes, he's unstable, but he's not a killer, she thought.

"Do you have any idea who may have wanted to hurt Fr. Hart?"

Farrah's question implied that she was open to the possibility that Christopher was innocent, and he allowed himself to feel a small glimmer of hope for the first time since being arrested earlier that afternoon.

"I know he wasn't too popular in the bishop's office, but aside from the feathers he would ruffle in Fall River, I don't know of anyone here who would want to hurt him."

Farrah was hoping for something more. The thought of a conspiracy within the diocese would certainly make for a good story, but she felt it was improbable someone in the church was involved with the priest's death.

"And just so I know, Christopher, where were you when the priest died?"

"I was in the church; it was the first Mass I have attended in over twenty years."

"And did you have any chance to see Fr. Hart before Mass?"

"I stopped by to see him in the vestibule right before Mass, and then we talked for a few minutes in the sacristy. He gave me a big hug."

"So you were alone with him before Mass. That's not good."

"Tell me something I don't know. Between that and my history of writing threatening letters to those in the Church hierarchy, Detective Nickerson thinks this is an open and shut case. But I didn't do it."

Farrah tapped her pen on the table as she thought. "Christopher, I'm afraid that our only hope of getting you out of here is for us to find out who really killed Fr. Hart."

The thought of spending more time confined in jail was almost too much for him to handle. "What about bail?"

"You're supposed to be arraigned at the courthouse in Bourne tomorrow. Tell your public defender that you wish to enter a plea of not guilty. After that, bail, if offered, will be set."

Christopher looked stunned for two reasons; he thought Farrah would be his lawyer and shuddered at the thought of not being granted bail. "What do you mean, 'if offered?' I can't spend time in prison – I'll die in there."

Because of his background as an abuse victim, Christopher was frightened he would be a target for other inmates, and he couldn't bear the thought of being abused again.

"There's no telling what the judge will decide. Whether or not he or she offers bail will depend on how strongly the prosecution feels you are a threat to others."

"Aren't you going to be there tomorrow as my lawyer?"

"I don't practice law anymore. My first priority will be to find the person who really killed Fr. Hart. Please, just hang in there, and I'll advise your court-appointed attorney to the best of my ability."

Farrah's words did nothing to comfort Christopher. It felt as though he was going deeper and deeper into a hole he could not climb out of.

A knock on the door meant that Farrah's time with Christopher had come to an end. While his hands were being un-cuffed from the table and then re-cuffed behind his back, Farrah couldn't help but see that Christopher Mitchell was as tormented a man as she had ever met. She worried about what the next few days would bring. The more fragile something is, the more likely it is to shatter.

CHAPTER NINE

A Confrontation

Jimmy Doubts sat in the waiting room at the police station while Farrah conducted her interview with Christopher Mitchell. The TV in the waiting room was tuned to the World Series of Poker, and Jimmy thought he just might be stuck in one of Dante's rings of hell. The only thing more boring than watching fat guys play poker on TV was watching someone else fishing; he was less than thrilled to find that coming up next was a show called Bass Masters.

Letting out an audible sigh, Jimmy turned his attention to the main desk where Arlene, the woman who greeted him and Farrah, was talking to a tall, white-haired man wearing a brown suit. While it was well after hours, Arlene refused to leave until all her "boys" had gone home for the evening, and Detective William "Nick" Nickerson refused to leave until after his collar's attorney left.

Eager to hear what they were talking about, Jimmy decided get a cup of water from the dispenser by the door to the waiting room. They could be talking about rhubarb pie for all he knew, but at least it would be more exciting than watching fat dudes wearing dark sunglasses indoors play poker.

"Did he call the attorney?" the man asked.

"No, Nick, he hasn't called anyone since we booked him.

Wanting to hear more of the conversation, Jimmy drank a second cup of water, and then a third.

"Then how would this attorney know he was here? We have yet to make it public that Fr. Hart was murdered, and we certainly haven't let it slip that Christopher Mitchell was arrested for it. How the hell did some popular podcaster attorney find out about it?"

"Beats me, Nick, but why don't you ask that fella in the waiting room? He came in with her."

Jimmy finished a fourth cup of water and made a beeline back for his seat when he saw the man leave the front desk and walk toward the waiting room. Suddenly watching fat men play poker on TV didn't seem so bad.

Detective Nickerson entered the waiting room and sat right in front of Jimmy, who feigned interest in the play-by-play going on about a river card — whatever that was.

"Are you with Farrah Graham?"

"Excuse me?" Jimmy said, pretending to be caught up with the action on the TV.

Nick got up and turned the TV off. "Are. You. With. Farrah. Graham?" Nick asked slowly and deliberately, with the intention of intimidating Jimmy. It worked. Jimmy started squirming in his chair, partly as a result of feeling intimidated, and partly because the four cups of water he drank were putting pressure on his bladder.

"Yes, Farrah and I work together. I'm a law school

student, and she is . . ."

"I know exactly who she is," Nick retorted. "What I want to know is why she is here in Chatham."

"She has a house here, right on Harding's Beach. Her brother is a priest who was friends with Fr. Hart – someone in the diocese told him Fr. Hart's death was going to be investigated as a murder and he asked Farrah to look into it."

Jimmy was nervous and, as such, was talking quickly. He took a few deep breaths to try to regain his composure, but it wasn't working.

The detective thought that Jimmy's explanation was plausible, but it still didn't explain how they knew that someone was arrested for the priest's murder. The only way to find out was to ask directly; Nick wasn't one for games or Jedi mind tricks.

"That's all well and good, but how did you know we arrested someone in the priest's death? We haven't told anyone about that yet, not even anyone in the bishop's office." While he said this, Nick looked intently into Jimmy's eyes.

"We were having dinner at a restaurant in town, and after our waitress found out who Farrah was, she let it slip that someone had been arrested in the murder of a priest. We were surprised that she knew the priest was murdered, so we asked her how she knew. She told us that her boyfriend's mother works here, and the boyfriend was asked to do some digging on the guy you locked up."

Nick looked away from Jimmy toward the desk where Arlene was sitting. He shook his head but quickly realized that if he hadn't asked for her son's help in finding information on Christopher Mitchell, he might not have made an arrest.

"I see." Nick was eager to know what Christopher and Farrah talked about, but he knew the conversation was protected by attorney-client privilege. He was about to ask Jimmy another question when Farrah walked into the waiting room.

"Making friends, Doubts?"

Nick got up and walked toward Farrah.

"Mrs. Graham, my name is William Nickerson, and I was the one who arrested Christopher Mitchell for the death of Fr. Gregory Hart."

The detective's tone was courteous, but Farrah could detect a hint of anger in it. He over-pronounced his words and talked through his teeth, which Farrah took to mean that he didn't appreciate the wrench her presence caused his investigation.

Farrah, sensing she wasn't about to make a new best friend, corrected the detective's assumption that she was married. "Ms. Graham, not Mrs., and you've got the wrong man in that cell."

"Excuse me?"

"I'm not married," Farrah quipped.

"Got it," Nick responded. "Why do you say we have the wrong man in the cell?"

"Look, Detective Nickerson . . ."

"Call me Nick," the detective interrupted.

"Why? I thought your name was William."

"Everyone calls me Nick."

"Well, everyone calls me Farrah."

This exchange caused Jimmy to laugh and, while doing so, he realized just how badly he needed to go to the rest room. He began to fidget with his legs and let out a grunt.

"Why are you dancing, Doubts?"

"I have to pee."

Farrah knew of Jimmy's notoriously small bladder; it had gotten them into trouble during the Sonny Michaels case when a casual conversation in a men's room tipped off a hit man about Farrah's identity.

The detective interjected, "Go down that hall, make a left, and it's the second door on your right."

Jimmy walked stiffly out the door, and the detective turned his attention back to Farrah. "You were saying?"

"Look, I know you are probably under pressure to solve this murder, but I'm telling you Christopher Mitchell is not your guy."

"And why are you so sure? Because he told you?"

"No, because he had no motive."

"No motive? He's been arrested for threatening priests before!"

"His ire was directed toward Church hierarchy, not local priests. In that regard, both Christopher and Fr. Hart were very similar."

"What do you mean?"

"Fr. Hart was a reformer. He upset the powers that be in Fall River over his outspokenness on the abuse scandal as well about other things. That's the whole reason he was sent to Chatham to begin with."

This was news to the detective, yet he stood firm. "Mitchell himself said he was alone with the priest just before Mass yesterday morning."

"Access doesn't prove anything. I am sure a lot of people saw him before Mass yesterday. You are going to need something more than that to make a case against Christopher Mitchell."

Nick knew that sooner or later Farrah would find out about the formal cause of death, so he reasoned it couldn't hurt to mention it now.

"According to the medical examiner, Fr. Hart died from cyanide poisoning. Only someone with an advanced degree in chemistry could create that poison and, in case you didn't know, Christopher Mitchell is a pharmacist. Adding that to the fact he has a history of making threats to men of the cloth, it's reasonable to assume we got our guy."

Farrah was stymied; the detective's argument was sound from a legal perspective, and the reveal of cyanide poisoning as the cause of death was a bombshell. Farrah wondered if she could have misjudged Christopher Mitchell simply because she wanted to believe that he didn't kill Fr. Hart.

"What if you are wrong?"

"I'm not wrong, Ms. Graham. And I suggest that you turn your attention to enjoying your vacation here in Chatham and not getting involved in this case which, as of tomorrow morning's arraignment, should be closed from our point of view."

Farrah didn't appreciate anyone telling her what to do, but she knew that continuing to push the detective's buttons wasn't going to help convince him that he had the wrong person in custody. She tried a different tactic. "You are right, detective, I shouldn't get involved in this case. I should just go back to enjoying my vacation."

Jimmy Doubts entered the waiting room and caught the end of Farrah's sentence. He was surprised that his boss was conceding so quickly.

"That's a good idea, Ms. Graham," the detective said

in a kinder tone than before. "Perhaps after all of this is over, you would like to have a drink with me sometime?"

Farrah was floored; the detective went from arguing with her about Christopher Mitchell's innocence to flirting with her in just a few seconds. While she was livid at his conceit, she decided to give him a false sense of security with the hope that it could help her manipulate him later.

"Maybe," she said, while biting her lip and winking at him. If he were like every other man she knew, the detective would let the wrong head do the thinking and not consider for a moment that she gave up too quickly.

Jimmy was beyond confused as to what was happening, and the expression on his face said as much.

"Come on, Doubts, we'd better call it a night."

Farrah walked out of the waiting room, and Jimmy followed. Detective William "Nick" Nickerson remained in the waiting room, feeling good about himself.

The feeling wouldn't last long.

CHAPTER TEN

The Death of Christopher Mitchell

Christopher Mitchell sat in his cell, once again rocking back and forth; he knew that sleep wouldn't come anytime soon and he would have to suffer in silence and darkness with his thoughts. That's when the ghosts that haunted him for so many years started to come back.

The abuse started when he was ten years old, the same year his father died of liver cancer. After the textile mill where he worked closed due to pressure from foreign competition, Charles Mitchell took to drowning his sorrows in a half a gallon of whiskey every day. After his passing, Christopher's mother, Karen, turned to their local parish for help, and Fr. Carrier was happy to oblige.

At first Fr. Carrier was a lifesaver to Christopher and his mother; he helped stock their pantry with donations from the parish and covered the tuition so that Christopher could stay in the school attached to the church. Months later, though, things started to change.

Come spring, Fr. Carrier asked Christopher's mother if the boy would like to stop by the rectory after school to earn some money taking care of the yard work. At first Christopher was excited to help, but then things started to get weird. After he finished his work outside, Fr. Carrier would invite Christopher into the rectory to have a cold drink and wait for his mother to pick him up. Christopher didn't think much of it when the priest started telling him dirty jokes because it made him feel a bit more grown up. However, not long after that Fr. Carrier started exposing Christopher to pornography, telling him it was their little secret. This made Christopher uncomfortable, and he asked his mother if he could stop working at the rectory. She said no because, after all, the family needed the little money Christopher was making and they couldn't afford to lose the donations they had come to depend on from Fr. Carrier.

On a particularly hot day, the priest offered Christopher a drink, and Christopher thought it tasted funny. It turns out that Fr. Carrier had spiked it with alcohol. Sensing that the boy's defenses were down, Fr. Carrier asked Christopher to pleasure him orally. When Christopher refused, the priest forced himself on the boy and raped him. Afterward he warned Christopher not to tell his mother — or anyone else for that matter.

Too ashamed to tell anyone, and afraid that his family wouldn't survive without the meager income he was bringing in, Christopher succumbed to the abuse, which went on for another two years until Fr. Carrier was transferred to another parish in the diocese. While the abuse had stopped, the damage had already been done. Christopher withdrew from his friends, started failing in school, and began experimenting with drugs and alcohol to numb the pain the trauma of abuse left behind.

For a period of time, Christopher was fixated on killing himself and attempted to take his life by overdosing on over-the-counter sleeping pills. After swallowing an entire bottle, though, he ran to the bathroom, stuck his fingers down his throat, and vomited them up. He never told anybody about this episode, another secret he kept hidden.

Ironically, he didn't begin to feel better until the sexual abuse scandal broke and he realized that he wasn't alone. He started attending survivor's meetings and, after years of therapy, he was able to turn his life around. He finished high school, went to college, and became a pharmacist.

While he was in a better place emotionally, he was still quite fragile and had a hard time relating to other people. Especially with women, he came across as weak and frail.

He also remained angry at the Church for its role in the abuse scandal. That it would simply move priests around after requiring them to get psychological treatment was inexcusable. He felt as if those with power in the Church were just as guilty as the abusers; they were aware of what was happening and could have put a stop to it but chose not to. Christopher became an outspoken critic of the Catholic Church.

Now, sitting alone in a cold, dark jail cell, the dark thoughts that haunted him years ago returned. He simply couldn't face the prospect of spending his life locked up in prison. He heard stories about the abuse weaker inmates suffered at the hands of other prisoners, and the prospect was too much to bear. The thought of suicide came back like an unwelcome relative he thought he'd seen the last of years ago. It was now three o'clock in the morning, and Christopher Mitchell started to panic.

There was no one else in the neighboring cells; Chatham, Massachusetts, after all, wasn't exactly known for its high crime rate. As Christopher pondered his options, he became more and more desperate. At mealtime, he had been given a plastic "spork" to eat with, but it wasn't sturdy enough to use as a method of self-mutilation, much less self-destruction. Feeling hopeless, an answer came to him as he sat on his bed: his sheets.

After being in the dark for so long, his eyes had adjusted to the lack of light. He noticed that his ceiling was actually made out of steel bars; this amounted to him being in a glorified cage. With the intensity of a man possessed, he stripped the sheet off his bed and made it into a noose. He pushed the desk in the corner of his cell to the center of the room and, while standing on it, attached the noose to one of the top bars. Now trembling, Christopher Mitchell placed his head through the makeshift noose and tightened it until it was snug against his neck. While a single tear ran down his cheek, he kicked the desk out from under him.

Since he wasn't that high in the air, the force of his fall wasn't strong enough to break his neck, but it was enough to cut off his airway. After a few minutes of intense suffering, Christopher started to blackout. Then the struggling stopped, and he was finally at peace.

He wouldn't be found until 6:30 later that morning when a guard came to bring his breakfast. The guard dropped the tray when she saw Christopher, whose bloated face was more purple than blue, swinging in the middle of his cell from the bedsheet noose. The sight of his tongue protruding from his mouth would give her nightmares for years to come.

She immediately ran down the hall, threw up her breakfast, and went next door to the fire department where the paramedics on call sprinted over to see if there was anything they could do. After seeing the state of his body, the paramedics determined that he was deader than a doornail and called the medical examiner who, in turn, called Detective Nickerson.

The detective believed wholeheartedly that Mitchell's suicide was an admission of guilt.

"I guess he couldn't bear the thought of life in prison," Nick said to the medical examiner.

Charles Stemper wasn't paying attention to the detective as he had other things on his mind. "Always hard to tell with these things, but I'd say he did it three to five hours ago."

"Excuse me?" the detective asked.

"I'd say he did it after midnight. You may want to look into a different type of cell to prevent this sort of thing from happening again."

"If his guilt got the better of him, I'm glad he did it," Nick said coldly. "It will save me a lot of time and the taxpayers a lot of money."

"Even before I got the call about Mitchell this morning," Stemper said, "you were going to be my first call."

"Why's that?"

"Because I don't think he did it."

Floored, Nick questioned, "Really?"

"Yep. We found trace amounts of poison in the cruet used to hold the sacramental wine."

"So?"

"So the person who poisoned the priest had to have

access to the wine before Mass."

Nick thought back to Christopher Mitchell telling him yesterday that he saw the priest just before Mass. A person looking to spike the wine with poison would have had to have been in the church much earlier.

"Nick, you got the wrong guy."

Detective William "Nick" Nickerson now had a bigger problem on his hands than he did yesterday. Instead of one death investigation, he now had two.

CHAPTER ELEVEN

A Confession

Bishop Robert Hurley sat alone in a confessional. While he had a few priests under him assigned to the Cathedral in Fall River who could hear midweek confessions, doing so helped him stay close to his flock and served as a reminder of why he became a priest to begin with. If he was being true to himself, though, that morning he was enjoying the quiet time.

Generally speaking Tuesday mornings were not popular days for confessions. The past six Tuesdays Bishop Hurley had only heard one confession; the real action happened on Saturday afternoons before the evening vigil where, on any given Saturday, the bishop listened as people confessed to drunkenness, impure thoughts, and adultery. Little did he know that in ten minutes, his quiet morning was going to change.

Before the fireworks began, though, Bishop Hurley had time to reflect on his path to religious life; something he did more frequently now that he was in his sixties. As a young child, he had been different than other boys his age.

While other boys were content pursuing sports or girls, Robert Hurley was more scholarly and introspective. His father was tough on him about this; as an only son, Robert was expected to be an athlete like his father. That Robert favored the arts was a bone of contention between them.

The future bishop attended Trinity High School in the upscale town of Newton, Massachusetts, and had been offered a full scholarship to attend another school run by the Jesuits in nearby Chestnut Hill — Boston College. It was there that he double-majored in theology and psychology, and it was during this time that he started to contemplate religious life. Upon his graduation Robert entered a seminary in Fall River, Massachusetts, where he spent the first year discerning his calling. He had never second-guessed it and was ordained a priest seven years later after earning advanced degrees in theology and counseling.

Thinking back on his almost forty years of religious life, Bishop Hurley remembered being the happiest during his first assignment at St. Cecilia's, a small parish in the town of Fall River, not too far from where he was right now. In contrast to the Cathedral he currently presided over, St. Cecilia Parish had been a poor parish serving the needs of mostly blue-collar workers and immigrants. While there he performed countless baptisms and celebrated weddings and, on the more sorrowful side of life, administered last rights and presided over funerals.

Back then his free time was spent serving those in need, whether it was making a house call to a family with a child too sick to attend Mass or walking the halls of the hospital, visiting sick parishioners and praying with anyone who asked. Those were the days, he thought to himself. In contrast, now his time was filled with addressing the administrative needs of the diocese. His days were filled with budget meetings, disciplinarily procedures, and meetings to decide which school or parish to close next. He longed for the old days.

Robert Hurley never had goals to be part of the Church hierarchy, but his superiors had other intentions. In Hurley they saw a leader, someone who could speak with conviction and make decisions with authority. His joyous nature and charisma were appealing to parishioners, higher-ups, and especially young men discerning a call to the priesthood. That there were no rumors of impropriety with members of the same or opposite sex also worked in his favor; while celibacy was a promise that priests made, it was widely accepted in religious circles that keeping that promise was more myth than fact.

Father Robert Hurley was given the honorary title of Monsignor shortly after his fortieth birthday. When he turned forty-five years old, the pope himself appointed him bishop of the Fall River diocese. Now sixty-five, there were some who believed Bishop Robert Hurley might very well become the first pope from North America. While there was a certain amount of pride that came with his current state, Bishop Hurley worked hard to keep it in check. Part of doing so was spending time each week listening to confessions and counseling his flock.

He looked at his watch and saw there were only fifteen minutes left before he would stop hearing confessions for the day; if history was a reliable guide, it was highly unlikely that someone would walk into his confessional between now and then.

He was wrong.

At five minutes before nine in the morning, he heard the door to the church open. A moment later he heard the door to the confessional open, and someone entered. The penitent began with the customary, "Bless me, Father, for I have sinned. It has been one week since my last confession."

Bishop Hurley recognized the voice immediately, and an ache formed in the pit of his stomach. *Oh no*, he thought.

While he had heard the confessions of this person only twice before, both times murder had been on the menu.

In both cases the penitent in question believed that absolution from the highest-ranking priest in the area was required due to the severity of the sin confessed. Unless His Holiness the pope was visiting, Bishop Hurley was the only one who could fit bill. In this situation, though, there was another reason for confessing to the bishop: It was ordered by the mastermind behind Fr. Hart's death.

The bishop couldn't put the voice to a face, but he was confident that the person kneeling on the other side of the screen was not a member of his parish.

Due to the seal of confession, Bishop Hurley had been unable to tell the authorities that he had counseled a murderer. Doing so would be grounds for immediate excommunication, so powerful was the seal of confession.

"Tell me your sins, my child," Bishop Hurley said in spite of the large lump forming in his throat.

"Last week," the penitent began, "I killed a man who I believed was a danger to me and my community, but I guess you could say that I acted in self-defense."

Bishop Hurley was silent for a moment. "The taking of a life is a grave sin. Have you considered turning yourself into the authorities?"

"A suspect has been arrested. Someone named Christopher Mitchell."

Bishop Hurley gasped audibly. This was unexpected and concerning; his mouth went dry.

"Did you know him, Father?"

Bishop Hurley remained silent. The person continued, "Unfortunately, he took his own life early this morning. The police are taking that as an admission of guilt, so I see no need to make their lives any more interesting."

"That would be a lie of omission. Are you confessing that as well?"

"Don't you see? I helped solve a problem for both of us; I got rid of a troublesome priest for you as well as another person who was a thorn in your side. You should be thanking me, don't you think?"

The penitent knew things that weren't common knowledge, and Bishop Hurley wondered how. He was also frightened by the coldness that emanated from this person who seemed to believe that what had been done was anything but murder.

"If it's all the same to you, Father, I must be going now."

"I cannot offer you absolution for your sins because you have not expressed sincere contrition."

While the penitent was, in fact, a deeply religious person, absolution was not today's objective.

After the penitent left the confessional, Bishop Hurley waited to hear the doors of the cathedral open and close. Before leaving the confessional himself, he listened for the faint sound of an engine turning over and a car driving away. He then returned to the rectory, asked his secretary to clear his calendar of evening obligations, and went straight to his room where he prayed for a while before retiring for the evening.

Bishop Hurley was a careful planner, but a plan he had recently hatched took a left turn with the suicide of Christopher Mitchell. He felt the pangs of regret settling in and turned to his bed for comfort.

It would be some time before he would emerge from his bedroom.

CHAPTER TWELVE

Mistakes were Made

After leaving the police station the evening before, Farrah and Jimmy decided it would be wise to get a good night's sleep. Farrah's house had three bedrooms in addition to the master, and Jimmy selected one on the first floor with a view of the ocean. He slept like a rock and woke up to the smell of Farrah frying bacon in the kitchen.

As they were eating breakfast, Farrah told Jimmy that she wanted to keep a low profile; she didn't want to ruffle the feathers of the local police department any more than she already had. She knew that it was always better to cooperate with police than to work against them, so she explained to Jimmy that they were going to take the day off. Her plan was to lay low for a while and wait for Detective Nickerson come to her for help should he need it.

After retrieving the local newspaper from her driveway, Farrah got the shock of her life when she read the lead article on the front page: "Pharmacist Accused of Killing

Priest Commits Suicide." The article went on to say that Christopher Mitchell had been arrested for the murder of Fr. Hart and the police viewed his suicide as an admission of guilt.

"Do you know of any firms in the area that might need a summer intern?" Jimmy asked.

Still stunned over what she had just read, Farrah didn't even hear Jimmy's question. "Did you say something, Doubts?"

"Don't worry about it."

Before Farrah could respond, a knock at her door caused Mulder to start barking. She opened the door to find tall, white-haired Detective Nickerson jumping away from the doorstep upon being confronted by Mulder.

"What's the matter, Detective, don't you like dogs?"

"I like dogs plenty," the detective said, "but dogs don't like me. Can you calm him down — and can I come in?"

"Doubts," Farrah called into the kitchen, "can you take Mulder upstairs and put him in my bedroom?"

"Who's here?" Jimmy asked.

"Detective Nickerson has paid us a visit."

Jimmy called Mulder, and the dog came right to him. The two went upstairs, and Jimmy left him in Farrah's room where he jumped up onto the bed and curled up next to Scully, Farrah's orange-haired cat. Back in the kitchen he found Detective Nickerson sitting at the table with a steaming cup of coffee in front of him.

"Cream and sugar, Detective Nickerson?"

"No. But you can just call me Nick," he replied.

"I'm dying to know why you are here, Nick, but first tell me how you found out where I was staying. My home was purchased in the name of an LLC, and none of my personal mail is sent here."

"That's easy — he told me last night in the waiting room at the station." Nick said, pointing directly at Jimmy.

Farrah looked at him and raised an eyebrow.

"What?" Jimmy asked. "The guy was squeezing me for information and I didn't know that your summerhouse was akin to a state secret."

The detective interrupted. "Besides, this is a small town. It wouldn't have taken me long to figure it out."

"Fair enough," Farrah said, letting Jimmy off the hook. "To what do we owe the pleasure of your company?"

Nick picked up the newspaper in front of him and handed it to Farrah. "This is why I am here."

"Based on that article it seems as if your case is open and shut. I believe you were the one quoted as saying that you are taking his suicide as an admission of guilt, or were you misquoted?"

"That was actually a well-crafted diversion; I no longer believe that Christopher Mitchell killed Fr. Hart." Nick went on to explain what Charles Stemper, the medical examiner, told him earlier that day. "I figured that positioning the suicide as an admission of guilt would give the real killer a false sense of security while we hunted him down."

Farrah contemplated what the detective had just told her, and suddenly the expression on her face changed as if a lightbulb went on in her head. "Let me guess, everyone in town knows you, and you want to be quieter about this investigation."

Nick took a deep breath as though he were swallowing his pride along with the air. "I know we got off on the wrong foot last night, but you are the only person who can help, given the circumstances. Everyone knows everyone in this town. If I go around asking questions, people will talk."

"And if I go around asking questions?"

"People will think you are doing research on another season of your show."

"Won't that raise suspicion that I'm not satisfied with your investigation?"

"It's really our only option if we want to find out who killed Fr. Hart. Besides, if it becomes an issue, I will publicly denounce you, thereby giving the killer more of a false sense of security." Nick ran his fingers through the white hair that fell in front of his eyes. "Give it some thought."

Farrah had made up her mind immediately, but she wanted to string the detective along as a consequence for being so rude to her last night, and then having the nerve to ask her out.

"I don't know detective; I was just starting to enjoy my vacation. In fact, Jimmy and I were going to go on a tour of Chatham Light today, weren't we?"

As book smart as Jimmy was, he was not great at improvisation. "I don't remember you say anything about that, Farrah. Besides, I heard the lighthouse only has tours on Wednesdays."

Detective Nickerson laughed.

Farrah rolled her eyes. "You are piece of work, Doubts."

"Aren't you the least bit curious about who would want to kill a priest?"

Farrah was beyond curious, and more than that, she had to keep the promise she made to her brother — that she would find his friend's killer.

"If I'm going to do this, it will be important that you and I aren't seen together," Farrah said.

"Agreed. But we'll need to keep the lines of communication open," Nick responded.

"How about you leave messages for each other in the classified section of the local paper?" Jimmy suggested.

"Or we could just text each other," Farrah said, stating the obvious.

"I was thinking along the same lines," Nick said. "You've seen one too many movies, kid."

Farrah was eager to get her investigation under way so she stood up, assuming the detective would follow her lead and do the same. She was surprised when he remained seated.

"If that's all, detective, I'd like to get my day started."

"Aren't we going to discuss a plan of attack?" Nick asked.

"If we are doing this, we are doing it my way. This is not a democracy, nor is it a collaboration. I'll keep you updated on my progress, but I'm not interested in your point of view regarding my strategies and tactics. Is that understood?"

Detective Nickerson sat there with his mouth open. He clearly had underestimated this attractive woman.

"I think she's telling you it's time to leave now, detective," Jimmy Doubts said. "It isn't personal — it's just business."

"Very well," Nick said, standing up. Before leaving, he gave Farrah his phone number, and she sent a text message from her phone to his so he would have her number.

Before closing the door behind him, Nick turned and asked, "Can you drop me a text tonight to let me know how you are progressing?"

"If I feel like it," Farrah said and closed the door. She had to stifle a laugh as she did so.

"Come on, Doubts, vacation is over! We have some work to do."

CHAPTER THIRTEEN

A Meeting Comes to Order

While Farrah and Detective Nickerson were making a deal, The Order of John the **XXIII** was convened at their private club in Fall River. Membership in the Order was by invitation only, and the qualifications of membership were quite strict; one had to be male, a cradle Catholic – no converts allowed — and one's political and social views must be conservative. These alone were not difficult criteria; it was the next that was the kicker: One had to be able to trace one's lineage back to a prominent family in medieval Europe, all the way back to the time of the great schism in the Church. Finally, a prospective member had to believe that the Church was wrong in its decision to move forward with the reforms of Vatican II. It was this last requirement that terminated most prospects; not that they even knew they were up for membership – all of this was carried out in secret.

Once a man's name was nominated by another member, the vetting process began. The first part of the process involved an audit to identify a prospect's net worth; the Order only wanted wealthy individuals in its ranks. The work it carried out was expensive and the members couldn't exactly conduct fund-raising campaigns. The auditing team would pour over years of a prospect's tax returns and financial statements obtained by the Order's intelligence wing. In addition to calculating net worth, the other purpose of the audit was to determine whether or not the prospect made any donations to organizations, charities, or political candidates that the Order deemed antithetical to its views. Most prospects cleared this hurdle with ease, given that their names had been nominated by a like-minded individual who knew the prospect personally. It was the second level of the vetting process most men had difficulty passing.

After one cleared the financial audit, the social audit began. A member of the Order was assigned to tail the prospect for no less than six months to make sure he did not cavort with any questionable elements of society. If married, the Order wanted to ensure that the prospect was living his vows; therefore, anyone having an extramarital affair was no longer considered for membership. This is where many prospects' names were crossed off the list; if a man couldn't keep a promise to his wife that he made before God, he could not be trusted with the secrets of the Order.

After a prospect cleared the social audit, a DNA test was administered to trace ancestry. If a prospect made it this far, one final test was given. Two members of the order would casually approach a prospect after Mass and nonchalantly try to ascertain his view on the Second Vatican Council. Typically they would pose it as a friendly tiebreaker to an argument, saying, "My friend and I need help settling a bet. He believes that Vatican II was good for the Church, but I think otherwise — who do you think is right?" Based on the response given, a prospect was earmarked to receive a bid to join the order or removed from consideration.

Bids were always delivered at night by an executive member of the Order. He would approach the prospect with a business opportunity and an invitation to discuss it in more detail over dinner at an exclusive members' only club owned by the Order. This was carried out very much like a seduction; the evening started with cocktails at the club's bar, where the prospect observed a who's who of the city's elite. Next came dinner in a "white-gloved" dining room, where the prospect was treated to a five-course meal. After dinner, the conversation moved to the club's game room; here the true intentions of the evening were divulged over a game of billiards.

While prospects were typically caught off guard when asked to join the Order, most considered it an honor. When they accepted their bid, they were immediately asked to remove their shoes as a sign of humility and agree to be blindfolded. The member of the Order who had suggested the prospect for membership would then lead him to the Order's temple, which was accessed via a hidden doorway through the game room of the club. Once in the temple, the prospect, still blindfolded, experienced a virtual tour of the old cities of Rome and Avignon. After the tour ended, the prospect was left in the middle of the room, where he was asked to state his name and formally request admission to the Order. After making a profession of faith and swearing allegiance to the Order — which included a blood oath and a promise to both die for as well as kill for the Order — the prospect's blindfold was removed, and he was welcomed as an official member.

Fr. Cossa, Chancellor of the Diocese of Fall River and founder of the order, was its senior-most member, and he ran every meeting. The group always convened midweek, since Fr. Cossa's other responsibilities kept him quite busy on the weekends.

Attendance at all meetings was mandatory; not showing up was considered a voluntary resignation from the Order, upon which the former member would be ostracized from his former brothers. Fr. Cossa was pleased to see he had 100 percent of the sixty-six members assembled that afternoon. They were arranged along a very large U-shaped table; as leader of the group, Fr. Cossa sat alone in front of the opening of the U. To his left was the Master of Ceremonies, and to his right was the Master of Finances. Directly in front of him was the Procurator, the member assigned to maintain order and discipline, both inside and outside of meetings. Two men in robes served as guards at the only door into and out of the room.

Before officially calling the meeting to order, Fr. Cossa turned to the Master of Ceremonies to lead the group through a brief ritual where members, in unison, restated the oath they took upon initiation. After that was concluded, everyone took their seats, and Fr. Cossa banged his gavel down three times.

"I formally call this meeting of The Order of Pope John the XXIII to order at 12:00 Eastern Standard Time on Tuesday, July 2nd, 2016. Mr. Secretary, please read the minutes from our last meeting."

Each meeting followed Robert's Rules of Order, and the first order of business was to read the minutes from the last meeting, invite a motion to pass them, and then vote as a group.

"Our last meeting was held on Tuesday, May 24th, and the following items were discussed: troublesome news coming out of Chatham, concerns about Church leadership in Fall River, and fund-raising ideas for the Republican candidate for president of the United States. A motion was presented to table the discussion on leadership in Fall River and fund-raising ideas so the group could devote its time and energy on the matter in Chatham. The motion was seconded and passed by a two-thirds majority."

"Motion to accept the minutes," came a voice from the left side of the table.

"Seconded," came a voice from the right.

The Procurator said, "All in favor of passing the minutes from the last meeting, say aye."

The motion passed by a unanimous vote.

Fr. Cossa banged his gavel down again. "Do we have any old business we wish to discuss?"

"Motion to move directly to new business and table old business so we may discuss the events that have transpired in Chatham," came a voice from the left side of the table.

"Seconded," came a voice from the right.

Fr Cossa spoke up. "All in favor, say aye."

The motion passed unanimously. All were eager to hear their leader's views on Fr. Hart's untimely death. During their last meeting, they had spoken about Fr. Hart, and the damage he was causing the Catholic Church, at great length. They were particularly concerned that his podcast and blog were reaching a critical mass of people who were demanding reform in the Church, and they had openly debated about how to put an end to it.

"Very well. As you all know, last Sunday Fr. Gregory Hart dropped dead during the closing prayer during the 10:00 a.m. Mass at Our Lady of Healing Church in Chatham. The following day, Christopher Mitchell, also a topic of discussion during our last meeting, was arrested for the murder of Fr. Hart. He committed suicide hours later while in a holding cell. The police have taken that to be an admission of guilt."

"Is it a coincidence that the concern we mentioned in our last meeting is now dead?" asked a newer member.

Fr. Cossa took a deep breath and chose his next words carefully. "I can assure everyone in this room that absolutely no one present had anything to do with the death of Fr. Hart or the subsequent suicide of Christopher Mitchell."

This reassurance seemed to appease the concerned member. Fr. Cossa continued, "I do believe that both deaths, though, are part of God's plan to eradicate the progressives amongst His ranks and restore balance and order to our beloved Catholic Church. While some view these deaths as a tragedy, I believe they are answers to our prayers."

Fr. Cossa looked around the room to see if each member agreed with him. Everyone seemed to nod their heads in the affirmative.

"Very well, now that we have that little bit of nasty business behind us, I'd like to open a discussion around a topic we didn't get to last month, and that is the issue of leadership in the Diocese of Fall River.

"Motion to discuss leadership in Fall River," came a voice from the left side of the room.

"Seconded," came a voice from the right.

The remainder of the meeting was spent discussing Fr. Cossa's concerns about Bishop Hurley and whether or not he was still fit to lead the diocese.

CHAPTER FOURTEEN

The Ex-Girlfriend Angle

Jimmy and Farrah were sitting at Farrah's kitchen table, making a list of people to interview, when they were interrupted by Farrah's brother. Fr. Michael had just come back from the funeral home that was taking care of the arrangements for Fr. Hart's wake. Bishop Hurley had asked him to take over the pastoral responsibilities at Our Lady of Healing Church, as the diocese had no other priest to spare. Fr. Michael had agreed immediately, and working at the parish kept him preoccupied for the last day and a half. Farrah had almost forgotten he was in town since he was staying at the church rectory.

"Well, if it isn't the infamous Jimmy Doubts! I figured you'd be back in New York by now."

"Why's that?" Jimmy asked.

"Didn't you hear? The case has been closed. They got their man."

"Except we don't really believe that they did," Farrah piped up.

"Of course you don't," her brother said with a laugh.

"Wouldn't be much of a story for you if you did."

"Hey," Farrah said defensively, "you're the one that asked me to look into this. Well, I did, and I don't like what I found."

Farrah brought her brother up to speed on yesterday's meeting with Christopher Mitchell and this morning's conversation with Detective Nickerson.

"Someone poisoned the wine?" Fr. Michael asked in disbelief.

"That's what the medical examiner told the detective," Farrah replied. "It was an inside job."

"There are only a few people who would have access to the sacramental wine before mass — the altar server and the Eucharistic Minister."

"Is there any way to find out who those people are?"

"Yes," her brother replied, and then typed a quick email to the secretary back at the rectory who, no doubt, had a record of this on her computer.

"That would be helpful," Farrah replied.

Her brother stared out the window, apparently lost in thought.

"What are you thinking, Michael?" his sister asked.

"I know in the Diocese of Bridgeport where I work, all sacramental wine purchasing is done in bulk. It's ordered through the bishop's office and shipped to each parish individually."

"So?" Jimmy asked.

"So," Farrah replied before her brother had a chance to respond, "we know that Fr. Hart wasn't very popular with the hierarchy in Fall River. If the wine came from Fall River, it's possible that it may have been tampered with before being delivered to Chatham.

"Is that something you could check out when you get back to the rectory?" Jimmy asked Fr. Michael.

"Yes. And the more I think about it, it's plausible that the bishop's office had something to do with this."

Farrah's ears perked up. "Why do you say that?"

"I called the bishop's office earlier to see what time we could expect the bishop and his entourage tomorrow for the funeral and the chancellor told me that no one from Fall River would be coming down."

"What is a chancellor?" Jimmy asked. "Sounds Germanic."

"The chancellor is basically the bishop's right-hand man. He has many administrative responsibilities in a Diocese, including managing the finances. The chancellor in Fall River is a priest by the name of Peter Cossa; he's old-school and actually says a high Mass in Latin once a month at the Cathedral in Fall River."

"Sounds charming," said Farrah.

"I've never met him since he doesn't oversee my diocese in Connecticut, but from what I read he seems exactly like the type of priest who would have had an issue with a progressive guy like Fr. Hart having such a powerful voice in the Church."

"Better put him on our list of people to interview," Farrah said to Jimmy, who nodded in response.

She was then distracted by a beep coming from her phone signifying that she received an e-mail. Farrah looked at her phone and then turned her attention back to her brother and Jimmy Doubts.

"We have to add to our to-do to our list," Farrah said.

"What's that?" Jimmy and Michael asked in unison.

"Detective Nickerson just went through some security

footage from the camera outside the church. It seems that an hour before Mass, a mystery woman entered the church carrying something in a brown bag. He sent me a still frame from the video. Apparently we have to track her down."

Farrah handed her phone to Jimmy, who in turn handed it to Michael.

"The Lord works in mysterious ways," Fr. Michael commented.

"How's that?" asked Farrah.

Michael handed the phone back to his sister. "Remember how I told you yesterday that Fr. Hart had a relationship with a woman named Amanda Brooks in Wellfleet?"

"Yes," Farrah replied.

"Well, now you have a face to put with the name."

CHAPTER FIFTEEN
Amanda Brooks

Amanda Brooks was working the lunch shift at Pal's Captains Table restaurant in Wellfleet. She typically only worked evenings during the tourist season, but she was pulling a double shift; money was tighter than usual that month. Plus, the work helped keep her mind off all that had been going on with her friend and former partner, Fr. Hart.

She chose to think of him as a "partner" — he technically hadn't been her lover because things didn't progress physically between them. He wasn't a "boyfriend," either, because that term implied that the priest was someone she could go out with socially, which hadn't been the case with them. No, Fr. Hart had been someone with whom she shared a very personal, emotional connection, and the only term she could think of to use was "partner"; "emotional friend" seemed too long and New Agey.

The two met six months ago in January when Fr. Hart had first been assigned to Our Lady of Healing Church in

Chatham. A parishioner had recommended that he have lunch at Pal's, as it had access to some of the most fantastic ocean views on the Cape and was well known for its fresh seafood and live entertainment.

He had been dressed in street clothes, looking more like a surfer longing for summer than a priest having lunch six months prior to tourist season. He had been seated in Amanda's section and became tongue-tied when attempting to order. Amanda, sensing that her customer was attracted to her, started to flirt with him — a trick she learned to get better tips.

He flirted back against his inner judgment, and by the end of the meal, he brazenly asked her out for coffee; while he knew he was treading into dangerous territory, it almost seemed as if he couldn't control the impulse to do so.

As a single mom of a twelve-year-old boy, Amanda's dating prospects were few and far between on the Cape. She would typically have a fling here and there during the tourist season, but nothing of any consequence. The truth is, most men got cold feet after finding out Amanda had a soon-to-be teenager.

From their early dates, she knew there was something different about the man who showed up at her restaurant in the dead of winter; he had a gentle manner about him and didn't seem to have a one-track mind; she was quite surprised when he declined her offer to come back to her place after their third "date." While he was different than any other man she had ever met, she never assumed for a moment that the lack of physicality between them was a result of his trying to keep a vow of celibacy.

A few weeks into their courtship, however, it appeared

as if something was bothering him, and that's when he had confessed to her that he was a priest. Up to that point, she believed that he worked for a Catholic ministry – which he had told her when they first met – and the fact that he was a priest was initially unsettling. Amanda didn't know if it was her lack of prospects in town or the fact that she was captivated by his charisma, but she continued to see him — even though she knew the relationship couldn't go anywhere unless he was willing to break his vows.

Eventually Fr. Hart told her he couldn't go on seeing her. Amanda did not take the breakup well. While she had known deep down that the relationship would come to an end, she had fallen hard for Fr. Hart, and her ego had a hard time reconciling the fact that a man she loved had chosen to continue a life of celibacy over being with her.

Her anger came to a boiling point last Sunday morning. That's when she decided to go to the church an hour before Mass, intending to get him to change his mind. She carried a brown bag with a picture her son, Patrick, had drawn of her and Fr. Greg because she thought it might tug at his heartstrings and cause him to reconsider his decision. It didn't work, however, and she left the church in tears as the early worshippers started to come in.

Even though she did not live in Chatham, word of his death reached Wellfleet by mid-afternoon Sunday. Amanda was so devastated that she could not bring herself to come into work on Sunday or Monday, and now she was pulling double shifts to cover lost wages.

She looked at her watch and saw that it was 2:30; at any other restaurant, that would mean the lunch rush was over, but given Pal's atmosphere and location, the rush never ended. So she was not surprised when she saw a beautiful blonde woman enter the restaurant. What did surprise her, though, was the younger man she had in tow. He was too old to be her son and given that they looked nothing alike, she didn't think they were siblings. *More power to ya,* she thought as she nodded at the hostess, indicating she would like them in her section. She waited for a minute to give them time to consult the drink specials before going over to their table.

Farrah and Jimmy were seated at a booth and both reached for the table tent advertising the drink specials at the same time. Jimmy saw the intensity in Farrah's eyes and decided to give up his claim. While Farrah decided on what to medicate herself with, Jimmy looked around, amazed at how crowded the place was well after the lunch rush. The large bar in the center of the room attracted an eclectic crowd of surfers, boaters, college kids, and a fair number of cougars — older women dressed provocatively and preying on younger men. Then, looking out at the water crashing against the rocks down below, he remarked, "This place is the GOAT."

Hearing these words, Farrah switched her attention from the drinks menu to Jimmy's face. "Huh?"

"This place is the goat," Jimmy repeated.

"What the hell are you talking about, Doubts? 'The goat'? What's your sudden fascination with livestock?"

"No, GOAT is an acronym: Greatest of All Time. That's what my friends and I call something we think is super spectacular."

"Doubts, do me a favor," Farrah said in a deadpan

voice. "Don't ever say that word again." She handed the tent card to him. While he was still looking at it, their waitress came over to take their drink order. She was shorter than Farrah had imagined, about five foot four with blonde hair pulled back in a ponytail. She's very cute, Farrah thought. I can see how any man, celibate or not, might fall for her.

"My name is Amanda, and I'll be your server this afternoon. Can I get you two something to drink while you look over the menu?"

"I'll have one of your original margaritas," Farrah said. Amanda turned to Jimmy, who just stared at her blankly; he often became tongue-tied in the presence of attractive women.

"Do you need more time, sir?" Amanda asked.

Farrah started to giggle. "Doubts, wake up!" she said while snapping her fingers in front of his face.

"Wait, what?" Jimmy said as if being pulled from a daydream.

"Doubts, let me introduce you to Amanda, our waitress. She wants to know what you want to drink." Farrah slowed her speech as if she were talking to a foreigner. This caused Amanda to laugh.

"Oh, sorry," Jimmy said. "I'll have a Captain and Ginger."

"That wasn't so hard was it, Doubts?"

This caused Amanda to laugh again. "Do you know what you want for lunch, or are you good with drinks for now?"

Jimmy started to open his mouth, but Farrah interrupted. "I better field this one. We'd just like a few appetizers; how about some conch fritters and a dozen steamers to start. We'll take it from there."

"I'll put those right in for you, and I'll be back with your drinks shortly."

Amanda walked over to a computer terminal to enter the order. While she did, Jimmy couldn't stop staring at her backside.

"You men are all alike."

"What?"

"Doubts, you're practically in a hypnotic trance. Might I remind you that we're here to investigate her?"

"Sorry, Farrah, but it's been a while."

"Look, Doubts, I'm going to need more blood flowing to your brain and less flowing to your-know-what if we're going to have a meaningful investigation."

"I won't let it happen again," Jimmy said, blushing.

"I won't hold you to that, Doubts."

"What's your first impression of her, anyway?"

Farrah looked around to make sure their waitress wasn't in earshot.

"She doesn't seem like the killer type, but that's what everyone said about Ted Bundy."

After entering their order into the computer, Amanda checked on her other tables and then made her way to the bar to pick up Jimmy and Farrah's drinks. She didn't notice it when she saw the couple enter the restaurant, but when she got close to them while taking their drink orders, Amanda thought the woman looked very familiar; it only came to her when she returned to the table with their drinks.

"Can I ask you a question?" Amanda asked as she

handed Farrah her margarita. "Are you Farrah Graham?"

Farrah shouldn't have been surprised that someone recognized her, but at the time, she was caught off-guard at being recognized by one of the suspects in the current case she was working on.

"Yes," Farrah admitted after a moment's hesitation.

"I have to tell you that my son and I were hooked on the Sonny Michaels season. He's twelve now, and your podcast was the only thing that got him away from playing video games. What's next for you?"

Farrah considered whether she should lay her cards on the table now or string Amanda along a while longer and confront her in a less public place. She decided on the former course of action as she was eager to see Amanda's reaction to the news that her former boyfriend's death still was being investigated.

"Actually," Farah said, "Jimmy and I are looking into the death of a priest right down the road in Chatham." Farrah never took her eyes off Amanda as she made this admission. She saw Amanda's face turn from being cheery to being in anguish within a split second.

"I'm going to check on your appetizer order — I'll be back in a minute." Now it was Farrah's turn to watch Amanda as she quickly walked away from the table toward the kitchen.

"If she doesn't come back in five minutes, she's going to be number one on our list, Doubts."

Four minutes passed. Amanda came back with their food, as well as with a soft drink for herself.

"I'm taking my break now," Amanda said. "Can I talk to you guys for a few minutes?"

"Sure," Farrah said.

Amanda slid into the booth next to Jimmy, and he immediately felt the warmth coming off her body. Seeing him blush, Farrah kicked him under the table.

"Greg Hart was a very close friend of mine," Amanda began.

"Before you go any further," Farrah said, taking an audio recorder out of her purse, "can we record this conversation?"

"That's fine," Amanda said.

In Farrah's mind, this was good news for Amanda. A guilty person wouldn't readily agree to being recorded, and certainly not without a lawyer present.

"What was your relationship with Fr. Greg Hart?"

"This is difficult for me to say because we had to keep it a very tight secret, but he was kind of my partner."

"Kind of?" Farrah said, raising one eyebrow.

"I met him last January when he came into the restaurant. He wasn't dressed as a priest at the time, and we hit it off." Amanda went on to tell the details of their courtship and how Fr. Gregory Hart wound up choosing his calling over her.

"Why did you want to sit down and chat with us?"

"Because I read the paper this morning, and I saw what the cops said about that guy who hung himself in prison. I don't think he did it."

"Really?" Farrah questioned. "And why is that?"

"Before he broke up with me, Greg told me he had been receiving anonymous letters from someone threatening him."

Jimmy finally snapped out of the fog he was in and spoke up. "But how do you know Christopher didn't send those letters?"

Farrah gave Jimmy a look as if she were impressed with his ability to ask a question.

"Because," Amanda replied, "he showed me some of the letters. They cited Greg's homilies as evidence that he was leading the Church down the wrong path. According to the article I read this morning, Christopher Mitchell hadn't been to a church until the day of the murder, so how would he know what was said in Greg's homilies?"

"It was my understanding that Fr. Hart recorded his homilies and distributed them as podcasts. Couldn't Christopher have heard them that way?"

"Let's say he did," Amanda conceded. "Why would a lapsed Catholic shunned by the Church cite the homilies of a progressive priest as evidence that the Church is becoming too liberal for his taste? It doesn't make sense."

Farrah had to admit that Amanda had a point, but she also knew she needed to turn up the heat a bit. She took an envelope out of her purse and showed its contents to Amanda. "You were in the church the morning Fr. Hart died."

Amanda was stunned to see the picture of herself. She opened her mouth to respond, but the words wouldn't come out.

"This was taken from the security camera inside the church pointing at the entrance. Here you can be seen entering the church an hour before Mass, holding something in your hand. You exit ten minutes later without whatever it was. Maybe you are the one who poisoned Fr. Hart."

Amanda was utterly speechless at the notion that she was a suspect in her ex-partner's death. With her eyes filling with tears, she said, "I went to that church to try and get Greg to change his mind about us. He was furious when he saw me. I had never been to the church before because he wanted to be super careful about the potential of any impropriety. Hell, he wouldn't even be seen with me at any of the restaurants here in town. Imagine how he reacted when I showed up at his church."

"Seems like you may have had some motive," Jimmy said. "I can't imagine how I would have reacted if someone chose a life of celibacy over me."

The expression on Farrah's face was one of amazement. The Captain and Ginger must have given Jimmy some confidence.

"Was I upset that Greg broke up with me? Absolutely! Did I want to kill him over it? No! Look, I was realistic about the long-term prospects of being with Greg and that it likely wasn't going to go anywhere. Hell, we hadn't even slept together."

Without a polygraph, there would be no way for sure to tell if Amanda was lying, but Farrah considered herself a good people reader. She sensed that the waitress was telling the truth, but she didn't want to let her off the hook too easily.

"If you didn't do it, and if Christopher Mitchell was innocent, do you have any idea who may have poisoned Fr. Hart?"

Wiping away a tear, Amanda replied, "I would look for someone in the bishop's office. Greg told me all the grief he received from Fall River over the years, and from time to time when he was with me, he would take calls on his mobile phone with someone up there who would chastise him for something he said in one of his homilies."

Just then Farrah felt her phone buzz. Glancing at the

screen, she saw it was a text from her brother. It read:

Looks like you have to make a trip to Fall River . . . turns out the wine for the church is purchased in bulk by the diocese and shipped to each individual parish . . . I'll come by later.

Their conversation was interrupted by a burly man wearing a coral polo shirt and a name tag that read Joe, Manager. He had long, straight black hair and a five o'clock shadow that was more gray than black. Either he dyed his hair black, or his beard grey; Farrah assumed it was the former.

"Amanda, is everything okay? We needed you back on the floor five minutes ago. Wait, are you crying?"

Everyone at the restaurant knew that Amanda had recently gone through a rough breakup, but of course no one knew it was with the priest who had been murdered two days before.

"I'm okay," Amanda said. It was a lie; she was far from okay considering all that was going on, both inside and outside her place of employment.

"Why don't you take the rest of the day off?" Joe said. "I can get someone to cover your shift tonight."

"No," Amanda replied. "I need the money."

"At least take a few minutes to clean yourself up. The way your mascara is running, you're starting to look like Alice Cooper."

"Who?" Amanda asked.

"Never mind," Joe replied.

Before Amanda headed to the ladies' room, Farrah handed her a business card with her phone number and email address on it.

"If you want to talk more, here's my number."

Amanda took out her cell phone and immediately sent

a text message to the number printed on Farrah's card. "And now you have mine." She turned and walked away.

"Can I get you guys anything else?" Joe asked.

"Just our check, please," Farrah replied.

When Joe left their table, Jimmy said, "I don't think she did it." And referring to the message Farrah had received on her phone, he asked, "And what was that text all about?" Jimmy asked.

"It was my brother," she replied, and filled him in on how the diocese shipped wine to the parish.

"Mike is coming over tonight to talk. We're going to need his help to set up a meeting with someone in the diocese."

"If the wine had been poisoned before being shipped from the diocese, it would mean that whatever is left in the bottle at the church would still have traces of poison in it, right?" Jimmy asked.

Before Farrah could reply, Joe was back with the check. Saying, "I can take that whenever you are ready," he walked over to check on another of Amanda's tables.

"You're right, Doubts. I'll text my brother and tell him to bring the remaining wine from the sacristy over to my house when he comes tonight."

"How are we going to test it?" Jimmy asked. "In my haste to come to Chatham, I forgot to pack my poison detection kit."

"We'll need Detective Nickerson's help with that. I'll ask him to join us tonight at the house. According to him, the medical examiner didn't believe Mitchell did it either; he won't be surprised if he's asked to test another sample."

Farrah looked at the bill and saw that it was thirty

dollars. Instead of leaving a 20 percent tip, she put two crisp one hundred dollar bills into the tray. She wanted to hand it to Amanda personally for fear that Joe, or whoever bussed the table, would pocket the cash. Farrah flagged Amanda down as she exited the ladies' room.

"I am sorry if we added to your stress today," Farrah said while handing her the tray. She and Jimmy then left Pal's and headed back to Chatham.

CHAPTER SIXTEEN

A Woman in Black

Fr. Michael Graham was about to leave the rectory of Our Lady of Healing Church when the doorbell rang. The parish secretary, Betty Conyers, only worked from 11:00 to 4:00, and it was just past 4:30 so Fr. Michael answered the door himself. He was surprised to see a diminutive fifty-something woman standing on the doorstep. He remembered seeing her at the daily Mass he celebrated that morning, but she did not approach him after Mass as most of the other people who attended the service did.

"Pardon me, Father," the woman said in a soft voice that somehow had a hard edge, "but I was wondering if I could have a word with you." She was dressed in black from head to toe as if she was mourning the loss of a loved one. Fr. Michael recalled that she had been dressed similarly that morning.

"I was just getting ready to leave, but I suppose we could chat for a few minutes. Come, follow me into the office."

Fr. Michael led his visitor down the hallway to the office where there were two desks, one for the pastor and one for the secretary, and a sitting area with a two couches facing each other with a round coffee table in between them.

The woman looked around, an expression of surprise on her face as she noticed the bottle of sacramental wine on one of the desks. She recognized the stain on the label; it was the same as the one on the bottle used at Mass the past Sunday when she had served as the Eucharistic Minister.

"I wouldn't suggest drinking that, Father," she remarked.

Surprised, Fr. Michael asked, "Why is that?"

"The Church isn't known for pouring the finest of wines. But if you don't mind, I'd love a glass of water."

"Of course. I'll be right back," Fr. Michael said, heading to the kitchen.

He returned with two glasses of water to find his guest looking at the books on the shelves that lined the walls.

Handing her the glass of water, Fr. Michael said, "I recognize you from Mass this morning, but I don't know your name."

"My name is Emily Rose, and I have been a member of this parish since moving to Chatham twenty years ago. I'm a Eucharistic Minister here — not that you needed my help this morning since there were only a handful of people at Mass."

Fr. Michael's ears perked up; in addition to the altar server, the Eucharistic Minister was the only other person who would have had a reason to be in the sacristy before Mass last Sunday — and therefore have access to the sacramental wine. He didn't want to raise her suspicions by asking her outright if she had been the Eucharistic Minister the past Sunday. Instead, he made a mental not to bring it up with Farrah later that evening.

"If you'd like to help me distribute Communion sometime, I'd welcome your assistance."

"I'm scheduled for Sunday Mass at 10:00 a.m. During daily Mass, I prefer to pray quietly after receiving the sacrament."

Fr. Michael began to realize that he wasn't dealing with your average Catholic. "How can I help you, Emily?"

"I'm going to attend Fr. Hart's wake tonight and his funeral tomorrow, and I wanted to see if you could use any help. I understand that the bishop cannot make it to the services."

Although Fr. Michael had received word earlier in the day that Bishop Robert Hurley had taken ill and no one else from the bishop's office would be attending either, he wondered how Emily would have known this. The bishop's schedule wasn't exactly common knowledge.

Seeing the look of confusion on his face, Emily said, "The bishop's schedule is posted online, and I checked it this afternoon."

"Fr. Gregory was well-liked here in town, and I expect to have a full church tomorrow for the funeral. If you're available to be a Eucharistic Minister, that would be a big help."

"I would be honored to serve at Fr. Hart's Mass," Emily replied.

"Were you close to him, Emily?"

"You could say that," Emily replied. "Why do you ask?"

"Are you aware of any enemies he may have had here in town?"

"Why?" she asked suspiciously.

"Just curious," Fr. Michael said, unconsciously looking at the bottle of sacramental wine. He saw that this did not go unnoticed by Emily, whose senses seem to be heightened.

"Father, there's one more thing," Emily said.

"What's that?"

"The day after tomorrow is the Fourth of July, and no one does the Fourth of July quite like Chatham. Every year members of the parish march in the parade to express our patriotism. Some of the ladies and I were wondering if you would like to march with us."

Fr. Michael had been hoping to go back to his parish in Connecticut after tomorrow's funeral, but he hadn't received word from Fall River about whether they could spare a replacement priest from the diocese. The Diocese of Bridgeport, where he worked, had a number of priests who could step in for Fr. Michael in Greenwich so his bishop had given him all the time he needed in Chatham.

"I would be honored to." After saying these words, Fr. Michael stood up to signal that he had to get going. Emily Rose started walking toward the door but stopped in front of the bookshelf after one book in particular caught her eye: a biography of Pope Francis.

"Have you read that book?" Fr. Michael asked after noticing his visitor staring at it.

"Heavens no!" Emily replied. "How such a liberal pope was elected is beyond my comprehension."

Fr. Michael was taken aback by her statement. He was always surprised by Catholics who criticized such a popular pope. Not responding, he walked her to the door and saw her out. He then returned to the office, picked up the bottle of sacramental wine, and placed it in a brown paper bag he'd found in the kitchen. He then made his way to his sister's house on Harding's Beach.

CHAPTER SEVENTEEN

True Colors

Fr. Peter Cossa was back from meeting with the Order and, having heard from the office secretary that the bishop had yet to leave his room, decided to bring the bishop's dinner upstairs. Fr. Cossa entered the bishop's personal chambers and shook his head as he looked at his superior's sleeping body. *He can no longer lead this diocese,* Cossa thought to himself.

If there was only one word to describe Fr. Peter Cossa, it would be ambitious. Since before his ordination twenty years ago, he had had one goal on his mind: to become a bishop. It was partly why he was so steadfastly loyal to Bishop Hurley in the first place. Cossa knew that a bishop was required to revise a succession plan every three years and present it to his superior; in the case of bishops in the United States, this was the Apostolic Nuncio based in Washington, DC, who served as the Vatican's ambassador to the United States.

This succession plan contained a short list of priests who would be suitable replacements. In the event of a bishop's death or retirement, the Apostolic Nuncio would present this plan to the Congregation of the Roman Curia, who would then study the report and eventually present a recommendation for the bishop's successor. The process could take anywhere between nine months and two years from the time of a bishop's death or resignation.

The priests on this short list would not become aware that they were under consideration until the Curia decided who to investigate more closely. But there was one other person in the Diocese of Fall River who knew the potential succession plan, and that was Fr. Peter Cossa; as chancellor he was privy to all communications between the bishop's office and the office of the Apostolic Nuncio in Washington. Bishop Hurley had recently completed his three-year update of needs of the diocese, and Fr. Cossa was pleased to see that his name, along with the names of three other priests, had been mentioned as potential successors.

The other priests were all based outside the Diocese of Fall River. They included Fr. Steven Capaldi from the Diocese of Bridgeport, Fr. Roger Gilmour from the Archdiocese of New York, and Fr. David Mason from the Archdiocese of Los Angeles. All were highly respected by United States Conference of Catholic Bishops, and any of them would make a good replacement for Bishop Hurley. Fr. Cossa, though, did not want to leave anything to chance so he had the intelligence arm of the Order looking into his competition to see if there was any dirt that could be unearthed and publicized. If not, there were other ways of limiting his competition, but Cossa hoped it wouldn't come to that.

Bishop Hurley began to stir, and Fr. Cossa put the tray

of food down on the table next to his bed. The bishop was still ten years away from the mandatory retirement age of seventy-five, and that left only two options for Fr. Cossa to become the next bishop: Robert Hurley's untimely death or voluntary resignation. While it was rare for a bishop to resign, it was not unheard of. As a matter of fact, Pope Benedict XVI, who was technically the Bishop of Rome, stunned the world when he resigned the papacy in 2013. Fr. Cossa had been devastated when the College of Cardinals elected to replace the conservative Benedict with a liberal bishop from Argentina. Jorge Mario Bergoglio, who took the name Francis upon his elevation to pope, had become a thorn in the side of conservatives who didn't care for his focus on the poor or the interfaith dialogue he encouraged. They would have preferred the leader of the Catholic Church to be the poster child for combatting the evils of abortion, homosexuality, and contraception.

As Bishop Hurley stirred, a pillow fell on the floor. As Cossa bent down to pick it up, he considered smothering the bishop with it, but thought better of it. It hasn't come to that yet, he thought.

Perhaps because he felt he was being watched, Bishop Hurley opened his eyes. He was startled to see his chancellor standing over his bed with a pillow in his hand.

"Peter, what are you doing here?"

Fr. Cossa pointed to the nightstand next to the Bishop's bed. "I brought you some dinner. Your secretary told me that you weren't feeling well, so I took the liberty of having the cook prepare some homemade chicken soup."

The bishop's eyes lit up upon hearing this. "Rabbi Blumberg calls it Jewish penicillin."

Rabbi Stephen Blumberg was the leader of the Jewish Community in Fall River and a close friend of Bishop Hurley's. The two had a standing lunch appointment every Thursday and genuinely enjoyed each other's company. Much to Fr. Cossa's chagrin, last year during Passover all employees at the bishop's office were invited to enjoy a traditional Passover Seder with the staff of Rabbi Blumberg's Temple Beth-El.

"Come, eat; you need your strength."

Bishop Hurley sat up in bed, and Fr. Cossa placed the dinner tray on his superior's lap. The bishop took a spoonful of soup and declared it to be delicious.

"What's troubling you, Robert?" In truth, Cossa knew the answer to this question, but he wanted to keep up the appearance of being concerned for his friend.

"I can't really say," the bishop replied. It was the truth; he couldn't admit that a confession he'd heard earlier in the day had troubled him. While making a general comment would not technically break the seal of confession, there was nothing to be gained by even hinting at the root of his malaise.

"You secretary tells me that you will not be going to Chatham tomorrow for Fr. Hart's funeral — and that you don't want me to go either."

"That's right. I don't think I'll be feeling well enough by tomorrow, and I'd like you here to take care of some administrative matters. The priest from Connecticut will be handling the service."

"What kind of administrative matters?"

"I need to appoint Fr. Hart's replacement, and my options are limited; I'd like you to put out a few feelers to find a suitable shepherd for the flock in Chatham."

"It would be my pleasure." Fr. Cossa was relieved to hear that he wouldn't have to attend Fr. Hart's funeral, and that he would be in charge of finding a successor for the liberal priest was the icing on the cake.

"I hate to bring this up," he said, "but Christopher Mitchell's mother called the office earlier to see whether or not we would grant her wish for a funeral Mass for her son."

For years, suicide had been looked upon as a grave sin, and those who committed the act were deemed unworthy of a Church funeral. In recent times, however, the Church took a different view on the topic and considered the taking of one's life to be a mental health issue and had relented on this stance.

In fact, though, Christopher Mitchell's mother had not called the Diocese's office; Cossa made this up to remind his superior that a man killed himself as a result of being wrongly accused of Fr. Hart's death.

His words had the desired effect. Hearing them, Bishop Hurley closed his eyes and sunk back on his bed, almost spilling his soup. "You can take this food away; I've lost my appetite."

The bishop dialed his depression up a notch, partly so Fr. Cossa would leave him alone and partly for more devious reasons.

"What shall we tell the mother?"

"Tell her whatever you like, Peter. Now leave me alone; I feel a migraine coming on."

As Fr. Peter left the room, Bishop Hurley took the covers and placed them over his head as he curled into a fetal position.

The Chancellor couldn't help but smile.

CHAPTER EIGHTEEN

A Signal to Melody

Farrah, Detective Nickerson, and Jimmy were sitting on the upstairs deck of Farrah's house waiting for Farrah's brother to arrive. Farrah was facing north with the waters of Nantucket sound to her right. The wind had picked up, and the beach was lined with kite surfers waiting for the lifeguards to leave so they could ride the waves, lest they be sent away for disobeying Chatham's strict rules about kite surfing. Hell, one couldn't even fly a kite on any of Chatham's beaches, let alone use one as a water sport, Farrah thought as she gazed at them.

From the second-floor deck, Farrah could see a lighthouse to the north; she was familiar with the famous Chatham Light located on Shore Road, but she had never noticed this one before; most likely because Melody typically sat facing north while Farrah sat facing south.

"See that lighthouse over there?" Farrah said, pointing toward it. "I've never noticed it before."

Both Jimmy and Detective Nickerson turned to see what she was pointing at.

"That's the Stage Harbor Lighthouse," the detective said. "It is the youngest lighthouse here on Cape Cod. Have you ever heard of Trick Evans?"

"The golfer?" Jimmy asked, his interest piqued.

"Yes," Nickerson said. "He bought the lighthouse and the house next to it a few years back to ensure that some wealthy developers didn't build a bunch of million-dollar homes there."

"Like they did in this neighborhood?" Farrah asked.

"Exactly," the detective confirmed. "To get to that lighthouse, you have to walk a mile down a sandy path, and the townspeople were afraid that even more of our precious beach space would be purchased by wealthy out-of-towners who are turning our quaint little fishing village into a playground for one-percenters. No offense, Ms. Graham."

"None taken," Farrah replied.

"Does he live there all year round?" Jimmy asked.

"No," Nick replied. "He spends most of his time now out in Southern California but this year he's going to be the Grand Marshall of our town's Fourth of July parade on Thursday."

Their conversation was interrupted when Farrah received a call from her brother; he was standing at the front door waiting for someone to let him in. Farrah had closed the French doors to the deck due to the wind, and no one heard the doorbell ring — or Mulder's barking, for that matter. Farrah told her brother to let himself in, and a moment later he joined them on the upstairs deck.

"I thought you got lost," Farrah said. "I expected you a half hour ago."

"A woman stopped by the rectory as I was leaving.

Actually, I want to talk to you about it — I got a funny feeling from her."

"From who?" Farrah, Jimmy, and Detective Nickerson asked at the same time.

"Emily Rose," replied Fr. Michael.

"Interesting," remarked Nickerson.

"Why?" replied Farrah, Jimmy, and Fr. Michael in unison.

"When I went to the rectory yesterday morning to meet with the parish secretary, Emily showed up to purchase a Mass card. She's actually the person who pointed me in Christopher Mitchell's direction. Why was she at the rectory tonight?"

"That's the strange thing about it," Fr. Michael replied. "I was just about to leave to come here when the doorbell rang. She wanted to see if I wanted any help at Fr. Hart's funeral tomorrow."

"What kind of help?" Nick asked.

"She's a Eucharistic Minister, and she wanted to know she could help distribute Communion tomorrow since the bishop won't be concelebrating the funeral."

"Why won't the bishop be there?" Farrah asked.

"Apparently he's taken ill."

"And how did Emily know that?" Jimmy asked.

"I wondered the same thing," Fr. Michael replied. "She apparently went onto the diocese's website earlier and saw that his schedule had been cleared."

"Didn't you say that the Eucharistic Minister was one of only a few people who had access to the sacramental wine before Mass?" Farrah asked.

"Yes. Oh, and I almost forgot . . ." Fr. Michael got up from his seat, went back into the house, and walked down the stairs. Jimmy, Farrah, and Nick heard the front door open and then close. A moment later, Fr. Michael was back on the second-floor deck with a bottle of sacramental wine in his hands. His breathing was noticeably heavier than a few moments ago.

"Sounds like someone needs to start running again," Farrah quipped.

"Very funny, sis," Fr. Michael replied. "This is the sacramental wine I took from the sacristy earlier today." He handed the bottle over to Detective Nickerson, who opened it.

"If you want a drink, detective, I have some better stuff downstairs."

Nick looked in her direction and snickered. He put the open bottle to his nose and took a deep breath.

"Good year?" Jimmy asked.

"When I was with the medical examiner on Monday, he had me smell a vile of Fr. Hart's blood, and it smelled like sour almonds. Apparently that's the smell cyanide gives off. This wine failed the sniff test."

"So what does that mean?" Jimmy asked.

"It means that this bottle wasn't the source of the poison; someone actually poisoned the wine in the cruet used during Mass."

"That kind of points to this Emily Rose woman, doesn't it?" Jimmy asked.

"What did you learn from Amanda?" Fr. Michael questioned.

"Who's Amanda?" Nick asked.

Farrah filled Nick in on Fr. Hart's ex-girlfriend and the meeting she and Jimmy had with her earlier in the afternoon. She explained how neither she nor Jimmy believed that Amanda had anything to do with the priest's death.

"This gets more interesting by the second," Nick replied. "We've got to get close to this Emily Rose woman without raising her suspicions, and I'm not sure how to do that.

"Farrah's too famous, for one thing; Emily will suspect something right away if she starts asking questions. I can't do it for obvious reasons, and, Jimmy, no offense, but you are not that good of an actor."

"How can you possibly say that?" Jimmy questioned defensively.

"You crumbled under the tiniest bit of pressure the other night when I cornered you in the waiting room of the police station."

"She may already be suspicious," Fr. Michael spoke up.

"Why?" Farrah asked.

"Because I'm pretty sure she saw the bottle of sacramental wine on the desk in the rectory's office where we were sitting. If she's the one who poisoned the wine, that would have raised questions in her mind."

"We're going to need someone confident, someone who isn't afraid to go into harm's way. Someone who can gain Emily's confidence."

"Shit!" Farrah exclaimed.

"What?" Nick asked.

"There's only one person I know who fits that description perfectly."

"Who?"

"Melody," Farrah, Jimmy, and Fr. Michael said at the same time.

"Who's Melody?" Nick asked.

"My girlfriend."

"Girlfriend?" Nick said quizzically, feeling foolish as he remembered the advance he made toward Farrah on Monday night.

"It's complicated," Farrah responded. She filled Nick in on how Melody had stormed out of the house on Monday after her brother arrived.

"Have you heard from her since Monday?" Jimmy asked.

"Nope, but I know how to get her up here quickly."

"This should be good," said Fr. Michael.

"Jimmy, take a picture of me getting cozy with the good detective."

Farrah went over and sat on Detective Nickerson's lap. She put her hands around his neck and stared longingly into his eyes.

"Put your hands on the small of my back — but so help me, if you go below the waist, you're getting kneed in the nuts," Farrah threatened.

Jimmy took the picture and handed the phone back to Farrah, who put it up on her Facebook page. In no less than two minutes, her phone was ringing.

"Aren't you going to answer that?" Nick asked.

"Nope," Farrah replied and then looked at her watch. "I estimate she will be here in three hours . . . maybe less."

CHAPTER NINETEEN
Message Received

Melody was at a dojo in Stamford, Connecticut, working with the dojo's owner, Manny Escriva. He was giving her a private lesson to help her prepare for her first-degree black belt test. She referred to him using the Japanese title Shihan which translates to "Master Instructor."

"Let's just warm up with a little jab cross," Shihan said.

"Osu," Melody replied, using the focus word he taught all the students who walked through the doors of his dojo. It was the only acceptable response to a command in Manny's school.

Melody jabbed with her left hand and followed with a cross with her right. Even though Shihan was wearing mitts, he felt every punch.

"Nice and strong! What are you doing back here anyway? I thought you were going to be on the Cape all summer."

In a normal class, discussion between students was prohibited during warm-ups, but during private lessons Shihan would often engage his students in some casual banter as they eased into the lesson. Besides, Melody was a model student. She never missed a class when she was in town, and she trained in her home gym on non-class days. As a result of her skills and dedication, Shihan often used her as a teaching assistant for lower-level classes at his dojo.

"Farrah decided to take on some extracurricular activities."

"Now add you elbows to the warm-up," Shihan instructed. "What do you mean by extracurricular activities?"

"A priest died in church last Sunday, and he was a friend of Farrah's brother. He asked her to look into it."

As Melody spoke these words, Shihan noticed the power and intensity of her punches and elbow strikes increase significantly.

"Now add your knees," Shihan instructed. "I know Chatham is a small resort town," Shihan said, "but I have to imagine they have cops there."

Melody struck Shihan's mitt with her right knee so hard it made his hand throb. "That's why I'm here."

"Okay, take a short break," Shihan said, more for his benefit than hers.

"Osu."

Melody was a handful of classes away from being able to test for her first-degree black belt, and she had been working through the packet Shihan gave her to ensure she would be prepared. In addition to proving a mastery of different techniques, Melody would have to prove her endurance, and Shihan reminded her of this fact.

"From here on out, I want you to pretend that the concerns you brought into this dojo today have fallen from your body like the beads of sweat that are now on the mat. They no longer exist for you until you walk out of this dojo. Face the eastern wall of the dojo and read the words above the mirror to me."

"Osu, Shihan," Melody replied. "'In the moment, at your best.'"

"When you are here, you need to be in the moment. Nothing from the outside world has any importance within the walls of my dojo when you are training. Now get into plank position."

Melody said, "Osu," and dropped to her hands and knees.

"Begin," Shihan commanded.

"Osu," Melody replied and made a fist with her hands. She then balanced herself on her fists and toes with her body, straight and taut as an arrow, approximately three inches above the mat.

Shihan touched the timer he held in the palm of his hand; it was set for three minutes which was the amount of time she would have to stay in plank position during her black belt test.

"You will find that the body will begin to question its ability to push on. It will lie to you and tell you that you have to give up, but don't listen. Your mind must be strong. If you have a strong mind, the body will obey. Persistence, perseverance, patience, and determination will be required for you to earn your black belt in my school."

Shihan saw Melody's body start to tremble and bent down so he was face-to-face with her. "Your body is lying to you, Melody; don't give in. Think about your goals and focus on them. Show your body that you arc stronger than it thinks you are."

Shihan's timer went off. "Time," he said.

Melody remained in plank position for another two minutes and thirty seconds.

"Osu," he said after she finally lowered her body to the mat. As she sat, Shihan lit some incense and gave her a final lesson.

"The true warrior only uses the skills learned in this dojo for self-defense or for developing oneself in a positive manner; anyone who is abusive or offensive has failed in my school. As a student in my school, you must avoid anything that may harm you or others."

"Osu," Melody whispered.

"You must be dedicated. You must be motivated. You must be on a quest to be your best."

"Osu," Melody whispered again.

"Please stand and face me."

"Osu," Melody said confidently, bowing.

"Great job today. I'll see you on Saturday."

As she walked to the car, Melody fished her towel out of her bag, intending to wipe her face with it. Her hands brushed against her mobile phone, and she saw a notification on her home screen that Farrah Graham had added a picture to her social media profile. Melody's curiosity was piqued since Farrah wasn't that active on Facebook. Once inside her car, she swiped the notification to the right and saw a picture of Farrah sitting on a man's lap. He had long white hair and very large hands that were resting right above her waist. The picture appeared to be taken from the second-floor deck of Farrah's beach house.

"What the . . ?" Melody said out loud.

The sense of peace and exhaustion that came over her body after her private lesson with Shihan Manny was overtaken by a wave of jealously and rage. Melody immediately called Farrah's mobile phone to demand an explanation. There was no answer.

"Aw, hell no!" Melody exclaimed. She turned on the car's engine, fastened her seat belt, and pulled out of the dojo's parking lot. Instead of making a left-hand turn onto Long Ridge Road to head back to the home she shared with Farrah, Melody made a right turn toward the northbound entrance of the Merritt Parkway.

Traffic was light for a Tuesday night, and she would make it up to Chatham in just under three hours.

CHAPTER TWENTY

Detective Nickerson does some Digging

Detective William "Nick" Nickerson left Farrah's house and went back to the station; his mind was working overtime and he wasn't ready to go home yet. He was interested in this new revelation about Emily Rose, and he wanted to check to see if she had a record on file at the police station. It's a shot in the dark, but just maybe I'll get lucky, he thought.

Employees entering the police department after hours were required to use a card reader outside the main door. Visitors and those without an ID badge would have to use a keypad and pray that the desk sergeant on duty felt like answering his phone. As Nick was about to swipe his ID badge, the doors opened automatically in front of him. As he walked in, he was surprised to see Arlene sitting at the front desk; her presence explained why the doors opened.

"Arlene, what are you doing here so late?"

"Getting caught up on some paperwork," she responded. "Besides, Bobby asked if he could use the kitchen tonight to cook for his girlfriend. I'm meeting some friends from church for a Tuesday night prayer group that doesn't start for another hour, so I figured I would just hang out here instead of micromanaging my son in the kitchen. What are you doing back here? And where have you been anyway?"

Nick was hesitant to tell Arlene that he had been with Farrah, her brother, and Jimmy. He didn't want anyone to know that there was an ongoing investigation into the priest's death, but he trusted Arlene and decided he had no reason to hide anything from her — though he did leave out the part about Emily Rose being a suspect.

"Well, that certainly is interesting," she replied after hearing his admission.

"You said you were going to a prayer group. What church do you go to?"

Arlene replied, "Our Lady of Healing."

"So Fr. Hart's church. I would think your group would be canceled considering the circumstances."

"I suggested that to our group leader, but she was against it. She said that Fr. Hart would have wanted us to meet, although she did agree to a later start time so others could go to the wake."

"Are you going to the wake tonight?"

"No, but I'll be at the funeral tomorrow. I hate wakes. I'm not sure why people are so fascinated with paying respects with an open casket. It creeps me out."

"What did you think of Fr. Hart?" Nickerson asked.

"He wasn't everybody's cup of tea, but I liked him. Some of the ladies in my prayer group, though, would swear he wore the mark of the beast on his forehead."

This reference was lost on the detective, who did not count himself amongst the religious set. Seeing the look of confusion on his face, she clarified her comment.

"Scripture tells us that the antichrist bears a mark on him that will distinguish him from followers of God. The mark, in this case, is the number 666."

"And people actually believe this stuff?"

"I don't judge you for your lack of belief, Nick, so don't judge me for mine."

"I meant no disrespect, Arlene," Nickerson said, offering her a sincere smile. "Who runs this prayer group of yours anyway?"

"A woman named Emily Rose. She's a bit old-school in her beliefs, but she's kind of an authority on all things Catholic."

Nick had to control the expression on his face so his surprise wouldn't show. "What do you mean old-school?"

"Back in the 1960s, there were a number of major reforms in the Catholic Church as a result of the Second Vatican Council, or Vatican II as it has come to be known. Among them were reforms designed to modernize the Church, including having greater layperson participation in the liturgy — which really meant that Mass could be celebrated in a vernacular language versus Latin. Some people disavow Vatican II, and Emily Rose is one of them. But given how much that poor woman has been through, I let her conservatism slide."

"All she has been through? What do you mean?"

"I'll tell you over a cup of coffee."

Nick and Arlene walked down the hall to the kitchenette where the station kept an industrial quality single-cup coffee brewer. Nick selected a French Roast pod while Arlene opted for Italian Roast. Once they both had their coffees, they sat down at a table. Given the hour, they had the entire kitchenette to themselves.

"I hope I never have to know the pain that woman has had to endure in her life," Arlene began.

Nick raised his left eyebrow and waited for Arlene to expand on her comment.

"About thirty years ago, Emily's husband, Todd, didn't come home from work. He was a fisherman here in town and would leave early in the morning to chase his catch, but he was always home by 2:30 or 3:00 in the afternoon after selling whatever he caught to the wholesalers at the pier here in Chatham."

"What happened to him?"

"I'm getting to that. Well, there was a rumor going around that he was having an affair with a widower; Emily had heard these rumors for some time but refused to believe them. On the day her husband went missing, she decided to pay a visit to this woman's house to see if there was a chance that he might be there. Sure enough, his car was in the driveway. Emily barged into the house, expecting to catch them in the act, and when she got to the bedroom, she had the shock of her life..." Arlene paused for dramatic effect.

"Don't leave me in suspense."

"She saw her husband and his lover stabbed to death!"

"A double murder?"

"No, the medical examiner deemed it a murder-suicide. He determined that the widower, a woman named Mary Francis, stabbed Emily's husband and then slit her own wrists."

"Any idea why she would do that?"

"Rumor has it that Todd was going to break up with her and Mary couldn't accept it, and she did what she did so they could be together forever."

"I can see how discovering her husband and his lover dead would be traumatic."

"But the tragedy didn't end there…"

"There's more?"

"This is going to require a second cup." Arlene got up and took another pod of Italian Roast out of the dispenser. After her cup was brewed, she returned to the table.

"She and her husband had a son named Connor. About fifteen years ago, his body was found washed up on Lighthouse Beach here in Chatham. It was initially thought that he had been involved in a boating accident and drowned offshore, but the coroner determined the cause of death could not have been drowning; there was no fluid present in his lungs during the autopsy."

"This sounds familiar. I think this case happened when I was still in the police academy."

"A toxicology screen came back showing Connor had trace amounts of heroin in his system. The department's subsequent investigation led to a drug dealer in Hyannis. The working assumption was that Connor had been in debt to the dealer and apparently paid the price with his life, but it was only an assumption. There was not enough evidence to arrest the dealer, so the case remains open."

"So Emily lost her husband and then her son. I guess that would make someone a little crazy."

"I never said she was crazy, just conservative."

"Same difference," the detective joked.

Arlene looked at her watch and got up from the table. "I need to finish some work before my prayer group," she said, heading back to the front desk.

The detective, on the other hand, went back to his desk, fired up his computer, and started reading the department's files on the deaths of Todd and Connor Rose; this kept him busy to well past midnight.

One thing he learned would have been startling if he had been more up on Church hierarchy in the Diocese of Fall River: Emily Rose's maiden name was Cossa.

CHAPTER TWENTY-ONE

A Rose by Any Other Name

Emily Rose entered the funeral parlor where Fr. Hart's wake was being held. She'd been there before: once for the wake of her son, Connor, and before that for the wake of her husband, Todd, not to mention the wakes of the many friends and townspeople who entrusted the Randolph Lightbody and Sons Funeral Home for their final arrangements. Todd and Connor's deaths were both so tragic that the funeral director had refused to allow an open casket in either case. He had recommended cremation, but Emily would not accept that; at the time it went squarely against Church teaching.

As she walked into the main room where the visitation was taking place, she noticed that there were many people in line waiting to kneel before the coffin and say a prayer. While Fr. Hart did not have a large family locally, many people in the community considered him a friend. *Stupid sheep*, she thought to herself.

Emilly would rather have not come to the wake, but given her high profile in the parish, she assumed others would think it strange if she didn't show up. She didn't intend to stay long, however, as a number of women from the parish would be coming to her house for their Tuesday evening prayer group. She got in line and strategically waved to certain fellow parishioners who, having already paid their respects to the deceased, were sitting on folding chairs in the center of the room and talking quietly.

As Emily got closer to the casket, the smell of the flowers became overbearing. She read the card from one particularly ornate arrangement; it had been sent from Rabbi Blumberg of the Temple Beth-El community in Fall River. *It figures*, Emily thought with disdain.

Once she reached the front of the line, she knelt down in front of the casket, grateful it was closed; she couldn't bear the thought of looking at the priest's face while she pretended to pray. She closed her eyes and made a less than heartfelt attempt at prayer.

Heavenly Father, give me the strength to do your will. Use my talents to serve your greater glory and restore the Church to what it should be rather than what it is becoming. In Jesus' name, I pray, amen.

Emily opened her eyes, looked down at the casket with a self-satisfied smile, and left the parlor. Out of the corner of her eye, Emily saw Fr. Michael Graham, the visiting priest from Connecticut, consoling a woman Emily didn't recognize. She was young, petite, and stunningly beautiful. Emily knew every parishioner in the parish, and was sure that this mystery woman was not a member of Our Lady of Healing. Emily assumed she must be a member of Fr. Hart's family and didn't give it any more thought.

Emily arrived back at her modest home with fifteen minutes to spare before her ladies' prayer group was about to start. A few of the women had assumed she would cancel their regular Tuesday night meeting given Fr. Hart's death, but the thought had never crossed her mind. She agreed to hold it later than usual to allow her guests to attend the wake, but Emily made it clear that canceling was out of the question.

In the kitchen, she brewed a pot of decaf coffee and took out a tin of butter cookies from the pantry. She gathered some paper plates and small napkins and carried everything to her parlor.

She was arranging the refreshments when the doorbell rang.

"Are you expecting company?" The question came from Emily's father-in-law, Tyler, a veteran of the US Air Force who moved in with Emily five years ago after his wife died.

"I'm having my women's prayer group over tonight, Tyler. I told you that four times!" Emily said, heading upstairs to check on him. She made no attempt to hide her frustration at her father-in-law's quickly failing memory.

"You look like you just came from a funeral," Tyler said.

"I told you I was going to a wake."

"Who died?"

Emily became increasingly frustrated with her father-in-law. She had told him multiple times that Fr. Hart, the priest from her church, had died the prior Sunday, but the memory would not take root in Tyler's brain. These days the only thing he could remember in any detail were events from his days in the service.

"Fr. Hart from the parish."

"You don't say! He was a young fella — what happened?"

Emily knew exactly what happened, but wasn't about to divulge it to Tyler. "Heart attack."

"So young for that. Are you taking me to the parade on Thursday?"

The veterans were a big part of the Fourth of July parade, and Tyler had his well decorated Air Force dress uniform ready to go.

Before Emily could respond, the doorbell rang again.

"Are you expecting company?" her father-in-law asked.

Emily went downstairs without bothering to reply.

CHAPTER TWENTY-TWO

Melody Returns

After the wake, Fr. Michael wanted to go back to the rectory and get some sleep, as he had to be up early the following morning to prepare the church for a funeral. However, he had promised his sister he would come by for a beer before calling it a night. As a result, he found himself on her second-floor balcony overlooking Nantucket Sound for the second time that day. Joining them were Jimmy Doubts and Detective Nickerson, who wanted to share what he had learned at the police station about the deaths of Emily Rose's son and husband.

"How was the wake?" Farrah asked.

"Crowded," Fr. Michael replied.

"You had a crowded house?" Jimmy Doubts joked, referencing the name of his favorite 80s band. While the 80s were well before Jimmy's time, he had an unexplainable fondness for everything from that decade.

"Don't dream its over, Doubts," Farrah quipped.

"If you like Crowded House," Detective Nickerson spoke up, "you should try and meet Trick Evans while you're here."

Nick pointed toward the Stage Harbor Lighthouse he had told them about earlier in the evening.

"There's a mile-long stretch of sand leading from the north parking lot of the beach to his house. He named that patch of land Mt. Pleasant Street."

"Let me guess — his house is Number 57," Jimmy said.

"Bingo," Nick confirmed. The reference was to a Crowded House song called "Take the Weather with You."

"I always love a trip back to the 1980s, but can I bring you guys back to the present?" Farrah asked. "Michael, did Emily Rose show up at the wake?"

"She was one of the last ones to show up, but yes, she was there. Instead of hanging around to chat with the other people from the parish, though, she just paid her respects and left."

Detective Nickerson spoke up. "She was hosting her Tuesday night prayer group."

Farrah, Fr. Michael, and Jimmy all turned their heads to look at him.

"What?" The detective replied. "I know things."

"Care to expand, Nick?" Farrah asked.

"I went back to the station to do a little digging on Emily Rose and see if we had a file on her for any reason. One of my colleagues was still there — she was going to leave work and go right to Emily's house for the prayer group."

"Did you learn anything about Emily?" Farrah asked.

"As a matter of fact," the detective said, handing them each a piece of paper from the folder he was holding, "it turns out that she is no stranger to tragic deaths   her husband was found dead in an apparent murder-suicide, and her son died from blunt force trauma to the head."

Reading the obituary for Emily's husband, Fr. Michael said, "Holy shit!"

They were startled to hear foul language from the priest, and all three turned their attention to him.

"Emily Rose's maiden name was Cossa!"

"So?" Farrah said.

"The Chancellor of the Diocese of Fall River is a very conservative priest by the name of Peter Cossa; I wonder if they might be related."

"So what if they are?" Nick asked.

"Fr. Hart had been sent to Chatham because he was making too much noise about how the Church was in desperate need of reform. There were some in the hierarchy, including the Bishop of Fall River, Robert Hurley, that did not share his enthusiasm. Fr. Hart was reassigned more times in the past five years than most priests are in a career of service. The move to Chatham was a punishment of sorts."

"How do you know all this?" the detective asked.

"Fr. Hart and I were friends. We met when we were both in the seminary, and we stayed in touch over the years. He often confided in me."

Jimmy, who had been uncharacteristically quiet for the past five minutes, decided it was time to speak up. "There's one thing that's bothering me about Emily Rose. We know she had opportunity because she had access to the wine before Mass last Sunday, but what was her motive, and how could she possibly get hold of a rare poison?"

"You know, this kind of reminds me of the story of

Pope Paul I," Fr. Michael said.

Not being as familiar with the history of the papacy as her brother, Farrah spoke up. "In what way?"

Well, Pope Paul I died very suddenly in the early days of his reign as pope. The official cause of death was a heart attack, but there have been many conspiracy theories that believe he was poisoned, either by the Communists or by organized crime."

"Why would they have wanted him dead?" Farrah asked.

"Well, there was a lot of corruption in the Vatican Bank in those days, and the bank had known ties to organized crime. Some believe that Pope Paul wanted to expose that and paid the price with his life. Others believe that he planned on being even more outspoken than his predecessors about the dangers of Communism and so the Russians put a hit on him."

"Sounds like the stuff novels are made of," Jimmy quipped.

"There's another theory floating around, though — one eerily similar to this case."

Fr. Michael now had the group's full attention.

"Many saw Pope Paul I as the reformer the Church desperately needed in the late 1970s, and they believed he was going to pass even more sweeping reforms than the Second Vatican Council, including reversing the Church's stance on artificial birth control. There are some who still hold fast to the belief that he was murdered by someone inside the Vatican to prevent those reforms from ever seeing the light of day."

Everyone on the porch was mesmerized by Fr. Michael's story. They sat for a few moments, considering the parallels between Pope Paul I and the circumstances surrounding the death of Fr. Hart. The silence was broken when the French doors leading from the second-floor hallway swung open. When Melody walked through the doors, it felt as though the temperature had dropped twenty degrees.

"You made good time," Farrah said.

"A word, please," Melody countered.

Farrah followed Melody through the French doors, and the two of them headed to the master bedroom for some privacy. Jimmy decided to call it a night, Detective Nickerson and Fr. Michael followed suit.

While the Fourth of July was two days away, the fireworks were about to begin.

CHAPTER TWENTY-THREE
Two Can Play at This Game

"Who is he?" Melody demanded. She wanted to cut right to the chase and had no interest in small talk. The two were standing on opposite sides of Farrah's king-sized bed.

"Who is who?" Farrah asked. She knew exactly who Melody meant, but she never wanted to lose the upper hand in the conversation — and knowledge was always the upper hand.

"The Edgar Winter lookalike sitting with his arms around you in that picture on Facebook."

Farrah pretended not to understand the reference to the seventies' albino rock icon.

Melody took her phone out of her pocket, pulled up the aforementioned picture, and thrust her phone in Farrah's face.

"That's Detective Nickerson. He's leading the investigation into the murder of Fr. Greg Hart."

"What were you doing on his lap?"

Saying nothing, Farrah merely smiled.

"Why are you smiling?"

Farrah remained silent.

Something clicked inside of Melody. "You sneaky bi . . ."

Farrah interrupted her before she could finish. "Don't say anything you'll regret later."

"But you tricked . . ."

Again Farrah interrupted Melody. "You have not been returning my calls or texts, so I had to up the ante a little bit."

"I should leave right now and never speak to you again."

Farrah knew that in order to get Melody on board with her plan, she had to extend an olive branch to her. She walked over to the bureau in front of the bed, opened the top drawer, and pulled out a small gift box. She walked over to the side of the bed where Melody was standing and sat down. She then patted the top of the mattress, inviting Melody to join her.

"What's that?"

"Sit down and find out," Farrah replied.

Melody did as she was asked, and Farrah handed her the box.

"Don't think you can buy your way out of this," Melody said as she opened the box. She reached into it and removed a diamond tennis bracelet.

Farrah had known that her decision to pursue the case while on summer vacation would be costly — in this case, it had cost her five figures.

Melody appeared stunned; she had wanted a diamond tennis bracelet for most of her adult life.

"Do you like it?"

Melody had no words.

"Because if you don't, I can take it back . . ."

"Don't you dare!" Melody finally said, her voice heavy with emotion. "It's beautiful, but you can't buy your way out every time you upset me. I was so looking forward to this vacation and you not working."

Farrah grabbed the top of Melody's hand. "I know, babe, but one thing you need to know about me — which I have always been up front about — is that I may never be the type of person who can just sit around and hang out on a beach. I get too restless."

Melody knew the truth of this statement. Before starting the podcast that would make her famous, when Farrah worked as a partner in a New York City law firm, her workaholic tendencies caused a major rift in their relationship, leading Melody to give Farrah an ultimatum: the job or her. Farrah chose her and resigned her partnership. The two sold their Soho loft and traded it for a small home in the suburbs of Connecticut. A few months into their new life, Farrah took up podcasting as a hobby to keep herself busy. She never planned on having the success that she experienced.

"Yes, but you promised me a vacation, and the next thing I knew, you started working again. I can't keep up with you sometimes."

Farrah was truly upset that she hurt Melody, but she also had to be true to herself. "I can't promise that I will change completely," Farrah said, "but I can promise to have a better work/life balance if it means keeping you in my life."

Melody looked down at the tennis bracelet and then back at Farrah. "I'm sorry, I can't accept this."

Farrah was stunned — she had been certain Melody would accept her apology.

"I don't understand."

"No, you don't. The truth is, I've been unhappy for a while; the other day was just the straw that broke the camel's back. I just don't feel fulfilled in this relationship any longer. I don't even know where it's going."

It was a line Farrah was all too familiar with and one that infuriated her. Why did it have to go anywhere? They had been together in a committed relationship for almost a decade. They owned a home together. Hell, Farrah thought, I even changed careers for her. To use the "I don't know where it's going" argument at this point in their lives was maddening. Farrah expressed as much to Melody.

"What if I want to be married?" Melody countered. "What about kids?"

Marriage and family was not something Farrah had ever been interested in. For one thing, until recently marriage hadn't been a possibility. And regarding kids, Farrah had always made it clear that she never wanted them.

"Why do you need some legal document to affirm my love for you?" Farrah protested. She went from sitting on the bed next to Melody to standing up.

"Maybe I just want more of a commitment."

"What more of a commitment would marriage provide?"

"If you are fully committed to me, why not formalize it in marriage?"

Farrah ran her fingers through her hair and felt her jaw tighten.

"There's the face," Melody said.

"What face?" Farrah said, exhausted.

"The face you make when you get angry and frustrated. You clench your jaw and look like Faye Dunaway in Mommy Dearest." Melody started laughing. "By tomorrow morning you'll be throwing out all the wire hangers."

"What the hell is so funny?"

"Two can play this game," Melody said.

"What game?"

"The game where one of us makes the other jealous by posting a picture on social media, and the other gets back at her by starting the "where we are going" talk."

Farrah looked Melody in the eyes. "Oh, you are going to pay, Melody Note."

Melody stood up, put her arms around Farrah, and whispered, "Pay? What do I owe?"

Farrah walked over to the door of the master bedroom and made sure it was locked. She then turned off the lights.

"I like where this is going," Melody said.

Farrah's pitch to Melody about how she could help the investigation would have to wait until morning — they had some making up to do.

CHAPTER TWENTY-FOUR

A Snake in the Grass

Fr. Peter Cossa woke up early Wednesday morning with a lot on his mind. He hadn't slept well the night before; a call from his sister Emily made him concerned that questions surrounding Fr. Hart's death, seemingly answered with the suicide of Christopher Mitchell, might still be hanging over Chatham like the fog off its shores.

Even though he had played back his conversation with Emily multiple times before finally falling asleep the previous night, he couldn't help but start over again this morning.

"Emily, you sound troubled. What's the matter?"

"I have a bad feeling about this — call it a woman's intuition."

"I'm not an expert on women, dear sister. Give me something more to go on than a hunch."

"I went to the rectory earlier today to meet with the priest and he had a bottle of sacramental wine on his desk."

"How do you know he wasn't hitting the bottle?"

"Because it was the same bottle from the sacristy."

"How do you know?"

"It had the same stain on the label as the one in the church. The only reason he would have brought it from the church to the rectory is if the police suspected something."

"The medical examiner already knows Fr. Hart died by poisoning — they're probably trying to make sure the whole bottle wasn't poisoned."

"Still, it doesn't feel right, and I have to go to that man's wake tonight and see him lying in that coffin."

"Emily, listen to me closely — you are very involved in that parish and if you don't go, people might be suspicious. Why did you go to the rectory in the first place?"

"To volunteer my services for the funeral. Where did you find that priest anyway?"

"He's a friend of Fr. Hart's from Connecticut. We don't exactly have a large number of men to spare here in the diocese, so when he volunteered to help concelebrate the funeral, we asked if he could spend a few days in the parish to honor his deceased friend. He agreed, and we didn't want to look a gift horse in the mouth."

"What do I do if the cops track me down as one of the few people who had access to the wine before Mass on Sunday?" Emily asked nervously.

"Have a little faith my sister, all will be fine."

In truth, though, Fr. Cossa knew everything was not exactly fine. While the matter of Fr. Hart's death was apparently behind them, and Christopher Mitchell's suicide deflected suspicion away from anyone else who might have wanted Fr. Hart dead, Fr. Cossa had not yet achieved the end result he longed for.

Since he had been a young boy, his father had instilled in him a thirst for power. He was raised to be ultracompetitive in any sport he played; having lettered in soccer, football, and baseball in high school, he was as ruthless inside the classroom as he was on the field. He had no choice but to succeed because anything but achieving number one was akin to failure in his father's eyes.

His father, Baldassarre Cossa, was an Italian immigrant from the town of Bologna, Italy. Born in 1936, Baldassarre was too young to fight for his country in World War II, but he wasn't too young to experience the misery most Italians went through after the war. In order to make a better life for himself, he and his older brother, Fredo, moved south to Sicily where they did some odd jobs for a local Mafia don named Umberto Andolini. Having become members of his crime family, the two Cossa brothers made their way from Sicily to New York where, in the 1940s and 1950s, they started to accumulate both wealth and power.

Fredo remained in New York while Baldassarre saw greater opportunity in Boston, where organized crime was controlled by the Irish and not the Italians. Knowing that he wanted a family, Baldassarre decided to start one far enough outside Boston so that they would be insulated from his business dealings. After having courted the daughter of the local don, Baldassarre was married in 1963 at the age of twenty-seven. One year later his wife, Nicola, gave birth to a daughter, Emilia, known as Emily, and two years after that she gave birth to a son, Pietro, known as Peter.

If there was one lesson Baldassarre had imparted to his children, it was that one had to work hard in order to achieve anything in life. While that sounded noble, the way he reinforced it had been anything but. If either of his children received anything less than a perfect grade in school, the punishment involved a belt and a bare bottom. As they got older, the punishments had become more severe — more so for Peter than for his sister. While Emily might be grounded without food, Peter had been regularly challenged to boxing matches with his father in the basement. It was a no-win situation; Baldassarre had grown up poor on the streets of Italy and later made his bones in a crime family, while Peter had enjoyed a solid upper middle-class lifestyle. The best Peter could do was cover his head and body while his father punched him repeatedly.

The only solace Peter had found was in the comfort of his home parish where he heard stories of miracles, forgiveness, and redemption. He had been very involved with the church, and the parish priest, Fr. Danny Boyle, had taken an interest in him — too much of an interest in him. Peter, who had mistaken the priest's physical attention for love instead of the abuse it truly was, received the beating of his life when his father found out what had been going on between his son and the priest.

After the beating was over, the elder Cossa removed a gun from the safe in his home office, drove to the parish, and killed the priest execution-style in the rectory. Knowing that others had seen him storm into the rectory and that there was no reasonable defense against what he had done, Baldassarre then put a bullet into his own skull.

In the wake of her husband's death, Nicola had a nervous breakdown and could no longer care for her children. Peter had been sent to a seminary and Emily to a convent.

His sister left the convent at eighteen and went to college on a scholarship. To earn extra money, she worked summers out on Cape Cod where, one day, she met and fell in love with a local fisherman named Todd Rose. She dropped out of college shortly after, married him, and started a new life in the town of Chatham as the wife of a fisherman. At twenty-two, she gave birth to her only child, Connor.

Peter, on the other hand, finished high school at the seminary and remained there in lieu of going to college. Romantic relationships held little interest for him, and he eventually came to see the Church as a place where someone could have a position of authority in the community.

He excelled in the seminary and mastered Latin as well as Italian; the later had come in handy when he had the opportunity to study in Rome.

Upon his ordination, Fr. Cossa had been assigned to a large parish in Fall River, where he had served as a special advisor to its pastor, Fr. Robert Hurley, now Bishop Hurley.

Fr. Cossa knew that Fr. Hurley was going places, and he had hitched his wagon to the priest's rising star. Where Fr. Hurley was concerned, Fr. Cossa was the very definition of loyalty, so much so that, upon being named Bishop of the Diocese of Fall River, Fr. Hurley had only one name on his list for chancellor: Fr. Peter Cossa.

Now Cossa was at a crossroads; he had gone as high as he could possibly go in priestly life, but he was thirsty for more. He wanted to become a bishop — and later the pope. But such an appointment wasn't easy to come by, particularly as there were many people in line before him that were just as qualified as Cossa, if not more so.

Being aware of this, Fr. Cossa hatched a plan that would fast-track him to the title of "His Excellency"; he would earn the trust of the bishop in his own diocese, make sure his name was on the short list in the current bishop's contingency plan, and create a vacancy. With two-thirds of his plan complete, it was the last third Cossa was having difficulty bringing to fruition.

He had thought about taking a page out of his father's playbook and just murdering the bishop, but he had decided there was too much risk in that. Instead, he decided to try to influence the bishop to voluntarily step down by causing the bishop to have a nervous breakdown. Fr. Hart, Christopher Mitchell, and his own sister were the pawns Fr. Cossa put into play on this chessboard. Although it had only been a few days since Fr. Hart's death and his sister's confession, he was becoming impatient.

It was time to up the ante, he thought.

CHAPTER TWENTY-FIVE

The Funeral

While Fr. Cossa was ruminating over how to expedite his superior's resignation, Fr. Michael Graham was busy preparing the church for Fr. Hart's funeral. He filled the church's nickel-plated vat with holy water and submerged the matching aspergillum, a scepter-shaped device used for springing holy water, in it. He then moved the Paschal candle to the center aisle of the church directly in front of the spot where the coffin containing Fr. Hart's body would be placed. Next he put a piece of charcoal in the censor, but then had to spend some time hunting down the incense that would be used during the funeral. Thankfully an altar server showed up who helped him find what he was looking for.

Earlier that morning, he had spoken with Farrah. She told him she didn't think it would be a smart idea for her to attend the service. She had already been spotted a few times in town by fans of her podcast, and she didn't want to raise any suspicions about why she was attending the funeral of a priest she'd only seen once. Instead, she and

Jimmy were going to do some digging into Emily Rose as well as her brother, Fr. Peter Cossa.

Fr. Michael learned that Detective William "Nick" Nickerson would also not be attending for similar reasons; he wasn't a member of the parish, and his attendance at the funeral would raise some eyebrows. Instead, his plan was to research the death of Connor Rose. Finding something significant was a long shot, but Nickerson never let poor odds get in the way of accomplishing something he set his mind on — it was partly the reason he went gray prematurely.

Emily Rose walked into the sacristy just as Fr. Graham was looking for something to light the charcoal he had placed in the censor earlier.

"If you're looking for a lighter, it's located in the top drawer under the chasubles. Fr. Hart hid it there after one of the altar servers almost burned the church down with it a few months back."

Fr. Michael turned his head toward the doorway of the sacristy and looked at Emily Rose. She was wearing a black dress with a matching black veil covering her head and face.

"Thank you — I would never have thought to look there," he said, making sure his body language or tone didn't communicate his suspicion that she may have had something to do with Fr. Hart's death. He walked over to the censor, opened it, and lit the charcoal.

"I've always loved that smell," Emily commented.

"I've always enjoyed it myself," Fr. Michael agreed.

Stepping into a Catholic church is a sensory, as well as spiritual, experience. Candles are lit providing not only lighting but also some drama, an organist and choir provide sound, and in the cases of high holy days or funerals, a censor provides the smell of perfumed incense throughout the church.

"It reminds me of purity," she continued, her face obscured by the veil.

"Would you like me to fill the cruets with water and wine?"

"Please," Fr. Michael replied.

Emily walked over to the cabinet in the sacristy where the cruets were stored and removed them. She noticed that the cruets from last week were missing and in their place were some new ones. She figured that the old ones were at the police station; leaving the cruet with the poisoned wine for the police to find was part of the plan to frame Christopher Mitchell — she didn't count on it backfiring.

She then opened the bottom cabinet where the sacramental wine was kept and took out a new, unopened bottle of a different brand.

"I need to use a mustum wine when I celebrate Mass," Fr. Michael said, watching Emily examine the wine's label. He had been searching for a reason why the sacramental wine had been changed from Sunday, and the best he could come up with was to imply that he had an intolerance to alcohol. Under Church law, priests with alcohol dependencies or intolerances were allowed to use mustum wine, which is derived from the juices of freshly squeezed grapes and immediately frozen to halt the fermentation process.

She reached down to pick it up, twisted the cap open, and started to fill the cruet. Next she opened the bag of hosts and filled the ciborium. She then placed the hosts, water, and wine on a table adjacent to the altar.

The church had started to fill up with people eager to say good-bye to the priest they had only known for six short months. *We are better off without him*, Emily thought as she walked back to the vestibule. She saw that the hearse from Lightbody and Sons funeral home had pulled up as well as the truck that transported all the flowers from the funeral home. As the doors opened, the organ inside the church came to life as the organist began to warm up with Schubert's "Ave Maria."

Just a few hours and I'll never have to think of this man again, Emily thought. But she had been wrong before, and she would be wrong again.

CHAPTER TWENTY-SIX

Melody's Note

Farrah woke up to the sound of a car's engine turning over. She walked down the stairs and looked out through the bay window in her family room just in time to see Melody's car pull out of the driveway. She headed for the kitchen, and on the counter, next to the coffee pot, she spotted a note.

I shouldn't have come up yesterday. While the evening was wonderful, I know that I'll never be able to compete for your attention, and I just can't take a back seat to your life. I'm heading up to P-Town for a few days . . . come find me if you want to chat — Melody

Farrah knew from the moment Melody fell asleep last night that her plan had backfired. She intended to draw Melody back to Chatham in hopes of making amends and convincing her to play a part in her plan to corner Emily Rose, but Farrah failed to see the flaw in her thinking. It was based on two improbabilities: 1) Melody forgiving Farrah, and 2) Melody being open to playing a part in the investigation that sent her packing to begin with. Farrah kicked herself for even considering it.

"What's going on?" Having woken up after hearing the front door open and close, Jimmy's inner detective kicked into gear.

Farrah handed Jimmy the note Melody left.

"Again?" Jimmy asked.

Farrah nodded.

Jimmy could tell that Farrah was upset and trying not to cry. He followed his instinct and hugged her. She buried her face in his chest, held on tight, and let her tears flow. After a minute, Jimmy second-guessed his decision to not put on anything over his boxer shorts before leaving his room. At twenty-three years old, he had yet to master control of his anatomy.

Farrah pushed herself away from him. "Holy shit, Doubts, are you getting a boner?"

Jimmy's face turned as as red as a tomato, which was in stark contrast to the white undershirt he was wearing. To be truthful, Jimmy found Farrah extremely attractive, and he should have been more careful about his choice to comfort her with a hug, especially when Farrah was only wearing a nightshirt.

"I'm sorry . . . it's just . . ."

Farrah walked out of the kitchen and took a seat on the love seat in her family room. When Jimmy walked in, he saw that her head was buried in her hands and her body was almost convulsing.

"I'm so sorry," he pleaded. "Look, if you want me to leave..."

As Farrah lifted her head and removed her hands from her face, Jimmy could see that she was laughing. When she looked at him, she laughed even harder.

Jimmy looked down to see that the opening of his boxer shorts had exposed his now flaccid penis.

"It looks like a scared turtle!" Farrah said, howling.

Jimmy was mortified. He sprinted to his room at the end of the hall, put on a pair of jeans, and replaced the undershirt he had been wearing, which had become wet with Farrah's tears.

"Oh, Doubts, I needed that laugh!"

Jimmy, who didn't find the situation nearly as funny as Farrah did, made one more attempt to apologize to his boss. She placed her finger to her lips, indicating that he shouldn't bother.

After catching her breath, Farrah changed the subject. "We need to come up with a Plan B."

Jimmy was quiet, his face still red.

"Come on, Doubts, you have to admit it was a little funny."

Jimmy, who couldn't get the sight of Farrah pointing at his boxer shorts out of his mind, failed to see the humor of the situation.

Farrah, realizing that he was mortified, tried to diffuse the situation by using more humor.

"I mean, this is a hard problem to solve; I could really use your help erecting a plan."

She saw what appeared to be the beginnings of a smile.

"Come on, Doubts, I need your brain on this one — the big brain, not the little one."

That's all it took, Jimmy was once again bright red, but at least he was laughing.

"That's the Doubts I know."

"A scared turtle?"

"Look, Doubts, I'm over it. Now we have to figure out

what our next move is. The way I see it, there are two things we need to do; one is to figure out why this Emily Rose chick might have offed Fr. Hart, and the other is to dig into her brother a bit more."

Jimmy rubbed his temples. "Why don't we let Nickerson do the digging into Emily while we dig into the brother?"

"That works for me. Up for a trip to Fall River?"

"Fall River?"

"That's where the chancellor's office is."

"You intend to get a meeting with the chancellor?"

"Don't go all soft on me, Doubts — how else are we going to put this puzzle together?"

Jimmy threw his hands up in the air. "Why don't we just try and get a meeting with the bishop too?"

"Great idea! I'll see if my brother has any pull."

Jimmy looked at Farrah blankly.

"What, Doubts — did you think this was going to be a vacation? Listen, hop in the shower, but don't take too long or I'll assume the worst." Farrah made an obscene gesture with her hand. "Let's plan to leave here in twenty."

Farrah got up from the couch and walked out of the room. Jimmy felt as if he'd been hit over the head with a hammer.

Maybe that internship really wasn't all that bad, he thought to himself.

CHAPTER TWENTY-SEVEN

A Changed Man

Detective Nickerson spent the first part of the morning looking into the Connor Rose case, which the Chatham police department considered technically still open. The case file wasn't very thick, and he was able to piece everything together quickly.

On Thursday, August 30, 2001, a body washed ashore on Lighthouse Beach in Chatham; later that day it was identified as that of fifteen-year-old Connor Rose, the son of Emily Rose and her late husband, Todd. It was initially assumed that he drowned in a boating accident, but an autopsy showed no sign of water in his lungs, indicating that he had to have been dead before being thrown into the water. Interestingly, there was a note in the margin of a legal pad suggesting that his mother was against preforming the autopsy for religious reasons but had been overruled by the medical examiner, whose examination found trace amounts of heroin in Connor's bloodstream. The autopsy also confirmed that there had been blunt force trauma to his head. The medical examiner concluded that head trauma was the cause of death and pushed the detectives to investigate any known heroin dealers on the Cape.

Bill Jamison, the detective on the case, still had one big question: How did Connor get in the water? To answer it, he asked Connor's mother for any information she could provide on people her son hung out with. She came up with the names of some kids she considered to be bad seeds, and when questioned, one of them gave Detective Jamison the name of a small-time dealer in Hyannis named Fabio Morgan.

Nick read the notes of the detective's interviews with Morgan and found that he had an airtight alibi for the period of time when Connor's death likely occurred. He was "doing time" in a home for at-risk teens in Nickerson State Park, located in the Brewster, Massachusetts. The case went cold after that.

Nick wanted to ask the former detective on the case some questions, but he learned that Bill Jamison had died of a heart attack shortly after working the Connor Rose case. He was, however, able to track down Fabio Morgan, who was now a counselor at the same home for at-risk teens he had lived in fifteen years ago. Nick called his long-time friend Mary Christine, who ran the home, and she confirmed that Morgan would be working that morning. He decided to pay Morgan a visit.

The drive to Brewster from Chatham typically took no more than twenty minutes, but the Fourth of July holiday was prime tourist season, and it took twenty minutes just for Nick to navigate Main Street.

Ten minutes later, Nick made a right onto Route 6A in Brewster, and a few minutes later he made a right into the main entrance for Nickerson State Park. He asked a park attendant for directions, and after a few wrong turns, he found the driveway to the home, spoke to the guard at the gate who crossed his name off a list, and parked his car.

He walked into the house, where Mary Christine was waiting for him.

"When I saw your number come up on my phone this morning, I assumed you were going to ask me out again. I was dismayed to find you were calling on business."

With her long, chestnut-colored hair and hazel eyes, Mary was the object of every single man's affection. Over the years, though, she made it clear that no man could possibly compete with the devotion she felt to the young men placed in her care.

"I might be just a simple detective from a small town in Massachusetts, but I don't have an addiction to rejection. Besides, the rumor around town is that you have freckles on your toes."

This almost caused Mary to spit out her coffee. There was a running joke in town that she couldn't keep a man in her life because her toes, and no other part of her body, were covered in freckles. No one was really sure who started that rumor, but Nick had a hunch it was Mary herself.

"What's your interest in Morgan? He's the best counselor I've got."

"I'm researching an old case, and his name is in the file."

"How old?"

"Fifteen years."

"He's a different man now," Mary said.

Nickerson could tell she was concerned. "Look, I don't

want him for anything; quite the opposite really. I'm hoping he can shed light on some things, that's all."

Mary knew that Nickerson was as honest as they come, so his words reassured her. She picked up the phone in her office and punched in a four-digit extension. "Mia, can you tell me where Fabio's group is now? Okay, got it. Thanks." Hanging up, she turned to Nick and said, "He's playing basketball with his group. I'll show you to the courts."

Nickerson followed Mary out the door. His eyes focused on her body as she walked in front of him; he was honest, but he was still a man.

At five feet five inches, Fabio Morgan was a little too short to be a basketball superstar, but he never let that get in the way of his love for running the rock. He first discovered his love for basketball as a resident of the group home, and now as a counselor he shared his passion for the game with the young men under his supervision. The kids quickly learned that playing with Fabio was part athletic competition and part motivational lecture. Before playing, he always lined "his boys" up and imparted some knowledge to them. He had just finished sharing some words of wisdom about winning and losing and the importance of dealing with obstacles when he saw his boss walking toward the court with a tall, white-haired man trailing behind her. It was clear they were coming to talk to him, so he threw the ball back to the group.

"Play a little five on five — I'll be back in a few minutes," Fabio said, walking over to Mary. He shook her hand and then extended it to the stranger.

"Fabio, this is Detective William Nickerson of the Chatham Police Department. He's an old friend of mine, and he'd like to speak with you for a few moments."

Fabio's demeanor changed as though someone flicked a switch. "What's this all about?"

Nickerson spoke up before Mary could answer. "You are not in trouble . . ."

"Man, I know I'm not in trouble; I haven't done anything. I just want to know what this is all about."

Nickerson understood that people had different responses to what they perceived to be threatening situations, and he wanted to put Fabio at ease. "I'm looking into a case from fifteen years ago, and I have some questions for you about the kid who died."

"Connor Rose," Fabio said.

"Yes."

"Did you know him, Fabio?" Mary asked.

"Met him only once. Sold to a friend of his, but the cops know that already. I had nothing to do with his death."

"I'm not here to question that, Fabio," Nick said.

"Then why are you here?"

"I'm curious — does this woman look familiar to you?"

Nickerson took a picture out of the folder he was holding and showed it to Fabio.

"I don't know . . . maybe. Why?"

"Look, Fabio, if you recognize her, it's important to say something," Mary said reassuringly.

"Man, I only sold dope twice in my life. I was just a small time pot dealer, but some guys out of Boston thought the Cape would be a good market for H," Fabio said, using the slang term for heroin, "and they told me I could make some big money if I got in that game. I sold it once to Connor Rose's buddy."

"That's consistent with the report. What was the other time you sold it?"

"I sold it to her," Fabio said, pointing at the picture of Emily Rose. "It was weird, though; she didn't seem like a junkie. She apparently had never bought drugs before — she was anything but discreet about the transaction."

"Are you sure it was her?" Nickerson asked.

"As sure as I am that this place saved my life," Fabio replied. "Can I go back to my boys now?"

"Yes. Thank you, Fabio," Detective Nickerson said.

Fabio went back to the group playing basketball, and Nickerson turned to Mary and asked, "How about dinner tonight?"

"Can't. Washing my hair."

"Worth a shot."

"You miss 100 percent of the shots you don't take," Mary said, quoting hockey legend Wayne Gretzky.

Nickerson shook his head with a small smile. He walked back to the main building with Mary, said good-bye, and got in his car, and drove back to Chatham.

CHAPTER TWENTY-EIGHT

Upping the Ante

Farrah pulled onto Route 137 on her way to Route 6 — otherwise known as the Mid-Cape Highway. As she was driving away from Chatham, she could have sworn she saw Detective Nickerson's car driving toward town; this prompted her to call him.

"Siri, call Detective Nickerson," Farrah spoke out loud into her iPhone. She was hesitant to give her phone to Jimmy to dial as there were some pictures in her photos from the night before that were for her eyes only.

"Calling Darlene Nickerbocker," the disembodied voice from her phone replied.

"Shit!" Farrah fumbled to get to her phone to end the call before it could connect. Darlene was an old flame who would have thought it strange that Farrah were calling her in the daytime instead of the middle of the night.

Farrah tried her luck again. "Siri, call William Nickerson."

"Okay, calling William Nathanson."

"Mother of pearl!" Farrah screamed, once again

ending the call before it could connect — Farrah wasn't exclusively into women, and William was the last man she had been with.

"Wouldn't it be easier if I . . ." Jimmy started to say, Farrah cut him off as she suddenly realized her mistake.

"Siri, please call Nick."

"Okay, calling Nick."

"This is Nick," came the voice of Detective William Nickerson after two rings.

"Nick, this is Farrah and Jimmy. You are on speaker."

"Hey, I'm just on my way back to the station; there's been a development. Can you guys meet me?"

"So that was you we passed on the way to Route 6!"

"Yeah, I'm just back from Brewster. Would it be easier if I came to your house?"

"Actually we're on our way to Fall River," Farrah replied. "I want to find out more about Emily's brother, the chancellor, as well as try and talk to the bishop — I have a hunch that his life may be in danger."

"What makes you think that?" Nickerson was eager to tell Farrah about the conversation he had just had with Fabio Morgan, but he wanted to hear what she had to say first.

"I had a thought last night before I went to bed. We have a suspect in Emily Rose but we don't yet have a motive. Why would she possibly want to kill her priest?"

"What are you thinking?"

"At first I thought the bishop might have had something to do with it, but that really doesn't make much sense. Why would he want to off one of his own priests?"

"By all accounts, he was a problem child for the diocese," Nickerson replied.

"Still, this isn't the Middle Ages," Farrah replied.

"And it can't be a coincidence that the chancellor's sister is our prime suspect," Jimmy added.

"About that," Nickerson said, "I just found a bit of information that is disturbing."

Farrah and Jimmy listened as Detective Nickerson recounted his meeting with Fabio Morgan. When he came to the part where Morgan recalled selling heroin to Emily Rose, both she and Jimmy said, "No way," simultaneously.

"So she staged the death of her own son as a murder? Why would she want to do something like that?"

"That's what I'm going to devote my entire day to find out."

"How are you going to do that?"

"With some good old-fashioned police work!"

"Keep us in the loop of with what you find out. We'll call you later with anything we learn in Fall River."

"Sounds like a plan."

Farrah hit a button on her steering wheel to terminate the call.

"This just gets more and more interesting," Jimmy said.

"So we have a dead priest and a dead kid, both who we think were killed by Emily Rose, sister of the Chancellor of the Diocese of Fall River. What the hell could those two deaths have in common?"

"Hey, shouldn't you call your brother to see if he has any pull with getting us a meeting with the bishop?"

"Thanks for the reminder, Doubts."

Farrah once again called out to her phone, "Siri, call Mikey."

The computerized voice replied, "Okay, calling Mikey."

Mikey answered and said, "Farrah, I'm just leaving the

church. Want to meet for lunch?"

"How was the funeral?"

"Sad. Church was packed, lots of tears. Listen, I'm really hungry and . . ."

"Can't. Doubts and I are heading to Fall River."

"Fall River? Why?"

"Your sister thinks she can waltz into the bishop's office and get a meeting with him," Doubts said before Farrah could answer.

"He's been sick, and I doubt he's seeing anyone. Why do you want to see him anyway?"

"Actually I wanted to see Fr. Cossa; the bishop was Doubts' idea."

"Let me stop you right there. Cossa won't see you — don't even try."

"But I'm Farrah Graham," Farrah joked.

"That's precisely why he won't see you. You don't fit the mold of someone he would want to be seen having a meeting with."

"What, because I'm bisexual?"

"No, because you are a bisexual burgeoning celebrity with the hottest podcast in the country, one that focuses on questionable deaths."

"Point taken. What about the bishop?"

"From what I can tell, he's a real man of the cloth, but when I called his office yesterday to let him know I was going to spend a few more days in Chatham, I was told that he was sick."

"What kind of sick?" Farrah asked.

"I didn't ask."

"I'm only asking because I think there's a bigger story here that we're not seeing." Farrah then told her brother what Detective Nickerson told them about Emily Rose and the death of her son.

"That woman really does give me the creeps."

"Do you have any way we can get in touch with the bishop?"

"You can't call his office because his gatekeeper will never put you through," Fr. Michael said. "But you could always try the rectory; if he's still sick, he might actually answer the house phone. It's worth a shot."

"Can you get me the number?"

"I'll look it up once I get back to the rectory. I'm almost there now. I'll text it to you."

"Thanks, Mikey."

"I hate it when you call me that . . ."

"Love you too," Farrah replied and terminated the call.

Farrah and Jimmy were passing through Centerville on their way west to the Sagamore Bridge. Traffic heading in the opposite direction was bumper-to-bumper as people made their way to the Cape's popular eastern towns for the Fourth of July.

"Too bad we can't fly back," Farrah observed.

"I could have flown us down," Jimmy replied. "My plane is fueled and ready to go."

"What did I tell you before, Doubts?"

"That you'd only fly with me if there's a life on the line."

"Exactly. We aren't there yet."

At the time, Farrah didn't realize just how prophetic her words would be.

Bishop Robert Hurley left his room just past 11:00 a.m.

and walked downstairs — it was the farthest he had been away from his room since hearing the confession of Fr. Hart's killer the day before. While he had regrets over what had happened in Chatham, he was playing a long game, and he knew that in order to win, he had to keep up the appearance that he was in a deep depression.

Truthfully, though, the bishop felt as if he had a tremendous weight on his shoulders. He knew that talking to someone about it would make him feel better, but since doing so would break the seal of confession, the bishop had no choice but to keep it to himself.

He looked at his watch and saw that it was a quarter past eleven. The funeral for Fr. Hart would be over by now, he thought.

He was alone in the kitchen of the rectory; the other priests who lived there were busy in the business offices, and the cook was not due to return for another forty-five minutes. He poured himself a glass of orange juice from the fridge and fixed himself a bowl of cereal. While he knew that other bishops insisted on having all their meals prepared for them, he was fine with taking care of his own necessities — it helped him stay grounded.

As he ate, the bishop reflected on his relationship with Fr. Hart and the regrets he felt over certain events that had transpired. Additionally, the fact that there was someone in his diocese that could kill without remorse scared him.

What's become of me? the bishop asked himself. Maybe it's time to retire — or go back to being a simple parish priest.

These thoughts were fleeting, however; there was no way his resignation would be accepted by the Apostolic Nuncio, let alone the pope himself. No, he would remain the bishop until he reached the mandatory retirement age of seventy-five, or until he died in office either naturally or unnaturally; the latter being a notion that he couldn't totally dismiss, all things considered. It was a sobering thought, and one that provided him with little comfort.

After he was done with his cereal, Bishop Hurley decided to have a cup of coffee and walked across the kitchen to where half a pot of coffee remained. Before he could finish pouring himself a cup, the house phone started to ring. Because all business calls went directly to the office line, only personal calls came through on the house phone. Since no one else was in the residence, Bishop Hurley decided to answer the phone himself. This, too, was a habit unique to him as the bishop — most bishops had a personal assistant, often a deacon, who answered their calls. That someone could call a rectory and reach a bishop directly was unheard of.

"Hello," the bishop said into the phone.

"Um, my name is Jimmy Rella, and I know this might sound strange, but I was wondering if I could speak to Bishop Hurley."

The bishop could hear the nervousness in what he imagined to be a very young man's voice. If he were in a joking mood, he would have tried to have fun with the person on the other end of the line. Now wasn't the time, though.

"This is Bishop Hurley."

"Wait, what?" the voice said on the other end of the line.

The bishop heard a bit of commotion on the other end of the phone and, although he wasn't sure, could have sworn he heard a woman's voice say something about having doubts. A second later, the woman's voice came on the line.

"Bishop Hurley, my name is Farrah Graham. My brother Michael is currently helping you out at Our Lady of Healing Church in Chatham."

Bishop Hurley felt a lump in his throat as he heard the caller speak her name. *Was this really THE Farrah Graham?* he wondered.

"How can I help you?" The bishop's voice came across with a fair amount of static, causing Farrah to speak louder into the phone.

"Bishop, it is very important that I meet with you immediately. My colleague Jimmy and I are heading to Fall River from Chatham right now. We are on Route 6, about ten minutes away from the Sagamore Bridge. We can be in Fall River in about an hour."

"This is very unorthodox, Ms. Graham."

"Please, Bishop Hurley," Farrah pleaded. "More lives may be in danger."

The urgency with which these words were said was not lost on the bishop; Farrah's sense of urgency reinforced his decision to see her.

"Fine," he replied, but then realized there were few places in the rectory or in the diocesan offices where he could find some privacy. He then had an epiphany. "Meet me in the confessional on the right-hand side of the cathedral."

Farrah felt her throat tighten — in season two of Uncorking a Murder, the wife of the main character was found dead in a confessional in a church in Pompano Beach, Florida.

"Is there any other place we can meet, Bishop Hurley?"

"I'm afraid it's the only place I can expect any privacy,

Ms. Graham."

"Is there a number I can call when I arrive?"

"Just meet me in the confessional, Ms. Graham. I'll be sure to be there in the next hour. If a penitent is in with me, which I highly doubt, just kneel in a pew close by and say a few prayers."

Bishop Hurley hung up the phone and was about to walk upstairs when he was startled by the sight of Fr. Peter Cossa in the doorway of the kitchen.

"I thought you would still be in bed," the chancellor said, sounding surprised to find his superior in the kitchen.

"I was hungry."

"I could have brought something to you."

"No need; I can take care of myself."

"Does this mean you are feeling better?" Fr. Cossa asked, not sounding the least bit happy that this might actually be the case.

"Better than last night, but still not 100 percent. How is the search for a new priest in Chatham coming?"

"I expect to have a short list of names for you by the end of the week. I'm just dotting my I's and crossing my T's, as they say."

"Excellent. I'm going back upstairs now."

"Before you go, Bishop, would you mind telling me why you were answering the house phone?"

Fr. Cossa wanted to find out who the bishop was planning to meet in the confessional. The bishop, hearing subtle urgency in Fr. Cossa's tone, decided to be confrontational.

"What's your interest in who I speak with?"

"You have to be careful not to answer the house phone. If word spread that one could reach the bishop on the rectory's line, I'm afraid it would begin to ring off the hook."

"It was someone who sounded distressed. The minute I forget that I became a priest to help those in need is the minute I should leave the ministry."

Fr. Cossa was taken aback by the bishop's tone. Perhaps he isn't so fragile after all, Cossa thought.

The bishop left the kitchen and went back upstairs, while Fr. Cossa poured himself a cup of coffee. He knew he had to do something.

"Bishop Hurley," Fr. Cossa called upstairs.

"What is it, Fr. Cossa?"

"There's something I think you should know," Fr. Cossa replied.

"Well, stop shouting from downstairs and come up and tell me. I have enough of a headache as it is."

Fr. Cossa took each stair slowly, careful not to trip over his long cassock. He entered the bishop's bedroom.

"I wanted to hold off on telling you this because you seemed to be in a fragile state these past two days, but now that I see you are feeling better, I feel as if I must."

"Spit it out, Peter; it's not like you to hold anything back."

"I received a call from a reporter at The Globe today."

The bishop's face went white. It was the same paper that broke the sexual abuse scandal in the early 2000s.

"And?"

"He called to check on the rumor that Fr. Hart's alleged killer, Christopher Mitchell, was exonerated of any wrongdoing after his suicide and the investigation into Fr. Hart's death is ongoing."

Any remaining color in the bishop's face was now gone.

"What did you tell him?"

"I told him the truth, that we have heard nothing of the sort. That's true, isn't it?"

Bishop Hurley closed his eyes. He knew that Christopher Mitchell wasn't the killer, but he couldn't divulge that for fear of breaking the seal of confession.

"Your silence troubles me, Your Excellency. Perhaps more troubling is the reporter's accusation that you had something to do with Fr. Hart's murder. I assured him that was preposterous, but he told me that, after piecing together some of your more public outbursts with Fr. Hart, he could craft a story pointing the finger at you."

Bishop Hurley thought the lack of anger in the chancellor's voice spoke volumes; the Machiavellian priest sensed opportunity.

"I'd like to be alone now, Peter."

"Shall I call Kenny Constantine?" Peter asked. Constantine was the lawyer whose firm handled all legal matters for the diocese.

"Don't be ridiculous. The Globe's accusations have no merit. Now let me be — you've just made my migraine worse."

"Would you like a glass of water, Bishop?"

The bishop nodded, and Fr. Cossa entered the master bathroom and retrieved a glass of water, but not before crushing a strong narcotic pill and mixing the powder in the water.

The bishop put it to his lips and winced. "Remind me to have maintenance check our water filters." Bishop Hurley then set the alarm next to his bed to go off in one hour so he could meet his visitor in the confessional.

Fr. Cossa waited outside the door until he heard Bishop

Hurley begin to snore and then walked quietly into the bishop's room and turned off the setting for his alarm. He went back to his office and immediately picked up the phone to dial one of the members of the Order who had connections at The Globe. Fr. Cossa told him exactly how to pitch an article about the bishop's rocky history with the recently murdered Fr. Hart as well as his connection to his suspected murderer.

Once that bit of nasty business was done, he made anonymous calls to the major newspapers in the Dioceses of Bridgeport, New York, and Los Angeles, spreading tales of corruption and impropriety about his short-listed competitors for successor to the Bishop of Fall River. When the time came for a new bishop to be named in Fall River, and that time was coming soon, Fr. Cossa was going to be sure that there was only one name left on it — his own.

The ante was now upped.

CHAPTER TWENTY-NINE

An Act of contrition

Emily Rose returned from the funeral relieved that she could finally put Fr. Hart's death behind her. While she did not feel the least bit remorseful about poisoning the priest, she was tired of being surrounded by the reminders of his death; between the wake and the funeral, she was eager to put the past week in the rearview mirror.

As Emily entered her house, the joy she felt coming home was soon interrupted by her ailing father-in-law, who had apparently fallen down the stairs and was sprawled out on the floor of the foyer.

"Tyler!" Emily screamed.

"Ohhhh," Tyler groaned.

"What happened?"

"I came downstairs to open the door, but I tripped on the last step."

"Why were you trying to open the door?"

"The doorbell rang, and I heard a voice outside say it was the police. I thought it was important."

Emily paused to consider why the police would come to

her house. She wondered if it could have something to do with the bottle of wine she saw in the office of the rectory the day before. Her concentration was broken when she heard the freezer door close and the sound of footsteps heading in her direction.

"I've got the ice — are you sure I shouldn't call for an ambulance?"

Emily was shocked to see Detective William Nickerson standing in her foyer.

"Ms. Rose, just in time! I'm afraid your father-in-law had a fall, although it doesn't seem serious."

Tyler, who was a proud veteran of the US Air Force, attempted to stand, but found that he couldn't put any weight on his left foot. Emily ignored her father-in-law and kept her eyes on Detective Nickerson.

"Why are you here, Detective?"

Ignoring Emily's question, Nick helped her father-in-law to his feet. The detective allowed himself to be a human crutch and walked with Tyler to the couch in the adjacent living room.

"Let's have a look," Nick said, rolling up Tyler's pants at the ankles. He saw that the old man's ankle was beginning to swell and become discolored.

"I don't know if it's broken or sprained, but I do know that you have to get that checked out. There's a new urgent care facility near the Rose Cottage Antiques shop on 137 . . ."

"I'll take it from here, Detective Nickerson," Emily interrupted. "Tyler, stay right here while I show the detective out."

Emily walked Nickerson to the front door, opened it, and followed him out.

"You didn't answer my question, Detective. Why are you here?"

It was a question Nickerson had considered on the drive from Brewster to Chatham; he knew he couldn't come out and tell her that she was a suspect the Fr. Hart's death for a few reasons. For one, any evidence he had was circumstantial; even though Emily had had access to the sacramental wine before Mass, he had yet to identify a suitable motive. And from what Fabio Morgan told him, Emily also might be a suspect in the death of her own son, and that presented another challenge for the detective; he wanted to figure out why she may have wanted to kill her own child. If he spooked her now, she might flee. He could tell she was a very proud woman, and he figured that to find the answer to these questions, he would need to get close to her and build her trust. To do that, he attempted to stroke her pride a bit.

"I know you and the entire community over at Our Lady of Healing have been through a lot these past few days, and I wanted to personally thank you for pointing us in the direction of Christopher Mitchell. Without you, we would still be looking for Fr. Hart's killer. Because of that, immediately after the Fourth of July parade tomorrow, the Chatham Police Department would like to formally acknowledge your role in helping us identify Fr. Hart's killer by giving you a citizen's commendation. In addition, the Mayor will be there to give you the key to the city. This will all take place in front of the Eldridge Library on Main Street right after the parade."

As Emily heard these words, a sense of warmth covered her body. After years of being treated like a nobody by her father and then later by her own husband and son, she was finally going to get the recognition she deserved. A feeling of pride bubbled up inside her chest. While she knew it was a sin to feel prideful, she brushed that inconvenient fact aside as the recognition she had been searching for since she was a little girl was finally within reach.

"I don't know what to say, Detective. I'm overwhelmed by this news."

"Are you planning to march in the parade tomorrow?"

"Yes, a group of us at the church always march in the parade."

"Main Street will be a bit of a madhouse after the parade ends, so we'll have a club car waiting at a parade route's end down by the health club. Someone will take you back to the library on Main Street. You'll have your very own police escort."

A groan came from the house. Upon hearing it, Emily was reminded that her father-in-law was still in need of medical attention.

"I'd better get back inside to take care of Tyler. I'll see you tomorrow, Detective."

"I'm looking forward to it."

Detective Nickerson left Emily's house and drove back to the station. He had two calls to make — one to the director of the Eldridge Library and another to the Mayor's office.

Emily walked back into her house, feeling elated at the prospect of being recognized by the police department and the Mayor for her role in the capture of Fr. Hart's killer. If they only knew, she thought to herself.

"Emily, who were you talking to?"

Her mood went from elation to anger as her father-in-law's dementia brought her back down to earth. The man could remember intricate details of spy missions flown over the USSR during the Cold War, but he couldn't remember the cop that was just in the house.

"It's not important," she told him as she didn't want to get into a back-and-forth about what Detective Nickerson told her. Tyler wouldn't remember the conversation anyway.

"My ankle is hurting. I must have done something to it. Can you take me to the doctor?"

"You really don't remember what happened to your ankle?"

Tyler looked at her, frustration evident in his eyes. He didn't realize how bad his memory was.

"If it's too much of an imposition, I'll call a cab."

Imposition? Emily thought. He's been imposing on me ever since his wife died.

Emily's late husband Todd had been an only child. His mother died of cancer five years ago, leaving his father a widower. Without much of a savings account, when his own health began to fail, Tyler had had no choice but to move in with his daughter-in-law, and she had no choice but to take him in, lest the townspeople consider her heartless. Appearances were very important to Emily, even if she didn't give a shit about her father-in-law.

"Fine," she said coldly as she grabbed her keys and helped him up off the couch. She slowly walked with him to her car, got him situated in the passenger seat, and then drove him to the urgent care center on Route 137.

The center was a state-of-the-art facility located adjacent to one of Chatham's most popular antiques stores. The growing number of families who vacationed in Chatham during the summer, combined with the increasing number of baby boomers who were retiring there, gave rise to the need for another medical facility. The building also housed an orthopedic practice which treated most of the broken bones from visitors and residents, and so, for Emily and Tyler, a visit to the center might be one-stop shopping.

After a painstakingly slow walk from the car to the front door of the building, Emily registered Tyler with the receptionist and was told to have a seat in the waiting room as there were several people ahead of them. A higher than usual number of people visiting town to celebrate the nation's independence plus copious amounts of alcohol consumed as part of the pre-celebration led to an approximate wait of forty-five minutes.

Emily walked over to a table and fished out a magazine for Tyler to read so he wouldn't rely on her for entertainment. As he dug into the pages of an outdated copy of *Fore!* Magazine, Emily searched for something to read herself. She came across an old edition of Highlights, a magazine designed for kids and found in doctor's offices throughout the country. Just seeing it caused Emily to think about her own childhood, which was anything but ideal.

Her earliest memories were of her mother, who always seemed to be on edge. Most likely this had been the result of Emily's father rarely being around; although when he had been around, he was always volatile. When Emily was younger, she had no idea that her father was involved in organized crime. She grew up believing he was a plumber, albeit one who worked until all hours of the evening. When she thought of her mother, Emily remembered how sad her eyes looked and how tired she always seemed. She never realized that the sadness was the result of an unhappy marriage.

When her father was around, he would constantly lecture Emily and her brother Peter on right and wrong, not to be confused with civics or morality. Don't rat on your friends, act for the good of the group, protect yourself at all costs — these were lessons of right and wrong as taught by a street thug. In fact, the worst beating she remembered her brother ever receiving at the hands of her father was after the principal of their grammar school, Sr. Elizabeth Collins, sent a letter home with Peter for his parents. The letter congratulated Mr. and Mrs. Cossa for raising a boy who had the courage to tell the truth about other boys in class who were cheating. Instead of being proud that his son did the right thing in the eyes of the Church, he gave Peter the belt while constantly repeating, "Nobody likes a rat."

After her father killed the priest who was abusing her brother, Emily came to view him not as a villain, but as an angel of vengeance who was strong enough and brave enough to right the wrongs of the world — and she vowed to continue his work.

She took to heart what the ultra-strict nuns taught during her days at the convent: The reforms of Vatican II were the root cause for all the evil the Church was facing in the modern era. The Church was getting too soft, they said, and needed to go back to the days when it held more authority. Emily, who did not feel a calling to religious life, vowed to do her part to bring authority back to the Church.

She married soon after falling in love with Todd Rose. To keep in line with Church teaching, their wedding night was the first time she had ever experienced sexual intercourse, and it was quite painful. When Todd suggested they try again the following evening, she pushed him away, informing him that she hadn't been put on earth for his pleasure. As their marriage went on, she would only share herself with Todd during those times of her cycle when the chance to conceive a child was at its peak, a fact that her husband had a hard time coming to terms with.

After the birth of their son, Connor, Emily made it clear that she never wanted to go through the pain of childbirth ever again. As a religiously conservative woman, she viewed the marital bed's main purpose as procreation, and since she didn't want any more children, Emily refused to share herself with Todd for years. Eventually, living in a sexless marriage became too much for Todd to handle, and he asked his wife for a divorce. Divorce was a sin, however, and Emily wouldn't be part of it. Feeling some guilt over her husband's feelings, she agreed to share herself with him when she knew her chances of getting pregnant were practically zero, but the lack of passion and physical interest in her husband only served to push him away even more.

"The only way you are leaving this marriage is feet first," Emily often told him.

Stuck between a rock and a hard place, Todd started to venture outside of his marriage for sexual fulfillment, and he eventually began having an affair with a widower named Mary Francis. Rumors of the affair spread through the small town, and Emily could feel the eyes of her friends and neighbors all over her. After driving by his mistress' house and seeing her husband's truck in the driveway, Emily barged in and heard moans of pleasure coming from the bedroom. She grabbed a knife from the kitchen, ran upstairs, and caught the two lovers off guard.

She would never forget the look on Mary's face — with Todd above her she was the first to see Emily barge into the room. Todd turned around when he heard the door open, but he couldn't remove himself from his mistress quickly enough when Emily came up from behind him and slit his throat. His body fell on top of his mistress, pinning her to the mattress. As her husband bled out, Emily whispered in his ear, "Thou shall not commit adultery."

She ignored the screams of her husband's mistress until she realized that she was in a rather precarious position — Mary could easily identify Todd's killer to the police. Emily knew there was only one way to take care of that problem.

She walked toward Mary, the knife in her hand still wet with her husband's blood, and sat down on the bed next to her. Todd was a heavy man, and his dead weight was too much for Mary to budge. Looking Mary in the eyes, Emily said, "Don't be afraid, I can release the burden of sin for you."

Mary looked in Emily's eyes, terrified at how cold and detached she seemed.

"Repeat after me: My God . . ."

"My God," Mary repeated with a quiver in her voice.

"I am sorry for all my sins with all my heart."

Once again Mary repeated Emily's words, wondering why she was being asked to do so.

"In choosing to do wrong and failing to do good, I have sinned against you, whom I should love above all things."

Mary started to cry uncontrollably.

"My dear woman, you must ask God for forgiveness," Emily said as she touched the blade of her knife to Mary's wrists. Emily repeated the phrase she asked Mary to say, and Mary said it, albeit through tears.

"Now here's the important part: I firmly intend, with your help, to do penance, to sin no more, and to avoid whatever leads me to sin."

Mary suffered through the final lines of the Act of Contrition and then felt a sharp pain in her wrist, followed by the feeling of warm liquid oozing out. A minute later she became lightheaded. She felt Emily get off the bed, but barely felt her other wrist being slit. A moment later, her world went black.

Emily's memory of that day was interrupted when she heard her father-in-law's name being called by a nurse with a clipboard standing in the doorway of the waiting room.

"Rose. Tyler Rose, the doctor will see you now."

Emily helped Tyler out of his chair and walked him to the exam room. She would have to finish her trip down memory lane later.

CHAPTER THIRTY

Every Rose has a Thorn

It had been thirty minutes since Farrah and Jimmy left Interstate 195 to turn onto Route 81. After getting off at Plymouth Avenue and making a series of left and right turns, they spotted the steeple of St. Mary's Cathedral. As usual, Jimmy had questions as they pulled up to the imposing all-stone structure.

"Do you really think the bishop is going to see us?"

"You never cease to remind me why I started calling you Jimmy Doubts," Farrah said as she pulled into a parking spot close to the church.

"I think it was Melody who started with the whole Doubts business," Jimmy clarified.

Hearing her girlfriend's name stung. Farrah hadn't figured out what she was going to do about her relationship with Melody; it appeared to be heading for the history books, and Farrah wasn't sure if she should let it wither on the vine, or go the extra mile and try to win her back.

"Ouch, Doubts."

Jimmy raised his eyebrow as he gave her a look. "It looks like there are some business offices in back of the cathedral. Are you sure he doesn't want us to meet him there?"

Farrah exhaled so forcefully that her breath blew her blonde bangs away from their resting place on her forehead.

"He was very clear, Doubts. He wants me to meet him in the confessional because he said it's the only place he can expect some privacy."

The two exited Farrah's car and walked into the imposing stone structure. As they entered the church, they were both hit with the scent of lit votive candles. Jimmy looked around and saw what appeared to be thousands of candles along the back of the church and extending up the sides. Each block of candles was located under the statue of a saint, with a sign saying the recommended donation for lighting a candle was five dollars. Jimmy approached the statue of St. Anthony, removed a five-dollar bill from his wallet, and placed it in the metal collection box. He then lit a candle, bowed his head, and said a prayer.

"What are you doing, Doubts?" Farrah whispered.

"St. Anthony is the patron saint of lost things. I ask for his intercession frequently so I figured a little donation in his honor wouldn't hurt."

Farrah shook her head and then looked down the side of the church and spotted what appeared to be an alcove for a confessional about halfway down on the right-hand side. She began walking in that direction.

"What am I supposed to do while you're in there?" Jimmy asked.

"Isn't there an Our Lady of Doubts you can pray to?" Farrah said a bit sarcastically.

She walked to the confessional and noticed that the red light above the door was not lit, which meant it was empty. She opened the door, knelt down, and remained in an uncomfortable silence.

"Do you have something to confess, my child?" came a voice from the other side of the screen that separated them.

Farrah wasn't sure that this sounded like the same voice she heard earlier, but she was willing to chalk up the difference to being in person as opposed to over the phone. Plus, never having seen the bishop before, insisting on seeing his face wouldn't have made a difference.

"Is that you, Bishop Hurley?"

"This is not how most people choose to begin the sacrament of reconciliation," the voice boomed from the other side of the screen.

Farrah replied with an exaggerated sigh. "Bless me, Father, for I have sinned; it has been one year since my last confession."

"And what are your sins, my child?"

Farrah assumed the bishop was playing it safe, and she decided this was code for her to tell him the reason behind her earlier call.

"Earlier I told you that more lives may be in danger. We have reason to believe that Fr. Hart's murderer is still on the loose."

Farrah heard the person on the other side of the screen take a deep breath.

"But the papers said that Christopher Mitchell was arrested for the death of Fr. Hart," the voice said.

"The police wanted to give the killer a false sense of security, so they published that article in the paper."

"Do they have any suspects in mind?"

"One in particular. A woman from the parish."

"What makes them believe she had anything to do with Fr. Hart's murder?"

"She's the only one who had access to the wine before Mass. We're just not clear why she did it."

Farrah heard the priest at the other end of the screen squirm in his chair. "I know this is a lot to handle, Bishop, but I thought you should know. Also, she has a brother who works here in the diocese."

Farrah could tell by the change in breathing pattern that the person on the other end of the screen was unnerved by this news.

"Who?"

"The chancellor, Fr. Peter Cossa."

"I see," the voice on the other end of the screen said.

"Bishop Hurley, you have to be careful," Farrah pleaded. "I can't say why, but I think your life may be in danger."

"Thank you, my child. I can assure you that Our Lord will protect me."

Farrah got up to leave, eager to get out of the confessional.

"There's just one more thing I have to ask you," the voice said.

Farrah thought this line sounded eerily like something from an episode of Columbo.

"What's that?"

"Please say your name again for me. I couldn't make it out on the phone earlier; our connection must have been bad. I want to add your name to my prayers this evening."

Farrah remembered that there had been some static on the phone when she spoke with the bishop earlier.

"Farrah Graham — I'm Fr. Michael Graham's sister."

"Well, may God continue to bless you and your brother, Farrah Graham."

Farrah took that as her cue to leave. She exited the confessional, met Jimmy in the back of the church, and together they headed back to Cape Cod.

Fr. Peter Cossa sat alone in the confessional, clearly disturbed about the news he just heard. He had assumed that Christopher Mitchell's background and subsequent suicide were more than enough to convince the police that he was Fr. Hart's killer — which was exactly why Mitchell's name had been fed to the police to begin with.

While Fr. Cossa tried to find out what went wrong, he knew he should call his sister to tell her she was under suspicion for the death of Fr. Hart. But as he reached for the phone in his pocket, he paused to consider that if his sister were caught, it might not be such a devastating thing. He had more than enough dirt on her to support the charges of murder that would be brought against her. Additionally, if she happened to implicate him at all in the death of Fr. Hart, he would claim that he could not address those charges or he'd be breaking the seal of confession. It would be a total lie and a sin, but one he was willing to commit to save his own skin.

As he pondered these things, he questioned if he had any love at all for his sister. During their childhood, she also had suffered at the hands of their father, but her punishments were mostly psychological, whereas his were always physical. Corporal punishment, his father had called it. The belt, the fist — over time he had come to expect them, so with each lashing and every punch, he had learned to feel nothing at all.

As he mulled over what to do about his sister, the phone in his hand started to vibrate. Looking at the caller ID, he saw that it was the member of the Order he had entrusted to pitch a damming article about Bishop Hurley. He flicked a switch inside the confessional, illuminating the red light on the outside so anyone seeking absolution would not interrupt his phone call.

"Did you speak with your connection inside the Globe?" Fr. Cossa asked.

"Yes." A gruff voice said on the other end of the line. "She wants to fact-check it with someone high up in the diocese."

Fr. Cossa had suspected this would be the case. And who better than he, as chancellor, to confirm the facts of the story being pitched?

"Very well, I will call her directly. What is her name and number?"

Fr. Cossa wrote down the reporter's name and phone number. He had one more request for the voice on the other end of the line.

"If I give you a name, can you do a little investigating for me?"

"Depends on the name."

"Farrah Graham. Ring any bells?"

"You're kidding, right?"

"Have you ever known me to kid?"

"She runs the hottest podcast in the country, Uncorking a Murder. Last year her podcast exonerated a guy in

South Florida for the death of his wife. The year before that, Brandon Nash, the former pro football player accused of killing his wife, was granted a new trial because of her investigation. The woman is relentless in her pursuit of the truth."

"Thank you. That will be all for now." Fr. Cossa terminated the call before the voice on the other end of the line could reply.

He looked at the reporter's name he had written down: Kathleen McKay. She had been a thorn in the side of the diocese ever since she came to Boston. Fr. Cossa knew she was a lapsed Catholic whose relentless criticisms of Church hierarchy made her a poster child of the liberal elite in a city where church attendance had been plummeting. On any other day he would have viewed her as the enemy, but today he viewed her as an unknowing ally in his quest to become bishop.

He dialed her number, took a deep breath, and exhaled slowly when he heard her New York accent.

"This is McKay — make it quick and make it interesting."

"Ms. McKay, this is Fr. Paul Cossa, Chancellor of the Diocese of Fall River. Is that interesting enough for you?"

"I'm listening."

"I believe you spoke with an associate of mine earlier about a potential story focusing on the bishop. Do you still need this to be quick?"

"I've got all the time in the world for you, Padre. I need you to confirm a few things."

I'll only talk on the condition of anonymity. If my name is associated with this story, I will deny every bit of it. Are we clear?"

"Crystal. I will quote you as someone high up in the bishop's office."

"I can live with that."

"I must admit, the story your associate told me was almost too good to be true. A problem priest, Fr. Hart, is reassigned multiple times in the Diocese of Fall River until he's finally assigned to a parish out on the Cape. I have to ask, why move around one of the good ones? I get it with the pedophiles, but this Fr. Hart guy seemed to be in it for all the right reasons, so to speak. Why play chess with the guy?"

Fr. Cossa did not share the same sentiments about the dead priest, but he didn't let on.

"The bishop had a personal problem with him; all that stuff about Fr. Hart being too liberal for the bishop was just a smokescreen."

"What kind of personal problem?"

"The kind that two men of the cloth aren't supposed to have with each other."

If Fr. Cossa had been able to see the reporter's face, he would have seen her jaw drop.

"Do you mean to tell me the bishop and Fr. Hart were romantically involved?"

"It was only after Fr. Hart ended the relationship that he started to get moved around. The bishop finally assigned him to Chatham so he wouldn't have to see him regularly around the diocese."

"Did the bishop play a role in the murder of Fr. Hart?"

"No doubt you've done your homework on Christopher Mitchell, the alleged killer of Fr. Hart?"

"What do you mean, 'alleged killer'? From what I can tell, the police were building a strong case against him, and his suicide all but confirmed he did it."

"This may shock you, but Christopher Mitchell had nothing to do with Fr. Hart's death — the two were lovers."

"What?"

Thanks to some information his sister gave him earlier in the week, Fr. Cossa knew that the dead priest had been meeting regularly in private with Christopher Mitchell.

"You can confirm with the parish secretary in Chatham. Fr. Hart always scheduled meetings with Christopher personally; the secretary didn't know anything about it until the investigation began."

"So if Christopher Mitchell didn't poison Fr. Hart, who did?"

Answering this question the way he did was proof that Peter Cossa would do anything to be named a bishop.

"Bishop Hurley hired a parishioner to poison the priest and then offered her absolution of her sins. He also instructed her to point the police in Christopher Mitchell's direction."

"Do you seriously expect me to believe that Bishop Hurley hired some kind of 'hit woman' to kill his ex-lover?"

"There's talk in the upper echelons of the Church that Bishop Robert Hurley may become the first pope from North America. He doesn't want an ex-lover out there who might ruin his chances. The fact that he was able to point the finger at the dead priest's current lover was the proverbial icing on the cake."

"How do you know all this, and why are you sharing it with me?"

Fr. Cossa had to be careful with his words, and while it

pained him to say the following, he knew it was necessary in pursuit of his goal.

"Like you, Ms. McKay, I want to see change come to my Church. I don't want anything hidden under the rug. The faithful deserve better shepherds, and I want to hunt down everyone who gives my Church a bad name." He hoped that he sounded convincing.

"I'm going to spend the rest of the day crafting this story. If my editor likes it, I expect it will run on the front page in tomorrow's Globe."

"I will say a prayer that God will guide your hand to write the truth," Fr. Peter said, and then ended the call.

All of his chips were now in the center of the table. He was all in.

CHAPTER THIRTY-ONE

Chatham's Favorite Son Returns

It was early evening by the time Farrah and Jimmy arrived back in Chatham. Being the day before the Fourth of July, traffic was barely moving over the Sagamore Bridge. Once over the bridge, traffic on Route 6 was at a crawl, and it took them over two hours before they hit Exit 11 and were on the road back to Chatham.

"All this driving has made me hungry, Doubts. How about you?"

"I thought you'd never ask."

"There's a popular inn on the north side of town that has a wicked good tavern inside. Sound good to you?"

"Did you just say 'wicked good'?" Jimmy asked.

"When in Rome, Doubts."

"Fine by me."

Farrah made a left onto Main street and then another left onto Chatham Bars Avenue. Parking for the Chatham Bars Inn was located in a lot on the right-hand side of the street.

Jimmy looked around and saw that the lot was

completely full, mostly with foreign luxury cars.

"Do you have a Plan B? I don't think we're going to find a spot here."

"No worries, Doubts, they have complimentary valet parking."

Farrah pulled into the driveway and waited for the valet to come out. When he approached the car, Farrah opened the door and got out.

"Are you guest of hotel?" the valet asked with a thick accent. His name tag read Jonas; he was part of the summer labor pool from Eastern Europe. Like many resort towns, Chatham had to import its seasonal labor pool from overseas since the town residents required year-round employment.

"Just here for dinner," Farrah replied, tipping the valet. While it was customary to tip when the car was returned, Farrah always tipped the guy who actually parked her car, assuming that it would hasten the retrieval process when she was ready to leave.

Farrah noticed Jimmy looking across the street.

"What do you see over there, Doubts?"

"I didn't realize the town had a golf course."

"It's a short nine-holer," Farrah replied. "Do you play?"

"Not as often as I used to, but I love the game."

"Well when this is all over, maybe I'll treat you to a round."

"I'll hold you to it."

"Now, come on, I'm starving."

Farrah and Jimmy walked into the inn, and Jimmy was immediately taken by the opulence of the interior. "That chandelier must have cost more than my mother's house!" he exclaimed.

"This is where the rich and famous come to vacation on the Cape, Doubts. Try to fit in."

"You're both — I'm neither."

"Fame isn't all it's cracked up to be, Doubts."

"I'll have to take your word for it."

They walked around the corner and saw the entrance to the Sacred Cod Tavern on their left. Farrah walked up to the hostess, whose name tag read Iggy.

"Cain I help you?" Iggy said in a stronger Eastern European accent than the parking attendant.

"Table for two, please."

"Do you have resyurvation?" Iggy asked.

Farrah looked around and saw that only one of no fewer than twenty tables was occupied. She saw a couple — a man and a woman — both who appeared to be in their early thirties. The woman was expecting.

"No, but it doesn't look . . ."

"Hmmmm," Iggy interrupted. "It may be deeficult to geet you in weethout resyurvation."

"Do you mean to tell me that . . ."

Iggy pretended to study the reservation book and tapped it multiple times with her pen. "Okay dookie. I cain squeeze you in. Fallow me, please."

Jimmy could see that Farrah was about to lose her cool.

"I hear they have a good borsht here," he whispered into Farrah's ear as they followed Iggy to their table.

It was clear that, even though the tavern was completely empty except for the other couple, Farrah and Jimmy were going to be seated right next to them.

"Would it be possible to be seated on the other side of the dining room?" Farrah asked. "We'd like a little privacy."

"Eyem sorry," Iggy replied. "This is the section of restaurant for peepole weethout resyurvation."

"You've gotta be fucking . . ."

"This is fine, Iggy. Thank you." Jimmy swooped in before Farrah could finish her sentence.

"I send waitor over soon, okay?" Iggy replied and walked back to her post in front of the restaurant.

"She's a piece of work, isn't she?" said the man sitting at the table adjacent to them. He wore his hair longer on top and shorter on the sides. Jimmy thought he recognized him but couldn't figure out from where.

"This place won't even be half full by the time we leave," the pregnant woman said. "Everyone's at the clambake on the beach."

"Are you guests of the hotel?" Farrah asked.

"No, I have a place here in town. We just didn't feel like cooking tonight."

"Do you spend your summers here?" Farrah asked.

"Not really," the man replied. "Our main home is in Westlake Village, California, but I grew up here in Chatham, and I always enjoy spending the Fourth here."

"That's a long way to come for the Fourth," Jimmy said.

"Where are my manners?" the man said. "My name is Patrick Evans, but most people call me Trick, and this is my wife, Casper."

"I'm Farrah Graham, and this is my associate, Jimmy Doubts."

"The podcaster?" Casper asked.

"That's me," Farrah replied.

"Oh my God, I love your show."

Trick and Casper took turns shaking Farrah's hands,

When they turned their attention toward Jimmy, they noticed his mouth was agape.

"What's the matter, Doubts? You've got that stupid look on your face you get whenever you meet a celebrity."

"Trick Evans," Jimmy replied.

"Yes," Trick said.

"You're Trick Evans — you won all four of golf's majors in one calendar year. You are a legend."

"What are you talking about, Doubts?" Farrah said, kicking Jimmy under the table.

"Sorry," Jimmy said, attempting to recover from his shock. "Farrah, Trick won each of the biggest tournaments in golf last season — golf's grand slam, if you will. It hadn't been done since the 1930s."

"I had a good year," Trick said humbly.

Their conversation was interrupted by a waiter ready to take Farrah and Jimmy's drink order. Unlike Iggy and Jonas, he did not have an Eastern European accent.

"A glass of sauvignon blanc for me," Farrah said.

"I'll have the same," Jimmy replied.

The waiter left to get their drinks, and Jimmy tried hard to not go full-on fanboy toward Trick.

"Shouldn't you be playing this weekend? Jimmy asked. "Isn't the tour in Phoenix?"

Trick looked at his wife and smiled.

"With Casper being pregnant with our first, I'm not playing as much this year."

Casper interrupted, "My husband is also being modest. The Mayor asked Trick if he would consider being the Grand Marshall for tomorrow's Fourth of July parade, and he couldn't say no."

"I could have said no, but I would never have lived it

down," Trick replied.

"Are you here for vacation or are you working on another season of Uncorking a Murder?" Casper asked.

"A little bit of both, I'm afraid," Farrah replied.

"Really?" Casper and Trick said at the same time.

"Trick, do you know Detective William Nickerson?"

"Nick? Of course. I grew up here — everybody knows Nick. He was a great football player for Chatham High. I looked up to him when I was a kid."

"Well, we're helping him investigate the murder of Fr. Greg Hart. I'm sure you heard about that."

"I was shocked to hear that he was murdered! I was very close with his predecessor, Fr. Paul Hewson, but I've never gotten to meet Fr. Hart in person because I've been spending most of my time on the West Coast. If you're involved now, that must mean that what I read about Christopher Mitchell wasn't true."

Farrah filled Trick and Casper in on the events of the case thus far, stopping just short of revealing that they were looking into a woman at the parish to pin Fr. Hart's death on.

"I lived in Chatham for most of my life, and stuff like this just doesn't happen here. I can only think of two murders in my own lifetime."

Farrah's ears perked up.

"Twenty years ago, a kid who was a bit older than me was found washed up on the shores of Lighthouse Beach. We all thought he drowned, but it turned out that he died of a head injury and was pushed into the water. No one knows what really happened, but we all assumed that he had been partying with friends, and the people he was with panicked when he OD'd and dumped him in the water."

"We heard it was a drug dealer who did it," Jimmy spoke up.

"That's what the police thought, but Connor wasn't mixed up with any hardcore dealers. He was a quiet kid who had a hard time dealing with the fact that his mother had killed his father."

"What did you say?" Farrah and Jimmy asked at the same time.

"Officially the story was one of murder-suicide, but none of us believed that Connor's father's mistress killed him. Connor's mother is batshit crazy."

Casper reached over and slapped Trick's hand. "Don't talk like that."

"Sorry. I'm just saying that the mother isn't playing with a full deck. I grew up in Our Lady of Healing Church — in fact, that's where Casper and I met. I've known the woman for years, and she's a few cans short of a six-pack."

Their conversation was interrupted by the waiter who brought Farrah and Jimmy their drinks and a check for Trick and Casper. Trick immediately handed the waiter his American Express card without even looking at the bill.

"I'll be back with this in a minute," the waiter responded.

"We got the early-bird special tonight," Casper explained. "Ever since I've been pregnant, I have to eat dinner early because I'm wiped out by 8:00 p.m."

"Do you play golf, Jimmy?" Trick asked.

"Who, me?" Jimmy asked.

"Yes, you, Doubts," Farrah said. "Is there another

Jimmy we don't know about in this restaurant?"

"Wait, I have a question," Casper said. "Why do you call him Doubts?"

"Here we go again," Jimmy said.

"When he first started working for me, Jimmy here questioned everything. Eventually he became known as Jimmy Doubts."

"Yes, I play golf," Jimmy replied.

"Well, I'm doing a fund raiser this weekend at the Chatham Seaside Links here in town. We are raising money for an organization called Arlene's Farm, a no-kill shelter for adult dogs. It's $125 for the round including dinner and drinks — $300 if you want to play in my foursome. Any interest?" Trick asked

Jimmy's eyes lit up.

"You look like a little kid on Christmas," Farrah quipped.

The waiter came back and handed Trick a receipt to sign.

"I'll take that as a yes," Trick said. "It was nice meeting you both. Maybe I'll see you at the parade tomorrow."

"I hope so," Jimmy said.

"Good luck, Farrah," Casper said. "And nice to meet you, Jimmy."

Farrah and Jimmy both took generous sips of their wine as they watched the two walk out of the tavern.

"If Emily Rose is as kooky as Trick says, and if she had something to do with both her husband's death and the death of her son, I don't have a hard time believing that she killed Fr. Hart, but I still don't understand why she would do it," Farrah said.

"Not to mention how she got the cyanide," Jimmy

added. "It's not like you can just buy that stuff on the street."

Farrah and Jimmy were startled when the waiter asked, "Do you need any more time to look at the menu?" Neither had realized he was in such close proximity.

Farrah thought they should be more careful about discussing these matters in public and made a mental note to change the topic of conversation after placing her order.

"I'll have the brick chicken," Farrah replied.

"And I'll start out with a cup of clam chowder and have the scallops."

"Very well," the waiter replied. "I'll put that in for you."

Chad Jackson had been waiting tables in Chatham for the past five years. Originally from the town of Brighton, just outside of Boston, Chad knew he could earn more waiting tables on the Cape in the summertime than he could working in any of the "college town" bars common on just about every corner in Brighton. The average dinner tab at the Chatham Bars Inn, for example, was $625 for a table of four. That same tab at the White Horse Tavern in Brighton was a quarter of that.

After years of working at Chatham's less exclusive restaurants, Chad finally earned the opportunity to wait at the exclusive Chatham Bars Inn, where, only halfway into the summer, he had already exceeded his income from the previous summer. On top of that, he had gotten to meet a fair number of celebrities who viewed the Chatham Bars Inn as the premier vacation destination on the Cape — a fact he was quick to share with the followers of his popular blog, aptly titled Celebs on the Elbow (a reference to the fact that Chatham was on the elbow of the Cape). As a journalism major at Boston College, his writing was strong, and at times the Boston Globe had featured his observations in its gossip column.

Chad had recognized Trick Evans immediately when he came through the door, but it took him a few minutes to figure out who Farrah Graham was, not being familiar with Uncorking a Murder. Thankfully he overheard Farrah introduce herself to Trick and his wife and did a quick Internet search of her name after taking her drink order. After eavesdropping on the two couples talking about the murder of a local priest and snapping a picture of them with his mobile phone, Chad knew he had an interesting story on his hands and tapped a quick blog entry summarizing what he overheard. What would have normally been buried on a gossip page, though, wound up becoming front-page news, given it corroborated the Globe's lead article written by impresario reporter Kathleen McKay.

Life for many people was about to change, and not necessarily for the better.

CHAPTER THIRTY-TWO

Lies in Print

Emily Rose woke up on the fourth of July feeling excited about the day that was ahead of her. She felt refreshed after having a good night's sleep and, while she knew it was sinful, she felt warm with pride about being recognized by the Chatham Police Department and the Mayor for her role in the arrest of Christopher Mitchell. Only in her twisted version of reality could she view pride as more sinful than murdering a priest or bearing false witness against another person. She was brought back to the reality of her life by the sound of her father-in-law's voice.

"Emily, can you wheel me to the bathroom?"

Yesterday the doctor at the urgent care clinic confirmed that Tyler did not break any bones after he fell down the stairs, but he did suffer a sprained ankle. He was advised not to put any weight on his foot, and when he found he couldn't balance on crutches, he was sent home with a wheelchair. He needed help getting from his chair to the toilet, but thankfully he could still manage to take care of his personal hygiene needs. *Thank God for small favors*, Emily thought, but she resented the fact that she would have to push him in the parade.

She got him to the half bath on the first floor, helped him stand up, and walked him to the toilet while he hopped on one foot and used her as a human crutch. She turned her head while he took down his pants and sat down. She quickly exited the bathroom before she heard any sounds emanating from his body.

Assuming he would be there for a few minutes, she went outside to retrieve the paper from the driveway. It was part of her morning ritual every morning to read the Boston Globe while sipping her hot tea. After coming back into the house, she went directly to the kitchen, placed the paper on the table, and turned on the electric tea kettle. She heard the water start to come to a boil just as the toilet flushed.

"Emily . . ."

"I'm coming," she barked. "Spray the air freshener before I open the door."

Tyler did as he was told, and Emily helped him into his chair and then wheeled him back to the family room where he had spent on the night on the couch; helping him up the stairs last night had not been in her game plan.

After he put his feet up on the couch and closed his eyes, Emily considered taking the pillow that had fallen onto the floor and smothering her father-in-law with it, but she decided against it, just as her brother chose not to smother Bishop Hurley with a pillow earlier in the week. Mercy was apparently a family trait.

The whistling tea kettle caused Emily to turn her attention back to the kitchen. She placed a teabag in her favorite mug — the one that read World's Best Mom — and then filled it with hot water and a few tablespoons of milk. She sat down at the kitchen table, removed the Globe from its plastic wrapper, took a sip of her tea . . . and nearly gagged on it when she read the front-page headline: "**Two Birds with One Stone: Murder in Chatham Linked to Bishop's Office**."

Emily went on to read the reporter's theory, citing support from an anonymous high-level official in the diocese, that Fr. Hart's death had been arranged by the bishop himself, who was in a jealous rage over the dead priest's choice to take a new lover, Christopher Mitchell. The article went on to argue that Mitchell wasn't the priest's killer, and that his suicide was not so much an admission of guilt as it was a sign of his mental illness as a result of past abuse. According to the article, the real killer was still on the loose.

This theory was corroborated by the story of a blogger whose post about celebrities having dinner at the Chatham Bars Inn also made front-page news because it mentioned the name of Farrah Graham. The blogger explained how she had been involved in two previous murder cases and had a knack for uncovering the truth in the most unlikely of places. The article contained a picture of two couples sitting next to each other in the dining room of the Chatham Bars Inn's tavern; Emily knew that one of the couples was Chatham native Trick Evans and his wife, Casper. By process of elimination, she surmised that the other woman in the picture was Farrah Graham; the article failed to mention the name of her dinner companion, whose picture was blurry.

Emily panicked, concerned there was a chance she

could still get fingered for the death of Fr. Hart. She reached for her phone and called her brother.

"Peter, did you read the paper this morning?" she asked. "What the hell is going on?"

"Such language, dear sister. It's just tabloid journalism, someone trying to make a buck. I wouldn't worry about it."

"But it's the Boston Globe, not the National Enquirer."

"They've been known to sensationalize the news just as much as anyone else. Just look at the sex abuse scandal."

If Emily could have seen her brother, she would have known that he was filing his nails as these words were spoken unenthusiastically into the telephone.

"Relax, Emily," her brother said. "When I find out who the Globe has been talking to, that person is going to wish he or she had never been born. The story will be retracted."

"What am I supposed to do until then?" Emily cried into the phone.

"Just go about your business as usual — don't do anything that would make them suspicious of you."

"How I am supposed to walk in the parade today knowing they may be looking for me? How can I possibly do that?"

"If you don't do it, my dear sister, they will have all the more reason to look for you. The best place to hide a pebble is on the ground."

Emily hated it when her brother became overly philosophical.

"And if they do try to arrest me?"

"Do what you do best," her brother said coldly. "Survive."

Emily heard the unmistakable click of the call being terminated. Having lost her appetite, she ripped out the picture of Farrah Graham and her blurry dinner companion, folded it, and put it in her purse.

"Tyler, we have to leave here in thirty minutes. I'll bring your dress uniform downstairs. Will you need help getting ready?"

"Where are we going?" Tyler answered weakly from the other room.

"Today is the Fourth of July parade in town. You're marching in it as an Air Force Veteran, just as you do every year."

"How can I march if I can't even walk?"

"I'll push you in your wheelchair."

The thought of having to wheel her father-in-law was painful, and Emily considered looking for a good Samaritan to push Tyler in the parade. The more she thought about this, the more it sounded like a smart idea, especially since she might have a need to get away quickly. Surely there would be a young man at the parade looking to help a vet in need.

Emily went upstairs to get herself ready. While standing in her closet, she unlocked the safe hidden behind some of her clothes and removed a .38 caliber Smith and Wesson "policeman's special" from the inside. The weapon had belonged to former Detective Bill Jamison, the cop who investigated the death of her son and had insisted on an autopsy, although he didn't live to investigate any other cases.

Emily hit the cylinder release and saw that there were still six bullets inside. After spinning the cylinder around, she closed it and placed the weapon in her purse. If she was going down, it wouldn't be without a fight.

Farrah was enjoying her coffee on the second-floor deck of her home. She noticed that the parking lot of Harding's Beach had already started to fill up, even though it was only 8:30 in the morning. July Fourth was going to be a beautiful day in Chatham, and those not going to town to enjoy the parade were already flocking to its beaches to enjoy the water.

She opened the French doors that led from the deck to the inside of her house.

"Doubts, what are you doing down there?"

Jimmy was sitting at the kitchen table and about to pull the newspaper out of its plastic wrapper.

"About to read the paper. What's up?"

"I'm bored, Doubts — come up here and talk to me. I must be entertained."

Jimmy got up from the table, grabbed his mug of coffee, and brought the paper upstairs.

"You're high maintenance, you know that?" Jimmy said to Farrah as he walked through the French doors onto the deck.

"You would look cute in a gladiator outfit."

"What?"

"Forget it, you don't look anything like Russel Crowe. Ditch the paper, Doubts! Who needs the news when we have a view like this?"

"I do," Jimmy said, spreading the paper in front of him. He picked up the front page without glancing at it and opened the first section to the middle to where he guessed the gossip pages were. This gave Farrah a clear view at the leading headline.

"Holy shit, Doubts!"

"What?" Jimmy said, not looking up.

"Did you bother to read the front page?"

"I always start with the celebrity stuff, and then work my way up to the hard news. It's like easing into a cold pool."

"You may want to take a look at the front page."

Jimmy closed the section of the paper and read the headline.

"What the what!" he exclaimed as he read the headline and skimmed the article. When he saw the picture taken at the Tavern last night he said, "What the . . . how the . . ?"

"I think we better call Nickerson. The cat is out of the bag."

Before she could finish dialing his number, Farrah heard her doorbell ring.

"Speak of the devil," she said, assuming the detective was at the door. Instead Farrah was surprised to see her brother, Fr. Michael.

"Hey, what are you doing here?"

"Did you read the paper?"

"Just now," Farrah said.

Fr. Michael walked through the door, and just as Farrah was about to close it, she saw an older car pull onto her street. Recognizing it as Detective Nickerson's, she decided to wait for him by the door.

"Go on up to the deck, Doubts is there. I'll wait here for a minute."

"Why?"

"I'm expecting more company."

Fr. Michael walked upstairs, and Farrah turned her attention back to the view outside her front door. She heard a car door slam and saw the tall, white haired detective walking toward her porch.

"Did you read the..." he attempted to ask on his approach to the door.

"Yep. Let's talk about it upstairs."

Farrah and Detective Nickerson joined Jimmy and Fr. Michael on the second-floor balcony.

"How could this story have gotten out? I thought you were being discreet about the whole thing."

"Why do you think we had anything to do about the leak?" Farrah said defensively. "Maybe someone at the station blabbed."

"The only person at the station who knows we are still investigating Fr. Hart's murder is Arlene, the office manager, and I know she wouldn't say anything to anybody."

"What about the medical examiner?" Jimmy asked. "Didn't you say he was convinced Mitchell didn't do it?"

"Yes, but he wouldn't say anything either; he knows how important it is."

"Wait a minute . . ." Farrah said.

Jimmy, her brother, and Detective Nickerson stared at her.

"Yesterday, in the confessional, I thought I was talking to Bishop Hurley. What if I wasn't?"

"Who else could you have been talking to?"

"Who did the paper say fed them the information for the article? Someone high up in the bishop's office?"

"That's right," her brother confirmed.

"What if I actually was speaking to that person? I

couldn't see his face, and I remember thinking that his voice sounded different than it did on the phone."

"It's actually irrelevant," Detective Nickerson said. "This may cause Emily to freak out; I doubt she'll even show up for the parade. She's likely already figured out that the little ceremony we planned for her is a sham."

"Maybe," Fr. Michael spoke up, "but maybe not. She might be smart enough to realize that not going to the parade would actually be more suspicious on her part. I bet she'll be there."

"I know her father-in-law will be there," Detective Nickerson added his opinion. "He's a Cold War-era Air Force vet who hasn't missed a Fourth of July parade since I can remember. This year, though, he'll have to be pushed since he hurt his foot yesterday."

"How did you come across this information?" Farrah asked.

"I was the reason he fell. I went over to Emily's house to sell the story that the town was going to recognize her efforts in the investigation into Fr. Hart's murder, and he slipped on the last step while coming down the stairs to open the door for me. Apparently he sprained his ankle, and I'm pretty sure he'll need to be pushed in a wheelchair during today's parade."

"Hmm," Fr. Michael said.

"What?" Jimmy, Farrah, and Detective Nickerson replied in unison.

"Jimmy, let me see the front page of the paper again," Fr. Michael said.

Jimmy handed the paper to the priest.

"Perfect," Fr. Michael replied.

His three companions stared at him anxiously.

"Care to elaborate, Mikey?" Farrah said.

"Look at this picture," her brother replied. "What do you see?"

"Looks like me, a professional golfer, his wife, and a big blur all having dinner."

"Exactly!" Fr. Michael said. "A big blur. A big boy scout-looking blur."

"Where are you going with this, Father?" Detective Nickerson asked.

"We can't make out Jimmy's face in this picture, meaning Emily can't either. What if Jimmy here volunteers to push Emily's father-in-law in his wheelchair? That way, we can ensure being close to him — and, by extension, her."

"That's not a half-bad idea," Farrah said.

"Agreed," replied the detective. "You up for it, Jimmy?"

"I've always loved me a parade," Jimmy replied.

CHAPTER THIRTY-THREE
The Parade

Few towns could compare to Chatham when it came to
the Fourth of July. Residents and visitors begin placing
their beach chairs up and down Main Street as early as
5:00 a.m. to mark their territory. When all was said and
done, no fewer than twenty thousand people would attend
the parade to see over one hundred local groups and
organizations march up Main Street and show their pride
on our nation's independence day.

Organizing such a large endeavor was no easy task, and
the town relied on a multitude of volunteers to ensure that
a such a large gathering was as safe and organized as it
could be. One of the hardest jobs was managing the
logistics of which local organizations should march when.
In years past, the parade committee had always allowed
any veteran groups to march first, followed by any groups
from Chatham's civil services, including the police
department and the fire department. These would be
followed by the Chatham Selectman, the Chatham Band,
and the Grand Marshall, who this year was Chatham's

current favorite son, Trick Evans. Chatham's many other civic organizations, retailers, and church groups would follow.

This year the members of Our Lady of Healing Church were placed fifty-ninth in line, sandwiched between a Boston College Alumni group and the employees of the Bleeding Seal Restaurant and Bar. This posed an issue for Emily, who now needed someone to push her father-in-law in his wheelchair much earlier in the parade.

"I can wheel myself, Emily," Tyler said as she navigated him through the crowd of people lining up on Shore Road.

"Who are you trying to kid, Tyler?" she replied. "Your arms will get tired after just one block. I need to find someone to help. Maybe one of the other veterans can push you."

When Emily and Tyler reached the place where the town vets were lining up, she realized the flaw in her plan. Most of the other guys were in the same condition as her father-in-law: in a wheelchair.

Just then a young man emerged from the crowd and approached Emily. "My name is Jimmy Rella, and I'm a former Eagle Scout. Do you need me to help wheel this hero during the parade?"

Emily looked him up and down and saw that he was tall, thin, and extremely clean-cut. If he was lying about being an Eagle Scout, his appearance certainly wasn't betraying him.

"Would you mind? I'm marching with my church group, and I need someone to watch my father-in-law until the end of the parade."

"It's no problem at all — that's why I asked."

Jimmy actually was an Eagle Scout. He had earned that honor when he was a junior in high school, and his Eagle Scout project had been to raise money and build handicap ramps for any veteran in his town who was confined to a wheelchair. He had a soft spot in his heart for vets, and he truly was honored to push Emily's father.

"I'm going to go line up with my group. Why don't we meet after the parade by the health club on Crowell Road?"

The town's Fourth of July parade began at the intersection of Main Street and Shore Road and headed up Main Street until it turned right on Crowell Road, right by the old cemetery, and came to an end near a local health club.

"That works for me," Jimmy replied.

"Let me give you my cell phone number just in case there are any problems."

Emily wrote down her number on a piece of paper she took out of her purse and handed it to Jimmy.

"I can't thank you enough for your generosity. God bless you."

Emily left to find the other members of Our Lady of Healing Church. She was surprised to see Fr. Michael Graham waiting with the others; she had forgotten inviting him to march with the group just two days before. Knowing that the investigation into Fr. Hart's death was still ongoing, his presence made her nervous. While she'd have felt better if he wasn't there, she knew that she couldn't afford to appear anxious.

"Emily, there you are," Fr. Michael said. "I've been talking with some of the other parishioners who agree that you should be in the front line of our parade group."

"You are too kind, Father, and I'd be honored."

Emily spotted a couple of the women from her prayer group and excused herself to go speak with them. As she got closer, it sounded like they were talking about the article from this morning's paper.

"Sounds like this bishop is no good," she heard her friend Margaret say. "And I just can't believe that Fr. Hart was that way," she continued, implying that he had been gay.

"I know," replied a woman named Denise. "I was convinced that he was dating a woman up in Wellfleet. I once saw them holding hands as they entered a restaurant. I didn't say anything because I'm not one to gossip."

Emily had to hold back a laugh as she heard Denise say these words. If you looked up the word gossip in a dictionary, Emily thought, you'd see a picture of Denise next to the description.

"It's best to move on," Emily chimed in. "Let the dead be, and move forward."

"I suppose you're right," Denise said. "Still, something seems funny."

Before Emily could respond, a volunteer came up to let them know that the parade was underway. The first of the groups, including the town's veterans, had already started marching, and the volunteer estimated that Emily's group would begin moving in the next few minutes.

As the parade began, Jimmy pushed Tyler Rose in his wheelchair while the later waved with both hands to the onlookers lined up on either side of Main Street. Tyler returned the salutes of anyone who offered him one and managed to smile at every young boy or girl who offered messages of thanks for his service.

Jimmy was curious to know more about Tyler, so he engaged the older man in conversation along the parade route.

"How long did you fly, Captain Rose?"

"I first started flying at the end of World War II; I was only eighteen at the time, and I was almost shot down once but my wingman got the son of a bitch before he could finish me off."

"Were you scared?"

"Scared? I didn't have time to know if I was scared or not!" Tyler said with a laugh.

"What did you do after the war?" Jimmy asked.

"I stayed in the Air Force and flew spy missions over the Soviet Union."

Tyler's memory about this period in his life were as clear as his words.

"That must have been something," Jimmy said with amazement.

"Now, that was scary. Whenever they give you a cyanide capsule to hide in a fake tooth, you know you're involved in some scary ass shit."

Jimmy stopped marching.

"What's the matter there, sonny, tired already? We've still got a ways to go."

"What did you say?"

"I said we've still got a ways to go. It's at least another three quarters of a mile before we reach Crowell Road."

"No, before that — something about a cyanide

capsule."

"Well, push me along young fella and I'll tell you."

Jimmy recommenced walking, and Tyler began to talk.

"Before accepting the opportunity to fly spy missions over the USSR, each of us pilots was given a fake tooth that included a cyanide capsule in it. In case we were ever shot down and captured, we were to quit the breathing habit by biting down on the cyanide pill so the Reds wouldn't get anything out of us."

"That sounds pretty extreme."

"War is extreme, son. Anyway, obviously I never had to take mine."

"What did you do with it?"

"You've sure got a lot of questions. What are you, a lawyer or something?"

"Not yet," Jimmy said with a sigh, rolling his eyes.

"Well, I keep it at home with my other keepsakes from my military service, including my sidearm, an old ration can, and a first-aid kit."

Jimmy was eager to text this information to Farrah and Detective Nickerson as it established where Emily had been able to acquire the cyanide that killed Fr. Hart. He couldn't just stop pushing Tyler in his wheelchair while the parade was in full swing, though. His text would have to wait until later.

Farrah and Detective Nickerson were on opposite sides of Main Street right before the traffic circle motorists navigated on their way in and out of town. Farrah stood directly outside of a cash-only diner, while Nick stood across from the Congregational Church. Their plan was to keep an eye on Jimmy and Tyler as they made their way toward the rotary; the parade had yet to make its way that far up Main Street, but by the sounds of it, the first marchers would reach Farrah and Nick's location shortly.

Nickerson planned to follow Jimmy and Tyler to the parade route's end while Farrah stayed behind to keep an eye out for Emily, who would be marching with Fr. Michael.

Farrah heard the unmistakable sound of a marching band playing "Yankee Doodle Dandee" and thought that she would be seeing Jimmy shortly. Sure enough, she was right. Jimmy looked tired as he pushed Tyler Rose in his wheelchair, while the veteran himself looked happy as a clam dressed up in his pressed blue officer's uniform and waving to the onlookers.

Farrah caught Jimmy's eye and saw that he was pointing to his mouth with his right hand, almost as if he were trying to pick something out of one of his back molars.

Jimmy became frustrated that Farrah obviously didn't understand the game of charades he was playing, and he quickly turned his attention to Detective Nickerson on the opposite side of the street.

The detective didn't understand what he was seeing either and admitted as much in a text message to Farrah. *There's something not right about your friend Doubts*, Farrah read.

Farrah agreed with the detective's assessment, but she chose not to respond because when she looked up a few seconds later, Jimmy and Tyler had passed by and Detective Nickerson was no longer in front of the church. He's good, she thought.

Farrah estimated that it would be another thirty

minutes or so before Emily and her brother's group would walk by, so she decided to go inside the diner to grab a cup of coffee. The diner was uncharacteristically empty as the usual patrons were lined up and down Main Street to watch the parade. After the parade, though, it would be a different story — the place would be mobbed along with all the other restaurants on Chatham's main thoroughfare.

Sandi, one of the waitresses, was drying some glasses behind the counter with an old-fashioned dishtowel. She had short black hair dyed from a bottle and wore an apron that covered her ample bosom.

"We don't have any public restrooms," she said without looking up.

"I don't need a restroom," Farrah said, "but I'd love a cup of coffee."

Sandi looked up and almost dropped the glass she was holding.

"You are Farrah Graham, aren't you? I saw you in the paper this morning. I love your podcast."

While being noticed was becoming a more frequent event, Farrah still didn't know how to act around fans.

"Thank you."

Sandi walked over to the coffee pot. "Large or small?" she asked.

"Large, please."

"Cream and sugar?"

"Just black."

"Like your men?"

"Excuse me?" Farrah said somewhat indignantly.

"Oh, sorry. Bad habit. It's a line from an old movie that I used to watch with my dad."

"*Airplane?*" Farrah asked.

"That's the one," Sandi said, handing Farrah her coffee.

"How much do I owe you?" Farrah asked.

"This one's on me," Sandi said. "Consider it a small gift for all the entertainment Uncorking a Murder has given me. I've always wondered, though — how did you come up with that title?"

A bell above the front door announced that the diner had another patron, but Farrah was too lost in thought to turn around to see who came in. She was remembering the day she and Melody had come up with the name; they had been struggling what to call the show when Farrah had trouble opening a bottle of wine. It was Melody who had suggested the title — Melody, who was now somewhere in Provincetown doing who knows what to who knows who. Farrah mentally kicked herself for not attempting to reach out to her since she left.

"It was a friend of mine who came up with the title."

"Just a friend?" came a voice from behind Farrah.

Farrah whirled around to see Melody standing in the doorway.

"How did you . . . ?"

"I've been tailing you since I spotted you near The Bleeding Seal. What's going on? You look like you are in the middle of an investigation or something."

Sandi decided to step in. "Didn't you read the paper this morning? She's helping the police find who really killed Fr. Hart."

"You never give up, do you?" Melody said with a sigh.

Farrah looked at Melody and smiled. "I can't stop being me." She then filled Melody in on what had transpired over the past day and a half.

"So this is almost over?" Melody asked.

"With any luck, it ends in the next hour," Farrah said.

She then looked at her watch and saw nearly twenty minutes had passed since entering the diner.

"We've got to get out of here," Farrah said. She said good-bye to Sandi, and Melody followed her out the door.

Amazingly, the spot where Farrah had been standing remained unoccupied. Farrah turned to the man next to her and asked if any church groups had passed by. The man replied that he didn't think so, and Farrah seemed satisfied with his answer.

"What do we do now?" Melody asked.

Farrah grabbed her hand and gave Melody a smile, "Now we wait."

Emily and the other marchers from Our Lady of Healing Church were just passing the Chatham Orpheum movie theater one block south of where Farrah and Melody were standing. As she walked in the parade, Emily felt as if all eyes were on her — especially when she passed by any of the many police officers stationed along the parade route. The tension in her body started to bubble up like a pot of water coming to a boil. She reached into the purse she had strapped around her shoulders to feel for the gun that she had brought with her. She allowed herself to relax just a little and continued marching.

Fr. Michael had managed to work up a decent sweat during the parade. While he rarely wore his clerics when not on official Church business, he thought it best to wear the characteristic black shirt and black pants combo so there was no mistake about what he did for a living. The extra twenty pounds he was carrying around his waist were not helping however. Looking up the road, he thought he spotted his sister standing outside a diner, and then he was taken by surprise to see Melody standing with her.

"What is it like having a famous sister, Father?" asked Nicole, one of the parishioners who had become friendly with Fr. Michael since he came to the parish earlier in the week.

"Excuse me?" Fr. Michael asked.

Emily Rose's ears perked up as well when she heard what Nicole asked.

"Your sister is Farrah Graham, isn't she? I saw her in the paper this morning; the resemblance is uncanny."

The relaxation Emily had allowed herself to feel minutes ago was now gone — flushed out of her system like a toxin leaving one's body.

"I just think of her as my sister," Fr. Michael blurted out, fumbling for something to say.

"I loved last season of Uncorking a Murder. The overall theme captivated me."

"And what was the theme?" Emily Rose asked, staring intently at the priest.

"I have to admit, that I don't follow what my sister does that closely."

"You would love it, Emily," Nicole said. "It's right from Scripture — "the truth shall set you free."

"Well, it usually does," Fr. Michael said, looking nervously at Emily.

After hearing this, Emily had had enough; the pot was about to boil over. In her purse, she always carried a light sweater in case she found herself in a restaurant with an overzealous air-conditioning unit. She reached in her purse, grabbed the gun, and wrapped the sweater around it. She then walked behind the priest and pressed it into his back.

It was a brazen move, considering the setting: thousands of onlookers lining up and down Main Street, not to mention those who were marching in the parade and all the cops scattered throughout the route. Emily decided to take the gamble, though, and whispered into the priest's ear.

"I have a gun at your back. At the rotary, you and I are going to take a right while the rest of the parade continues on. If you make a scene, I will shoot you."

Fr. Michael gave a slight nod. They were about to pass the diner and fortunately he caught his sister's eye; he winked at her twice. He then made a right at the traffic circle with Emily following immediately behind.

"Don't even think about running."

"Where are we going?" the priest asked nervously.

"To my car. We're going to take a little drive."

Farrah and Melody were standing outside the diner watching the parade when Melody tugged at her girlfriend's arm.

"I think I see Mikey," Melody was one of the few people who could refer to Farrah's brother by his childhood nickname.

Farrah turned her head to the right and spotted him. "Yep, there he is. Looks like he's sweating like crazy."

"Gotta get that boy back in the gym."

"Does something look funny to you?" Farrah asked.

"Like what?"

"Emily — she's walking directly behind Michael, and it looks like she has something pushing into his back."

Melody squinted, trying to see what Farrah was talking about.

"Looks like her hand is wrapped in a sweater."

"I think he's in trouble."

As her brother and Emily got closer, Farrah caught his eye in time to see him wink twice at her. This was a sign they devised when they were kids — if either of them were in trouble, they would use a double wink to signify it to the other. It had gotten Farrah out of a few potentially bad situations at high school parties, and now it was time for her to return the favor.

"Now I know he's in trouble. We have to follow them."

"Wait, how do you..."

Before Melody could finish her sentence, Farrah had ducked under the wooden barriers separating spectators from the parade and started walking toward her brother. She decided not to run to avoid calling attention to herself.

"Damn it, girl," Melody said as she struggled to follow Farrah.

They saw Fr. Michael and Emily make a right at the traffic circle while the rest of the parade veered left and continued up the parade route for the final quarter of a mile. Farrah and Melody tried to maintain a safe distance behind the priest and his kidnapper; fortunately, other people on the street provided them with some cover should Emily decide to turn around.

"Where do you suppose she is taking him?" Melody asked.

"I'm guessing her car," Farrah replied. "But from there, it's anyone's guess."

Farrah saw Emily and her brother walk across the street and onto the access road leading to the baseball field where the town's Cape League baseball team, the Chatham As, played.

"Odd time to take a tour of the field," Melody commented.

"I bet her car is parked around there," Farrah said. "There's some hidden parking by the cemetery, and I'm guessing that's where she parked."

"Wait, isn't the church around here?" Melody asked.

"Yes, it's just a quarter mile up this road on the right."

"Don't follow them," Melody said.

"Why the hell not? We don't have any time to lose!"

"You told me before that she was marching with her church group, right?"

"Right."

"Then don't you think she would have parked at the church? She's probably going this way to see if anyone is following them."

"What if you're wrong?" Farrah asked.

"Trust me," Melody pleaded.

Farrah nodded, and the two walked briskly to the parking lot of the church, which was full of cars.

There were some woods in an undeveloped area of the parking lot, just behind the back of the church. Melody and Farrah walked toward them.

"Let's hide in the woods over there and wait."

"I've got a bad feeling about this," Farrah replied.

"It's the only chance we've got," Melody said.

Emily couldn't be certain, but she felt as if someone was following her and the priest. She decided to test her hunch and told the priest to walk across the street and head toward the ballpark, even though her car was parked in the church parking lot.

"Make a left here," she said sternly.

"What do you want with me?" Fr. Michael asked.

"Shut up," Emily responded.

When they crossed the street and were the equivalent of a block away from the road they had exited, Emily looked back to see if anyone followed them. The only two people behind them were a mother and her young son; his face was bright red as if he had been crying.

"Is it much farther to the playground?" Emily heard the boy ask.

"It's just up there on the left. We'll be there soon."

"That parade was boring," the boy said.

"All parades are boring," the mother admitted, and the pair walked past the priest and Emily without giving them a second glance.

Emily then guided the priest to the end of the road, where they made a right onto the street and then another right on a bike path that would take them to the church parking lot. As they neared the rectory, the priest stopped walking.

"Emily, do you really want to do this? Why don't you come inside? I can offer you some counseling . . ."

"That's cute," Emily said. "But at a young age, I learned not to trust men of the cloth. Keep walking."

The two walked to Emily's car, a Toyota Prius with a bumper sticker that read "Let go and let God." It was parked adjacent the wooded area where Farrah and Melody were hiding.

Emily clicked a button on her car key, and Fr. Michael heard the unmistakable sound of the doors unlocking.

"Get in."

Fr. Michael knew that he could easily escape at this point; while it was true he was a little overweight and out of shape, he could easily dart into the wooded area and run away from Emily. Considering this option, he looked into the woods and suddenly saw movement — and that's when he caught his sister's eye. He then had a thought.

"Get in the car." Emily demanded again.

"Not until you tell me where we are going."

Emily saw no harm in telling the priest where she intended to go.

"We're going to take a trip to Fall River."

"Fall River," the priest said loudly, hoping his sister overheard him. "Why?"

"I need to see my brother. He'll know what to do. He always knows what to do."

Fr. Michael couldn't help but hear the sound of desperation in Emily's voice. To him, she represented a soul in trouble and for this reason, combined with the hope that his sister had heard where they were going, he did as he was told and got into the car — but not before saying a silent prayer.

Farrah and Melody watched Fr. Michael get into the car. After it left the parking lot, Melody turned to Farrah and asked, "Aren't we going to follow them?"

"No," Farrah replied. "I know where they are going."

"Getting to Fall River will take an eternity on the Fourth. We've got to leave now if we're going to catch up to them!"

"We've got some time," Farrah said, although she had to admit she was uneasy about the plan she just concocted in her head. "But we do need to find Doubts."

"Doubts?" Melody questioned. "Why?"

"Because a life is on the line," Farrah replied.

CHAPTER THIRTY-FOUR

A Life is on the Line

After leaving the wooded area, Farrah called Jimmy on his cell and learned that he was a half a mile away at the parade's end on Crowell Road. He was waiting there with Detective Nickerson when Farrah and Melody arrived. Thankfully, one of Emily's friends from the church had relieved Jimmy of the burden of caring for Tyler.

"Doubts," Farrah said, running toward him.

"Hey, boss," Jimmy said, and then saw Melody behind her. "When did you get back in town?"

"We don't have time for that, Doubts."

"What's going on?" Detective Nickerson asked.

"She kidnapped my brother," Farrah said.

"Who?" Jimmy asked.

"Emily. Looked like she's holding him at gunpoint."

"And no one saw it?" Detective Nickerson asked, reaching for his mobile.

"Don't do that just yet," Farrah pleaded. "I know where they're going."

"Where?" Jimmy and Detective Nickerson asked in

unison.

"Fall River. They're going to see Emily's brother."

"It will take them forever to get there today," the detective said. "Which means it will take us forever to get there."

"Not exactly," Farrah said, looking at Jimmy, who flashed a big smile to her.

"Seriously?" he asked.

"A life is on the line, Doubts."

"Will one of you two please fill me in on what you are blabbing about?" Melody asked.

"Doubts, why don't you tell Melody and Detective Nickerson how you arrived in Chatham."

"I flew into the airstrip in Chatham."

"Look, we aren't going to find a pilot willing to leave Chatham on the Fourth of July," the detective argued.

"We already have a pilot," Farrah retorted, looking at Jimmy.

Melody now understood what Farrah was referring to.

"There's no fucking way I'm going up in a plane with that boy behind the wheel."

"It's not a wheel; it's a yoke. Besides, do you have a better idea?"

"How confident are you that they are going to Fall River?"

"Very. We were hiding in the woods near their car and we heard their entire conversation."

"Here's what I'm thinking," the detective said. "You, me, and Doubts fly to Fall River. I'll radio ahead to a local contact I have there, who will put a watch on the cathedral. I don't want to spook Emily because we know how unstable she is, so it's best if she gets where she is going without incident. Then we can nab her in Fall River."

"Isn't that breaking some sort of protocol?" Farrah asked.

"Put it this way: If things go wrong, I'll be looking for a new line of work."

"What am I supposed to do?" Melody asked.

"Come along for the ride," Farrah said. "You always said you wanted more adventure in life."

"Come on," Jimmy said. "What could go wrong?"

The four of them walked back to the police station which was only two blocks away from where they were standing, got into Detective Nickerson's car, and drove to the airstrip.

Detective Nickerson parked his car in the small parking lot directly in front of the airstrip's main office. There was a group of kids on bikes hanging out watching the planes take off and land; they appeared to be in their early teens and apparently had no interest in the parade that was just ending downtown.

Jimmy went inside to speak with the manager of the airport and arrange for his plane to be refueled as well as file a flight plan to Fall River. On the drive over, he had read about a grass airstrip near the town and had some questions about landing on it. The manager, Lloyd Ryder, was happy to answer.

"Hey there, young fella. You'll have no problem landing there since it has been so dry; if we had gotten a good rain, you wouldn't be so lucky."

"Thanks."

"You look like an eager beaver. Why are you in such a rush to leave town on the Fourth?"

Detective Nickerson spoke up. "You're nosey, you know that, Lloyd?"

"I suppose I am, Nick, but most people are coming into town today, not leaving. It's just strange, that's all."

When all the office business was done, everyone followed Jimmy out to the tarmac and watched him complete his preflight check. After manually checking fuel levels and doing a visual inspection of the aircraft, Jimmy signaled for everyone to come over to the plane and get in. Farrah and Melody boarded first and occupied the two seats in the rear, Detective Nickerson took the front left seat, and Jimmy took the pilot's chair.

Jimmy placed a pair of headphones over his ears; they were the old-fashioned kind with a microphone extending from the left ear to his mouth.

"It's about to get really noisy in here. If you want to talk to each other, put on a pair of cans."

"Cans?" Melody asked.

"Headphones," Jimmy replied and pointed to his own.

Melody and Farrah did as they were told. Melody grabbed Farrah's hand and said, "I can't believe we are letting that boy fly us. I remember when he could barely figure out the phone system."

"I love you too, Melody," Jimmy replied.

Jimmy started the engine and checked the gauges in front of him. He was specifically concerned about his oil pressure, as it had seemed a little high on the way up from Connecticut. Once he was confident that everything looked good, he began his taxi to the runway.

"CQX, this is Murder One requesting permission for

takeoff."

"Interesting name for a plane," Detective Nickerson remarked.

Jimmy just smiled.

"Murder One, you have permission for takeoff. Winds are 15 knots out of the northeast, and visibility is four miles. Have a great flight."

"Roger that."

Jimmy lined up with the runway, making sure his directional indicators matched what he saw in front of him. He then advanced the throttle to full, and as the plane began its roll down the runway, he kept an eye on the oil pressure and oil temperature gauges to make sure they were still green. Once the plane hit 55 knots, he pulled back on the yoke, and the plane was airborne.

Melody was too scared to open her eyes during takeoff, but Farrah had no problem taking in the sights from a few thousand feet in the air. Once Jimmy banked over the water, the air got a lot smoother.

"If you look out to your left, you can make out the tip of Provincetown. It would only take us a few minutes to fly there, but a few hours to drive today based on what Route 6 looks like from up here."

"How long before we get to Fall River?" Detective Nickerson asked.

"Should be on the ground in about forty-five minutes," Jimmy replied. "Say, how are we going to get from the airstrip to the Cathedral?"

"I called ahead and arranged for an unmarked car to pick us up. We should beat them to the church by about an hour if not more."

Jimmy looked out the window. "Judging by the state of

Route 6 going west, maybe more."

He banked the plane toward the west and leveled off. "Sorry there's no in-flight movie or beverage service," Jimmy joked and continued flying west.

CHAPTER THIRTY-FIVE

Emily Makes a Confession

It took Emily an hour to drive from Chatham to Hyannis, where she stopped to get gas. During the entire ride, Fr. Michael did not utter a word; instead he sat in the passenger seat attempting to hide the fear that was building inside him.

As part of the curriculum to become a priest, Fr. Michael had to take a number of pastoral counseling courses, and he found that caring for people in this manner was very rewarding. Thus, with his bishop's permission, he went on to earn a master's degree and then a doctorate in clinical psychology. He knew from his experience that Emily was not a stable individual and sensed that she could snap at any moment. He also knew that trying to conduct an impromptu counseling session could easily backfire, so his strategy was to wait and see if she would volunteer any information. To do that, he needed to promote an environment where she felt safe, and he decided the best way to do that was to remain calm and quiet; it would be better if she started speaking first.

After refueling, Emily got back into the car and drove back onto the Mid-Cape Highway heading west. The traffic had eased up, and they made it to the Sagamore Bridge in twenty minutes and were on Route 25 moments after that. The priest noticed that Emily seemed to breathe easier as the traffic subsided, and he wondered if she was about to start talking.

"You seem more like a monk than a priest," she finally said.

"I apologize for being speechless; it's been a while since I've been kidnapped at gunpoint during a parade."

Fr. Michael thought that by using humor Emily would loosen up some more. It appeared to work.

"I never wanted it to get this far," Emily admitted.

"You never wanted what to get this far?"

"The thing with the priest, Fr. Hart. It was supposed to be a clean job, like all the others."

"Others?"

Emily reached between her legs to touch the gun that she had placed there after getting back into the car. She did this to signal to her passenger that she was the one in charge.

"People who cross me have a way of dying. Do you feel like crossing me?" Emily's tone was cold and detached.

"I can assure you, Emily, I have no intention of doing so."

"Because I'll end your life and not feel the least bit guilty about it."

"I'll take your word for that."

"Killing can always be justified," Emily responded.

"How do you figure?"

"I assume you are familiar with the ten commandments?"

"I've heard of them," Fr. Michael said sarcastically. "'Thou shall not kill' comes to mind."

"And what is the first commandment?"

"I'm a priest — is this Sunday school lesson really necessary?"

Emily pulled the hammer back on the revolver; this encouraged Fr. Michael to start reciting the first commandment.

"'I am the Lord your God; you shall not have any other gods before me.'"

"And what happened when the Israelites lost hope after the exodus and built a golden calf to worship?"

"God got angry and punished them with famine."

"And many of them died, didn't they?"

"I would assume so."

"Well, then, the punishment of creating a false idol is death."

"I don't understand," the priest admitted.

"Don't you see? Breaking a commandment is punishable by death."

"I think you're taking a big leap with that, Emily."

"Oh, am I? When my father found out that my brother was being molested by our parish priest, do you know what he did?"

Fr. Michael looked at Emily blankly.

"He shot the priest, and then he shot himself."

Fr. Michael was taken aback by this news. If her father had had that much anger inside him, there was no telling what kind of home life Emily and her brother experienced, but the priest guessed there was abuse involved, and he knew that violence begets violence. He decided to remain silent.

"My husband broke another commandment: 'thou shall not commit adultery.' When I found out he was having an affair, it caused me a great deal of embarrassment, so I did what had to be done — I killed that son of a bitch and his slut girlfriend. It was so clean no one ever expected me. I put on a good show for the funeral, but the truth is I didn't feel anything for that man after his death, and I wasn't the least bit sorry for what I had done."

The way Emily was talking, the priest suspected that she might be a true sociopath. Most people who commit crimes of passion feel some remorse for their actions, but if Emily were to be believed, she had felt nothing. As a result, the priest considered her more dangerous than he originally had thought.

"I didn't even feel anything after killing my own son."

The priest was shocked by this admission and couldn't hide the look of judgment that came over his face.

"'Honor thy father and thy mother,'" she replied. "On more than one occasion I smelled marijuana on my son's clothes. I warned him not to hang around with the bad seeds he fell in with after his father's death, but he didn't listen. I even followed them down to Hyannis where I saw them buying drugs with my own eyes."

The priest could only imagine how his father's death had affected Connor, particularly because he could not imagine Emily being all that nurturing. Given this, it was no wonder a teenage boy would want to self-medicate to fill the void in his life.

"When I confronted him about it that night, he called me a bitch, and that was it. The following day I paid a visit to his dealer, bought a bag of heroin, and brought it home. I went into Connor's room when he was sleeping, tied his arms and legs to his bedposts, and injected the heroin into his arm. I watched as his eyes rolled back into his head and the color of his skin changed dramatically. When I was sure he was dead, I took him down to the dock where we kept our boat, went a mile or so out into Nantucket Bay, and dumped his body. To add insult to injury, his head hit the side of the boat as he fell into the water.

Fr. Michael felt as if he were going to be sick. A mother who could kill her own son without feeling remorse was less than human, and at that moment he closed his eyes and said a prayer for her soul.

"I thought I was done killing for a while, but the truth is, I was just getting warmed up. After the police found his body, the detective on the case demanded an autopsy. I objected on the grounds of religious reasons, but due to the circumstances of the case, my objection was overruled. Once the medical examiner determined Connor was dead before he hit the water, I thought there was a chance I would be a suspect. In order to protect myself, I fed the names of the boys my son had been hanging out with to the cops, and I was never asked a question after that. Sloppy police work, if you ask me."

Fr. Michael decided to break his silence. "Why kill Fr. Hart? What commandment did he break?"

"Don't you want to hear about how I got my revenge on the detective who forced the autopsy?"

Fr. Michael had no desire to hear about another murder, but he realized that he had no choice.

"Detective Bill Jamison was a popular guy in town, but

he made the mistake of crossing me. I knew he had a bad heart, and I read somewhere that it is dangerous for very sedentary people with heart issues to physically exert themselves early in the morning. That's why I asked him to come over at 6:00 a.m. one day to help me remove some furniture from my home. After he went back to his house after helping me, he complained to a neighbor of dizziness. An hour later he was dead of a heart attack. I suppose you could say I killed two birds with one stone that day; the detective was dead, and I didn't have to pay anyone to help me move my furniture."

Fr. Michael closed his eyes and rubbed his temples. When he opened them again, he realized he had been so lost in conversation that he wasn't paying attention to where they were. After realizing they had crossed the town line into Fall River, he asked the same question as before, "Why Fr. Hart?"

"Fr. Hart was different. With Fr. Hart, I was just following orders."

Emily smiled and didn't say anything else until she parked in front of the rectory located adjacent to the cathedral.

"Ride's over, Father. Time to have a chat with my brother."

CHAPTER THIRTY-SIX

The Resurrection

Bishop Robert Hurley woke up on the morning of July Fourth feeling as if this would be his personal Independence Day. The diocesan offices were closed due it being a national holiday, and the bishop had encouraged all the other priests who lived at the rectory to take the day off and spend it with their friends and family; the only one who did not oblige was the chancellor, Fr. Cossa, who was getting some administrative work done in the offices adjacent to the rectory. Thus, when the doorbell rang, Bishop Hurley was the only one available to answer it.

He was surprised to see Farrah Graham and three others waiting on his doorstep so early in the day. He was a fan of her podcast and she had become a key player in the plan he put into motion the prior weekend. For that reason, her presence wasn't a surprise at all, but her timing was; not knowing she had access to an airplane, he didn't expect her so soon.

"Bishop Hurley, we have to talk right now."

"Come inside, Ms. Graham. I've been expecting you."

Farrah and her companions followed the bishop inside to a sitting room adjacent to the foyer.

"What do you mean, you were expecting me?"

"Sit down, Ms. Graham. There's something I have to confess to you, but before I get to that, Detective Nickerson, let me just say that you are highly respected by your peers here in Fall River."

The detective was taken aback by this admission. Why would the bishop know of his reputation?

"That's nice to hear, Bishop, but can you tell . . ."

Before the detective could finish, the bishop focused his attention over to Jimmy.

"You seem much more confident than I imagined, Mr. Rella. Based on the last season of Uncorking a Murder, I imagined you would be our comic relief, but you have proven yourself to be quite adept. I think your boss is going to have to change your nickname."

"Thank you . . . I think," Jimmy said, failing to hide the confusion in his voice.

"Melody, I must say, you were certainly the wildcard. I didn't think you would make it back, but I'm glad you did. I don't think Farrah could put the show together without you."

Melody looked at the bishop, stone-faced. She was as curious as the others as to what was going on, but she remained silent to hide her emotions.

"Look, Bishop Hurley, we believe Emily Rose is on her way down here right now. She kidnapped my brother at gunpoint and there's no telling what she is capable of. We need to be prepared."

"I'm counting on her being here in the next twenty

minutes."

Everyone gazed each other with puzzled glances. Detective Nickerson was the first to speak up. "What's this about a confession you had to make?"

The bishop reached into his pocket, removed his mobile phone, and dialed a number. In some distant part of the rectory, a phone began to ring, and a man answered.

"It's time. Come to the parlor."

A moment later, all eyes were on the French doors leading from the foyer into the parlor. When the doors opened, and Fr. Gregory Hart walked through them, Farrah couldn't believe what her eyes were telling her.

"But I watched you die," she said to the priest as he walked casually into the room and took a seat.

"Is this some kind of freaky Catholic shit?" Melody asked.

Bishop Hurley gave her a nasty look as if to reprimand her, but then smiled.

"Why don't I start from the beginning," the bishop began. "Over the past few years, it came to my attention that my protege, Fr. Peter Cossa, has been scheming to get my job. I always knew him to be a conservative type of priest and ruthless in his convictions, but to be honest, he balanced me out very well. He had strengths that I didn't, and I could always count on him to handle some of the unpleasant tasks that sometimes can't be avoided in a diocese."

"Please . . . cut to the chase and tell us how Fr. Hart went from being dead to sitting in this living room."

"I'm getting to that. It's no secret that Fr. Hart and I did not see eye to eye on many things; our disputes were quite public."

Fr. Hart interrupted the bishop, "I still think you're wrong on women clergy."

"We're not here to debate that, Gregory. Anyway, it was Fr. Hart here who clued me in to Fr. Cossa's true intentions."

All eyes shifted to Fr. Hart.

"We priests move in very small circles. I heard about an organization Fr. Cossa started called the Order of Pope John the XXIII, and, given what I knew about that particular pope, I thought it could be an extremist group.

"Gregory, you're being kind calling that an organization. It's more like a fraternity for grown men who are still angry at the reforms of Vatican II. Hell, I've heard that he crafted the organization's initiation rights after reading about a fraternity ritual on the Internet."

"May I continue?"

"Be my guest," the bishop said.

"When I had a parish here in Fall River, one of my parishioners confessed to being invited to join a secret society. He was a well-to-do married man who had conservative leanings. I encouraged him to join, and he has been feeding me inside information ever since. He's the one who told me that Fr. Cossa intended to take action against Bishop Hurley."

"When did this happen?" Farrah asked.

"About six months ago," Fr. Hart replied.

"So right about the same time you were transferred to Our Lady of Healing Church in Chatham," Detective Nickerson observed.

"It wasn't a coincidence that I assigned him there. I knew that Fr. Cossa had a sister who was living in Chatham. When the former pastor, Fr. Paul Hewson, decided to retire and move back to his native Ireland, I asked Fr. Hart to replace him."

"I wasn't happy about it," Fr. Hart admitted.

"I know," said Bishop Hurley. "Anyone who followed your blog and listened to your podcast is aware of that," he joked. "But it was an important sacrifice."

"But how did Fr. Hart come back from the dead?"

"There's only one man who came back from the dead, and He had nothing to do with my resurrection," Fr. Hart said.

A lightbulb went off in Jimmy's head. "Wait, Fr. Hart didn't come back from the dead because he wasn't dead at all."

"Bingo," said Fr. Hart.

"But I saw you in the morgue!" Detective Nickerson exclaimed.

"Did you see my face?"

Detective Nickerson thought about the visit he paid to Dr. Stemper's office that past Monday morning. He remembered that the medical examiner only lifted up the sheet covering the body to expose the dead man's legs.

"Was Stemper in on this?"

"Charles is an old friend," the bishop said, "and a good Catholic."

"But something doesn't add up," Farrah said, looking at Fr. Hart. "How did you know that Emily was going to try to kill you?"

"My guy inside the Order overheard Fr. Cossa talking to his sister one day and sent word to me. He heard enough of their conversation to make out they intended to spike the wine used for Communion with cyanide. Apparently she had stolen the capsule that her father kept as a keepsake from his flying days. From then on, I always smelled the wine to make sure it did not smell like almonds, which Dr. Stemper told me was a telltale sign of cyanide poisoning."

"But we saw you drink the wine last Sunday at Mass," Farrah said.

"I only pretended to drink it. And then tapped into my theater background to sell the story."

"According to the report, though, a doctor pronounced you dead at the scene."

"Let me guess," Melody spoke up. "That was Dr. Stemper, wasn't it?"

"Smart girl," Fr. Hart said.

"There's something I still don't understand," Farrah said. "Where does my brother fit into all of this?"

"Your brother and I are old friends," Fr. Hart replied. "No offense to Detective Nickerson here, but the Chatham police department hasn't been able to pin any of the other murders Emily has under her belt on her. We knew we needed a heavy hitter to help solve the case, and you were it."

Farrah instantly became furious, as did Detective Nickerson who didn't like being insulted by the priest.

"Now my brother's life is in danger," Farrah said. "I suppose that was part of your plan too?"

"That's where the plan fell apart," Bishop Hurley admitted. "We didn't anticipate Christopher Mitchell being arrested for Fr. Hart's murder, and we certainly didn't anticipate his suicide."

"The more I think of it, the more you two might be held liable for his death. If you didn't fake Fr. Hart's death, he would never have been arrested, and he would never have killed himself."

Before either Fr. Hart or Bishop Hurley could respond to Detective Nickerson's point, the doorbell rang.

"Gregory, I believe you have a visitor."

CHAPTER THIRTY-SEVEN
The 11th Commandment

Emily and Fr. Michael approached the door to the rectory. The priest was in front of his captor, and she reminded him of the fact that she was armed by pushing the nozzle of the gun into his back. While it was still wrapped in a sweater, anyone who observed the two would have known instantly that something wasn't right about the situation.

As they walked, the priest looked around and saw that there were very few cars in the parking lot.

"Are you sure he's here?"

Emily pushed the gun deeper into the priest's back. "I received a text message from him earlier telling me to meet him here. Apparently everyone, including the bishop, is gone for the Fourth of July holiday, and he's the only person at the rectory."

This, of course, was a bit of deceit crafted by the bishop himself who had grabbed the chancellor's phone earlier in the day and sent a misleading text to Emily. Before erasing the message and returning the phone to its owner, he sent another message warning her not to communicate by text any more given it could be used as evidence in court.

Fr. Michael faced the door to the rectory and debated whether to knock or use the doorbell. Apparently he took too long to make up his mind, because Emily pushed him out of the way and rang the bell.

When the door opened, Emily was expecting to see her brother and instead heard the words, "Hello, Emily," spoken by none other than Fr. Gregory Hart.

Emily immediately fainted, dropping the gun and falling backward. Luckily, Fr. Michael's instincts were quick, and he grabbed her arm and held her up before she fell down the stairs leading up to the rectory entrance. He was surprised to see his old friend in the flesh, but Emily's sudden loss of consciousness prevented him from fully processing what just happened.

"I have a thousand questions right about now, but I'm going to need your help to bring her inside."

Fr. Hart positioned himself on the opposite side of Emily and grabbed her under the arms while Fr. Hart moved toward her feet. They carried her inside and placed her on the couch.

"She's a lot heavier than she looks!" Fr. Hart remarked.

Fr. Michael looked around the room and saw his sister as well as her partner, Melody, Jimmy Doubts, and Detective Nickerson.

"Will one of you please tell me what the hell is going on?"

"Watch your tone," remarked Bishop Hurley, who Fr. Michael did not immediately see when coming into the room.

"I apologize, Your Excellency. I'm just very confused."

"Join the club," Farrah stated.

"Do you have any smelling salts?" Jimmy, who had been an EMT in college, asked Bishop Hurley.

"Let me get our first-aid kit," the bishop said.

"Hold on a second," Detective Nickerson interrupted. He walked over to Emily and handcuffed her hands. "We shouldn't take any chances."

The bishop came back with the first-aid kit and handed it to Jimmy, who found the smelling salts, broke open a capsule, and placed it under Emily's nose. He moved his hands back and forth a few times and stopped when her eyes shot open. She looked around the room and then tried to move her hands, which she quickly realized were cuffed. Her eyes then rested on Fr. Hart.

"Are you a ghost?" she asked weakly.

"No, Emily, I am very much alive."

"But how . . . the poison . . ."

Detective Nickerson spoke up. "Emily Rose, I hereby place you under arrest." He then proceeded to read Emily her Miranda rights.

"Emily is only half of the equation though," Farrah spoke up. "How are we going to make anything stick to her brother? He hasn't admitted to anything yet."

"I have a plan for that," Bishop Hurley said. He then nodded to Fr. Hart and said, "It's time."

Fr. Peter Cossa was working diligently at his desk, finishing the paperwork that would formalize a new priest taking over Fr. Hart's place in Chatham. While Fr. Cossa considered Fr. Thomas James to be a bit of a softie, he didn't have many options, as these days fewer men were answering the call to the priesthood. Fr. James, who was close to retirement age, expressed interest in finishing his ministry in Chatham, and Cossa was going to grant that wish.

He then began to think about all the other decisions he would be able to make after becoming bishop: where the money for the annual appeal would be spent, the parishes he would close due to declining membership, and the punishments he would dole out to those who had crossed him in the past.

This daydream was interrupted by the phone that began to ring on his desk. Surprised that someone would call his office on a national holiday, he glanced at the caller ID and saw that it was from the 202 area code, which he knew was from Washington, DC, where the apostolic nuncio lived. Thinking it could be important, Fr. Cossa decided to answer the phone.

"Chancellor's office, this is Chancellor Fr. Peter Cossa. How can I help you?"

"Fr. Cossa, please hold for the papal nuncio."

The priest allowed himself to feel a sense of excitement. Receiving such a call on a national holiday confirmed that it must be important.

A gravely voice with a thick Italian accent came on the line.

"Fr. Cossa, this is Monsignor Roberto Calibri, the apostolic nuncio to the United States. I am sorry to interrupt your holiday celebrations, but there is a matter of utmost importance that I must speak with you about."

Fr. Cossa's heart began to beat a little faster.

"I am here to serve, Monsignor."

"I received the documents you sent earlier this week

with the recommended succession plan for Bishop Hurley."

"If you have a question about those plans, Monsignor, it would be best to discuss them directly with the bishop."

"That's part of the reason I am calling. After reading the succession plan, I am not so sure we can trust Bishop Hurley's judgment. Out of the four recommended names on the list, three of these priests were recently implicated in some form of scandal in their respective dioceses. I have also heard word recently that Bishop Hurley has not been himself. Is that true?"

"He has been under a tremendous amount of stress after the death of one of our priests," Fr. Cossa said. "Mentally, he's not all there."

"This concerns me greatly, as it does the Holy Father. Therefore, I am going to make a recommendation to the pope that Bishop Hurley be removed from service immediately."

The excitement building inside Fr. Cossa had reached a fever pitch.

"But who will lead the diocese in Bishop Hurley's absence?"

"I think we both know the answer to that question," the Monsignor replied. "I will be speaking with the Holy See first thing tomorrow morning. I'll reach out with more information after that."

"Thank you, Monsignor."

"Congratulations, Bishop Cossa."

Fr. Cossa terminated the call and immediately called Bishop Hurley's mobile.

"Hello, Your Excellency. We need to talk."

Bishop Hurley felt his phone begin to vibrate in his pocket. Removing it, he checked the caller ID. "That was fast," he said to everyone in the room.

They all looked at the bishop with confusion plastered on their faces.

"Bishop Hurley," the bishop said into his phone. A few seconds later he replied, "Why don't you meet me in my private office at the rectory? Very well, I'll be there in five minutes." He put the phone back into his pocket.

"I need all of you to wait upstairs. This is a meeting I must have alone."

Fr. Hart led everyone else upstairs.

Emily protested, "What if I scream when I hear my brother come into the house?"

"I thought you might try and do something like that," the detective said. "Fr. Hart, can you get me some duct tape?"

The priest left and came back with a roll of tape. The detective ripped off a piece with his teeth and placed it across Emily's mouth. "Problem solved."

Bishop Hurley, meanwhile, walked across the first floor of the rectory and entered his private office. He removed a small audio recorder, turned it on, hit record, and then placed it under some papers on his desk. A moment later he heard the front door of the rectory opening and footsteps approaching his office. There was a knock at the door.

"Come in," Bishop Hurley said in a stern tone.

"Good afternoon, Your Excellency, I hope I am not disturbing you."

Under normal circumstances, Fr. Cossa would attempt

to sound sincere, but these weren't normal circumstances, and he came off sounding sarcastic.

"What can I help you with?"

"I just received an interesting call from the apostolic nuncio in Washington, DC." Fr. Cossa said, pacing across the floor with his hands behind his back.

"And?" Bishop Hurley said nonchalantly.

"And, Your Excellency, it seems that the diocese is going to make a few changes."

"What are you talking about?"

"It looks as if the papal nuncio has lost faith in you."

"Is that so?" Bishop Hurly said. He tapped his lips with the tips of his index fingers.

"And did he discuss with you who my replacement would be?"

"As a matter of fact, you are looking at him," Fr. Cossa said smugly, flashing a wide smile and extending his arms out wide.

"Is that so?" Bishop Hurley said again.

"I wouldn't lie to you, Your Excellency."

"Interesting," the bishop said, snickering.

"What's interesting — and why are you laughing?"

"I wonder what the papal nuncio would say if he knew you encouraged your sister to kill Fr. Gregory Hart."

The chancellor was taken aback. "How dare you suggest such a thing!"

"I've spoken to the police in Chatham," the bishop said. "They called me immediately after that article ran in the paper this morning; they informed me that they had a suspect in mind."

"What makes you think Emily had anything to do with it?"

"She had access to the wine before Mass, and she had access to the cyanide that killed Fr. Hart." Bishop Hurley could have also added that she confessed it to him earlier in the week, but that would be breaking the seal of confession. For the same reason, he also wouldn't admit to knowing that Fr. Hart wasn't the first person the chancellor's sister had tried to kill.

"Let's say she did it," Fr. Cossa said. "My sister is a very sick person. What makes you think I had anything to do with her actions?"

"I've been wrestling with that for some time now," the bishop replied. "At first I thought you told her to kill Fr. Hart because you felt he was a threat to the Church with his messages of reform and his growing platform through social media and his podcast. But then a lightbulb went off in my head."

"This should be good. I can't wait to hear it — should I make some popcorn?"

"Joke all you want, Peter, but you'll be the only one laughing. You see, I know how ambitious you are, and I've always known that you wanted to become a bishop someday."

"Ambition isn't a sin," Cossa said defensively.

"True, ambition in and of itself is not a sin, but what you do to pursue ambition can be sinful."

"And what have I done, Your Excellency, to pursue my ambition?"

"Speaking to a reporter as an anonymous source to spread lies about me and Fr. Hart as well as encouraging your sister to kill a fellow priest come to mind."

"Prove it."

"You thought you were so clever in this whole thing, but

there was something you didn't count on."

"And what's that?"

The bishop reached for the phone in his pocket, dialed a number, and then spoke. "Please come downstairs now and bring our guests with you."

"Who are you talking to?"

"All in good time," the bishop said.

A moment later there was a knock on the door. "Please come in," Bishop Hurley said in a loud voice.

Fr. Cossa's eyes were glued to the door to the bishop's office. He saw his sister walk into the room, handcuffed, followed by Detective Nickerson.

"Emily, what are you doing here?"

His sister couldn't respond since the duct tape was still covering her mouth. She simply made grunting sounds and started to cry.

"Was your conversation with Emily productive?" the bishop asked Detective Nickerson.

"She told us everything we needed to know."

Emily began to vehemently shake her head no, the tears falling more quickly.

"She's a very disturbed person," Fr. Cossa argued. "How else could someone kill her husband and only son? What — do you believe that I encouraged her to kill them as well?"

Farrah Graham then walked into the room with Jimmy and Melody in tow. When Fr. Cossa saw her, he sat upright in his chair.

"You know, Fr. Cossa, your voice sounds very familiar to me. Were you by any chance hearing confessions yesterday in the church next door?"

Fr. Cossa turned to Bishop Hurley and said defensively,

"Nice try, but you of all people should know that I cannot break the seal of confession. Anything she says would be inadmissible in court."

"I don't recall confessing any sins," Farrah said. "Besides, we can find some other parishioners to testify that you heard their confessions that day to establish that it was you in the confessional."

Fr. Cossa started to get nervous. While he couldn't divulge what happened in the confessional, there was nothing stopping Farrah from testifying what she had said, and from there it wouldn't take a lot of hard work to link Fr. Cossa to the leak at the Boston Globe. Even so, the case was circumstantial because there was no proof; aside from whatever his sister told the police, nothing linked him to Fr. Hart's death.

Sensing that Fr. Cossa was still resisting the notion that he was guilty, Bishop Hurley decided to play his trump card. He stood up, walked over to the door of his office, opened it, and spoke with someone on the other side. A moment later Fr. Gregory Hart was standing in the center of the office. The blood in Fr. Cossa's face drained.

"What the . . ."

"Surprised to see me?" Fr. Hart said, putting on a thick Italian accent. Immediately Fr. Cossa knew that he hadn't been speaking with the apostolic nuncio just minutes earlier. The fact that he had been fooled caused him to go into a fit of rage.

"You were supposed to be dead!" Fr. Cossa screamed. Turning to his sister, he snarled, "Can't you do anything right?"

Emily closed her eyes and continued to cry.

At that point, sensing that having her mouth covered

with tape could be dangerous given how hard she was crying, Detective Nickerson ripped the tape off her mouth.

"I didn't tell them anything!" she protested.

"And you," Fr. Cossa said, addressing the bishop, "you played me this entire time."

At that point, his anger enveloped him like a blanket, and he lunged across the desk and wrapped his hands around the bishop's throat.

Detective Nickerson sprang into action and tried to peel Cossa off Bishop Hurley, but the chancellor anticipated the attack and kicked the detective hard in the stomach. Just as the bishop's face was turning from bright red to deep purple, there was a loud bang, and everyone stopped to see Melanie pointing Emily's gun at the floor. It was smoking. She then raised it and pointed it toward the priest.

"You have three seconds to let him go. One, two . . ." She pulled the hammer of the gun back.

Fr. Cossa released his grasp on the bishop and put his hands up in the air.

"This is all your word against mine," Fr. Cossa said. "It won't hold up in court."

"I wouldn't be too sure about that," Bishop Hurley said after catching his breath. He then reached for the audio recorder that was hidden under the papers on his desk.

"This would make for a compelling ending for your next season, wouldn't you say, Farrah?"

"I believe it would, Your Excellency."

Detective Nickerson stood up and removed another pair of handcuffs from his pocket.

"Peter Cossa, you are under arrest. You have the right

to remain silent. Anything you say . . ." After he finished reading the priest his Miranda rights, Nickerson placed a call to the Fall River Police Department.

"You know what your problem is, Peter?"

"What's that?" Cossa asked as he was being led out the door.

"You broke the eleventh commandment."

"Which is?"

"Thou shalt remain obedient to one's bishop."

CHAPTER THIRTY-EIGHT

Loose Ends

Detective Nickerson waited for his counterparts from the Fall River Police Department to arrive and then escorted the disgraced Fr. Peter Cossa and his sister, Emily Rose, to the police station where they would be booked and later arraigned on charges of attempted murder.

Nickerson knew that he had his work cut out for him. He intended to prove that Emily killed her husband, son, and his former colleague Detective Bill Jamison; he would be a busy detective for the remainder of the summer.

While it was true that Emily was in hotter water than her brother, from a certain point of view, his punishment would almost certainly be more severe. He'd be laicized by the Church, meaning he'd no longer be a priest. After whatever prison term he was sentenced to was up, he'd be a lost soul once again looking for purpose in life.

Farrah, Fr. Michael, Melody, and Jimmy stayed at the rectory for a few minutes after the Detective Nickerson took Bishop Hurley's statement; they were eager for the bishop and Fr. Hart to fill in the details of how they were able to pull off faking the priest's death. Specifically they wanted to know where Fr. Hart had been hiding for the past few days.

"Wellfleet," Fr. Hart replied. "With my friend Amanda Brooks."

Fr. Michael raised an eyebrow as he looked at his friend. "Friend?"

"Yes, my friend. I couldn't be seen in Fall River, and I certainly couldn't hang around Chatham, so I stayed with Amanda in Wellfleet."

"Wait," Jimmy said. "That means she must have been doing an acting job on us when we interviewed her at the restaurant."

"She was a theater major in college," Fr. Hart said. "She could have been an actress, but an unplanned pregnancy changed all that."

"If she was in on this," Farrah piped up, "then what was she doing at the church the morning of your death?"

"What did she tell you?" Fr. Hart asked.

"That she was going to plead with you to reconsider your decision to leave her."

Fr. Hart laughed. "She wasn't misleading you. She actually did bring me a picture her son had drawn for me, hoping to get me to change my mind. She almost fainted when I showed up later that night after hearing I had died."

"How are you going to possibly explain this to your parishioners in Chatham?"

Bishop Hurley spoke up. "Well, Ms. Graham, we were hoping you could help us with that."

"How's that?" Farrah replied.

"One of the reasons we got you involved in this was to

help us tell the entire story once everything went down."

"Hold on a second — I was part of your plan the entire time?"

Farrah looked at her brother and gave him a stern look; her grandmother used to refer to it as the evil eye.

"Don't look at me — I didn't have anything to do with it," he protested.

"You were the one who asked me to look into this murder in the first place." When Farrah said the word murder, she placed it in air quotes with her hands.

"That's because I knew that my friend Greg over here had been receiving some death threats."

"Your brother is right, Farrah," Fr. Hart spoke up. "He had nothing to do with it. I actually used him to get to you."

"And I suppose it was just a coincidence that I happened to be in the church the morning you were supposedly murdered?"

"The Lord works in mysterious ways," Fr. Hart replied.

Melody, who had been holding in her anger since Detective Nickerson left, broke her silence.

"Not only did your ruin our summer vacation plans, but you put lives in danger. An innocent man is dead because of what you did, and Fr. Mikey over here was held at gunpoint by a crazy bitch who killed her husband and child."

Bishop Hurley said soberly, "Christopher Mitchell's suicide will be on my conscience for the rest of my life, but it was Emily who pointed the finger at him, not us."

"As for me," Fr. Michael spoke up, "I could have ditched Emily right after she tried to kidnap me during the parade, but my instincts told me to stay with her. I guess you could say I had faith that I'd be okay."

"Still seems like some crazy shit to me."

"Melody!" Farrah said in a warning tone.

"What? Look, I was hoping to have a relaxing summer, and now here we are with you involved in yet another case and me left wondering what I'm doing with you."

"Maybe we should have this conversation another time," Farrah pleaded.

"Damn it, Farrah, you never want to talk about anything in the moment. I don't care that all these people are around us — why do you?"

"It's a private matter."

"Private? Let me tell you something, girl, there's nothing private about us anymore because of that damn podcast. As far as I'm concerned, you waived your right to privacy the moment you started the damn thing."

"We started the podcast," Farrah said. "We did it together."

"Your memory is so damn short, girl. I wanted no part of that fiasco in Florida last year, and I made it clear I wanted nothing to do with this."

"I'm sorry but . . . ." Farrah cut herself off. "You know what? I'm not sorry. I won't apologize for my success. I never intended to be a happy homemaker. I enjoyed the stimulation of being a trial lawyer, and I gave that up when you handed me an ultimatum. I did that for you! Now I enjoy the excitement that comes with this, and you know what, I love the celebrity I am becoming. And if you can't handle that, then I suggest you pack your bags again and make your own goddamn decision. Stay or go, but there will be no in between."

Everyone in the room was speechless, and Melody

looked like a deer caught in the headlights. Farrah's brother actually felt some pride for his sister; he thought she had let Melody push her around for too long. As far as he was concerned, he had hoped Farrah would cut ties with her years ago. His opinion was that a partner is someone who was there to support you and build you up, while Melody was the exact opposite.

Farrah looked at Melody and saw that her lip had started to quiver. She walked toward Melody with her arms open, but Melody pulled back.

"You've said enough," Melody said. She pulled her phone out of her pocket and tapped the screen a few times.

"What are you doing?" Farrah asked.

"I just sent a prayer to Our Lady of Uber," Melody replied. "Good-bye, Farrah. It was nice while it lasted."

Melody then turned around, ignoring the others, and left.

"I'm sorry if we caused you any trouble, Farrah," Bishop Hurley said in an apologetic tone. "It wasn't our intention."

"This has been building for a while," Farrah replied numbly. "It was bound to happen sooner or later."

Jimmy went over to hug Farrah, seeing how upset she was. As she buried her face in his chest, she began to cry. He hugged her tightly, and as his body pressed against hers, he felt the heat emanating from their embrace and couldn't control his physiological reaction.

"I don't think the turtle is scared," Farrah whispered in his ear, but she didn't break their embrace.

Epilogue

Farrah and Jimmy spent the remainder of the summer in Chatham piecing together what would become season three of Uncorking a Murder, which began with the death of Fr. Gregory Hart but then took some unexpected twists as they dug into the deaths of Todd and Connor Rose as well as Detective Bill Jamison.

To fill out the story, they spent time in Fall River interviewing people who knew Peter and Emily Cossa as children. They also interviewed friends and family members of Christopher Mitchell, who was, after all, the sacrificial lamb of Fr. Hart's faked death. When all was said and done, they edited all the footage they had captured into ten one-hour episodes that would make up what Farrah considered to be the most compelling season of Uncorking a Murder to date.

Since Melody had formally left both the podcast and Farrah's life altogether, Farrah pleaded with Jimmy not to go back to law school and instead take over Melody's production responsibilities. It wasn't a hard sell; Jimmy actually hated the thought of becoming a lawyer. Signing a contract to split the profits from advertising 50/50 didn't hurt either.

Now back in Stamford, Connecticut, Farrah sat in the recording studio she had set up in an office building downtown. They were now deep into winter, with the previous summer well in the rearview mirror. Jimmy had done a great job of piecing the entire narrative together into a cohesive season, and all that Farrah had left to do was record her opening. As she looked over the words she had printed out in front of her, she couldn't help thinking about what had become of former Fr. Gregory Hart. After the full story broke, he asked Bishop Hurley to be removed from active service in the priesthood as he had discerned a calling that was at odds with his priestly vows: He had fallen in love with Amanda Brooks and intended to pursue married life as his new vocation. Amanda had accepted his marriage proposal, and the two were planning to get married next July in a small ceremony on the Cape.

As she thought of them, Farrah wondered if she would ever find love again. Unknowingly she stared at Jimmy Doubts, whose newfound freedom from the legal profession combined with an increase in personal confidence had caused her to see him in a new light.

"Why are you staring at me like that?" Jimmy asked.

Farrah, suddenly realizing that she had been staring, snapped out of trance that she was in.

Jimmy continued, "And why are you smiling? What's wrong with you?"

"Sorry . . . I was just reconsidering what I was about to say and I got lost in thought."

"Get your head in the game, Golden Graham," Jimmy replied. He had taken to calling her by her childhood nickname as a reaction to her consistently calling him

Doubts. While her father was the only person she usually allowed to call her that, she didn't fight Jimmy on it.

Farrah cleared her throat and said, "I'm ready when you are."

"We're rolling . . ."

Farrah inched forward so her mouth was an inch away from the pop filter that covered her microphone.

"Welcome to season three of Uncorking a Murder. Buckle yourselves in, because you're in for a roller coaster of a ride as we take a deep dive into the attempted murder of a progressive priest preaching the gospel in the resort town of Chatham, Massachusetts. Be warned — this season has more twists and turns than a David Fincher movie, and don't blame me if you spend the next ten hours binging on it. Wait — what am I saying? Of course you can blame me, because I put it together; just don't come to me complaining that your relationship has hit the skids since you started listening. I've got enough of my own relationship problems."

Jimmy heard a newfound playfulness in Farrah's tone. He thought it made her sound more relatable to the audience and made a mental note to encourage her to dial it up in the future.

Farrah continued, "By now you know the big-picture story of how Fr. Greg Hart was murdered last summer but then found to be very much alive, but what you know is only half of the story. Not only does this season focus on who did it and why, but we delve deeply into the backstories of the key players. The disgraced priest who took advantage of his sister's psychological problems for his own potential gain, the pious woman who killed without remorse, the detective charged with putting the puzzle together, and last but certainly not least, the bishop who was the mastermind behind the faked death. Ladies and gentlemen, put your tray tables up and make sure your seats are in the upright position; we are about to take off on what I can guarantee will be a thrill ride like no other you have ever been on before."

Acknowledgements

I did not anticipate the success of Uncorking a Murder. While I loved the characters, the nervous and slightly unconfident writer who lives inside me questioned whether anyone else would. Thankfully, people loved Farrah Graham and Jimmy Doubts and the quirky, twist filled mystery they got involved in. Even so, I did not intend to write the followup so quickly but as the saying goes, man makes plans and God laughs.

I was vacationing on Cape Cod in the summer of 2016 where I was finishing up the manuscript for Winning Streak, my third novel. After addressing my editor's comments and suggestions, I decided to go to Mass at a small Catholic Church located in the town of Chatham. As Mass begun, my mind started wandering to a dark place — the priest was on the older side and I started to think about what would happen if he dropped dead on the altar. I have a vivid imagination, don't judge me! Then I started to think, what if he was actually murdered? In that instant, the story arch for The Last Homily came to me. Upon getting back to the house I was renting, I sat down and wrote an outline and spent the next nine months putting pen to paper.

I need to thank my editor, Claudia Volkman, for her expert guidance in this project. Her developmental suggestions were spot on and her line editing, as always, made this novel much stronger. Thank you Claudia.

Robert Bartlett has graciously rented me his house in Chatham for the past twenty years and this story would not have been possible had I not been vacationing in Nana's Beach House. Thank you Bob for renting your house to me and my family, it will always hold a special place in our hearts.

In August of 1999, my wife Nicole had no idea that the man she was marrying was eventually going to become a novelist. As such, she was not prepared for the late nights and early mornings when she would find me writing or the constant waking up and writing of notes that no doubt disturbed her sleep. She puts up with my quirky habits and I love her for it. Thank you Nicole for being a source of inspiration for me.

Sue Oats was the first of my beta readers to get their hands on this manuscript and her keen auditor's eye helped get The Last Homily ready for publication. Thank you Sue!

Lastly, I want to thank you for buying this book and getting to know Farrah Graham. I can't wait to see where her next adventure takes her and I hope you share the same anticipation.

Sneak Peek into Michael Carlon's forthcoming novel

All the F*cks I Cannot Give

Confrontation Isn't My Strong Suit

One might think the worst day in a man's life might be when he finds his wife in bed with another woman, but I knew my wife Laura was a lesbian very early into our marriage. No, she didn't have a ring of keys clamped to one of her belt loops by a carabiner nor did she ever come out and say, "Kelly, I'd like to chow some box tonight," and invite me to an all you can eat buffet of beaver; come to think of it, the fact that my parents gave me a woman's name may have been what attracted her to me in the first place (apologies for the digression). No, I knew my wife was a lesbian because my twin sister, Josephine - who everybody calls Jo - spotted her in a gay bar shortly after we returned home from our honeymoon ten years ago. FYI Jo is a Lesbian and my father considers her the son he never had.

At first, I didn't believe her because the initial photographic evidence of Laura chatting with another woman at a bar appeared innocent. Sure, it was clear she was at a gay bar, as all the women were dressed as Schneider from *One Day at a Time*, but so what? I've heard that oftentimes women feel more comfortable at those places than straight bars because they don't get hit on as much. When Jo showed me the picture of my wife tongue kissing a woman who resembled Nancy McKeon from *The Facts of Life*, I chalked it up to Laura being a bit curious. I didn't confront her about it because, by nature, I hate confrontation. Nothing scares me more than causing conflict - so I tried to forget about it and buried it; as the saying goes, denial isn't just a river in Egypt.

When I caught Laura in the act with my eyes, that was different. It was on a day I came home from a business trip early. Instead of taking the early morning flight from San Diego to NY, I decided to take a red eye so I could get to our suburban Connecticut home early as a surprise to my wife. She was surprised alright, especially when I walked in on her and our handywoman Ella having a good old time in our bed. Holy hell, Laura's face was buried so deep in Ella's crotch she looked like a bear fishing for salmon swimming upstream.

A more aggressive man would have offered to join them, but part of being non-confrontational means I'm also not the least bit aggressive -- I simply coughed loudly to make my presence known. Ella opened her eyes and stared at me with a look of shock on her face. Laura unburied her face from between her girlfriend's thighs, turned around and simply said, "Oh fuck." She then rolled over, pulled our sheets over the two of them, and reached for the pack of cigarettes on our cherry wood nightstand.

At the time I wanted to say something other than, "Since when do you smoke?" but that was the only phrase I could muster.

"I didn't expect you until later," Laura said while

maintaining eye contact and exhaling a plume of smoke through her nose.

"I wanted to surprise you so I took the red eye."

"I told you never to take the red eye since you're always grumpy when you don't get enough sleep."

"Apparently that's not the only reason," I muttered under my breath.

I remember turning around so Ella could get dressed with at least a minimal degree of privacy. After she left the room, Laura told me she was in fact, drumroll please, a lesbian and that she only married me to appease her conservative parents who loved that their wild child of a daughter was settling down with a white-collar guy who had a good job; it certainly explained why we were on the quarterly plan when it came to sex! Incidentally, that was supposed to be a night of matrimonial congress, but congress decided to take a ten-year hiatus -- that's right, I have not had sex with another human being in ten years.

I remember being more shocked than angry and, since we've already established that I have a hard time dealing with conflict, I agreed to Laura's proposition that we live in an open marriage, which we've done for the past decade. She argued that I wouldn't survive in the modern world as a single man and that it would mean a lot to her if I kept up appearances around her family.

So while that was a pretty shitty day for Kelly Carson, that's me if you haven't guessed, it wasn't the worst day of my life. No, that would be today, the day my spineless boss fired me...over the telephone.

My Spineless Boss

I work in the field of marketing research and before I educate you more on what that means, let me just make something perfectly clear -- no one in this field says to themselves, "I want to study consumer opinion for the rest of my life." No one goes to school for a degree in market research; people who wind up in this field have dreams of becoming psychologists, sociologists, anthropologists or any of the other ologists one can become after almost a decade of higher education. For one reason or another, though, they wind up selling out and applying their research skills to marketing problems -- my story isn't unique in that regard.

I was all set to earn a Ph.D. in clinical psychology from a prestigious university but decided to take my father's advice and work for a year before returning to school. I took a job at a well-known New York based advertising agency and that's where I saw my first focus group.

The topic was what people would want in a website from their bank and the guy leading the discussion looked like he was having a blast engaging people in conversation and asking probing follow-up questions.

At the time, I thought it looked like a cross between group therapy and improvisational theatre and I knew right then and there that I wanted to do that for the rest of my life, so I turned down the opportunity to earn my doctorate and pursued running focus groups full time.

Seventeen years ago, I left the agency world to work for a research company called Stahl and Partners run by an inspiring woman named Michele Stahl who had a penchant for French wine, younger men, and a cocaine habit that would shock Charlie Sheen. She was looking for the next generation of moderators to run her business so she could retire early and spend her days in Hawaii with her collection of antique coke spoons and boy toys of the week. While she was, and this is putting it mildly, bat shit crazy, she had moments of lucidity when she taught me the ins and outs of leading group discussions and keeping clients happy. According to her, the key to the latter was offering sexual services after each night of research and submitting to their every demand. That's one of two bits of advice I didn't take from her, the other being never to believe a drug dealer when he says he'll be over in twenty minutes. I didn't take that advice because, well, I've never required the services of a drug dealer -- I'm as square as they come.

A little over two years ago, I walked into the office and Michele informed me and the rest of the staff that she had sold her firm to Omnivore, a large holding company, and that we would be integrated into their research division. She also informed us that she made twenty million dollars on the sale; even though she had a three-year earn out, I never saw her again and often wonder if she lived to see her mid-fifties. The following day I met my new boss, Pete Jackson.

You know Pete Jackson -- even if you've never met him, you know him. Why do I say this? Because he exists in every American high school. He was likely the captain of the lacrosse team, maybe the student council president. Always had a positive, go get 'em attitude even though you knew he was full of shit and said whatever he needed to in order to get ahead. Ring any bells?

My first meeting with Pete was one I'll never forget. He sauntered into a conference room 15 minutes late for an "all-hands" meeting he called. He was wearing a plaid sport coat and trendy green coke bottle glasses and was clearly trying to look younger than his fifty-seven years by dressing down with a pair of designer jeans and black sneakers, which, for all intents and purposes, looked orthopedic. As he walked into the room, he tucked the Nalgene water bottle he was never seen without under his arm and started clapping as if to suggest we should all clap when he entered.

"Team!" he exclaimed. "Thanks for coming. I've heard so many good things about all of you and I can only imagine what you've heard about me. I can assure you only half of what you heard is true."

Actually, what I had heard was that Pete was about one percent business man and ninety-nine percent bullshit, but that for some reason the board liked that ratio well enough to believe he could double the revenue in our department.

"I like to be scrappy so don't expect anything too formal from me, and the only thing I expect from you is that you kill it and crush it every day."

Right then and there, I knew this asshole had no idea what we did as moderators. We don't kill, we don't crush --

we talk to strangers and turn their stories into insights our clients can use to make better decisions. No killing required.

"Who here wants to take Pork Chop Hill with me?"

After he said "Pork Chop Hill," I made a mental note to revise my resume that afternoon.

Much to my surprise, the other people in the room all stood up and cheered; one even let out a hoo-rah with a little vibrato as if he were Al Pacino's understudy in Scent of a Woman, the Musical.

I remained sitting, unable to comprehend the shitstorm that just walked into the room.

"What's your name?" Pete said to me.

"Kelly," I replied.

"Kelly? That's a girl's name."

I could tell the minute he heard my name that this is what his response would be. Call it a would-be woman's intuition.

"It's the name my parents gave me."

I told you before that my parents named me Kelly, but I didn't mention why. Now's as good a time as any. Three months into her pregnancy, my mother was told she was having twin girls -- now in the 70's, ultrasounds were not a perfect science and the equipment my mother's doctor used couldn't pick up the dangling thing between my legs that's the telltale differentiator between boys and girls. As such, my mother and father told their friends they were having twin girls and planned accordingly.

My parents decided on the names Kelly and Josephine in honor of their mothers. When we were born, they were as shocked as anyone that I was, in fact, a boy. Because they already had clothes embroidered with the names

Kelly and Josephine, and because my parents are cheap bastards, they went with Kelly not thinking about the hell it would put me through. No one can fuck you like family.

"Your parents have a sick sense of humor," Pete said. "I have a question for your Kelly. Are you a hunter or are you a farmer?"

"I'm a moderator," I replied.

"Yeah, all of you are moderators, but what I want to know is, what kind of moderator are you. Do you hunt or do you farm? Do you chase after business looking to kill it, or do you sit on the sidelines waiting for it to sprout because I got news for you, I want hunters, not farmers."

"I billed 1.5 million last year, Pete. I'm not sure if I did that hunting or farming, but I ate pretty well." It would have been great if I actually said this, but true to my nature, I just thought it.

Pete turned around and left the room but not before looking back and saying, "Hunters." He then pounded his chest like Tarzan and walked down the hall.

Over the next year, he treated me like a red-headed stepchild; I knew he wanted to fire me because, well, he would often pass me in the hall and say, "I really want to fire your ass, Kelly." The problem was, I was his most profitable resource and firing me would have been like shooting himself in the foot. While I mean that metaphorically, the hyper-testosteroned goon actually did wind up shooting himself in the foot.

He invited himself hunting with some actual hunters and smartly, the people he was with only gave him a .22, which was barely enough to take down a squirrel, let alone a deer, but they smelled an idiot when they saw him and were nervous about giving him too much firepower. They didn't expect him to play with the trigger when the barrel was resting on his shoe. For this reason, he was working from home in the beginning of December.

My job requires a lot of travel and I see my fair share of airports every week. Just five minutes ago, my phone rang while I was enjoying a cup of coffee in the Delta Sky Club at Los Angeles International Airport. It's three weeks before Christmas and I'm making my way back to New York after leading a project to understand how recently divorced women in their forties approach dating. It was commissioned by a skin care client looking to market a new miracle in a bottle face care product. The caller ID read FuckFace. Because I am non-confrontational by nature, I get some revenge by giving people I don't like derogatory nicknames in my phone's address book. Petty? Yes, but definitely satisfying. I pick up the phone and here Pete's voice on the other end.

"Kelly, I'm glad I caught you."

He never calls me so I immediately know something is up.

"How did Project Beaver go?"

Since I was talking to recently divorced women, and since he's a complete sexist, he referred to the study I just wrapped as Project Beaver.

"Client is very pleased."

"Did you get any?"

"No, Pete, I didn't get any. What do you need?"

"Figures. Fucking farmers never get any."

My conversation with Pete is interrupted by an attractive woman who motions for my attention. She clearly sees I'm on the phone but doesn't seem to give a shit.

"Pete, can you hold on a second?"

"What the fuck, do not put me on hold. No one puts Pete Jackson on hold!"

As if you needed any more proof of his assholery, Pete Jackson talks about Pete Jackson in the third person.

I turn my attention to the woman; she's familiar looking but I can't place her.

"What?" I ask.

"Can you watch my bag while I go to the ladies' room?"

"We are in the Delta lounge, your bag will be fine."

"What's the big deal, just watch it okay?"

"Fine," I reply and watch her walk away. I notice the other people can't take their eyes off her and some begin to whisper. Then I hear Pete Jackson's voice again.

"Farmer Kelly, where are you?"

"Here, sorry. Why are you calling me?"

"Well I'll get right to it. There's no easy way to say this but..."

I immediately envision him sitting at home with his injured foot wrapped in maxi pads because he was too cheap to buy the bandages his doctor recommended.

"...the business has been soft lately and you are a lever I have to pull."

I can't believe what I'm hearing. Is this idiot firing me over the telephone three weeks before Christmas?

"What does that mean, a lever?"

"Let me put it in farming terms for you. Let's say you're a farmer right, which of course you are. Let's say that for seventeen years, your farming feeds you very well. Crops come up year after year, but then all of a sudden, there's a drought. No crops."

"But there hasn't been a drought. I've grown my

business 20 percent over last year. I'm on the road more than anybody else."

By this time, the familiar looking mystery woman returns to her bags and takes the seat across from mine.

Pete continues, "Right. The drought hasn't hit you yet, but it hit Heather, Laurie, and Brian."

He names three of my colleagues who haven't had a project since October.

"So why aren't you talking to them?"

"Because they are hunters."

I have seen porn with better plotlines than the story he's selling me.

"Apparently not very good ones." In true Carson form, I think it but don't say it.

"Listen, the fact is they're cheaper than you. I can actually hire three more hunters for what we pay you and I need more hunters. It's not personal, it's just business."

The Godfather is one of my favorite films and while normally I'd appreciate the reference, given the circumstances under which it was said, I don't.

"Look, we will honor your bonus and pay you a severance of two months. After that, Kemosabe, I suggest you learn to hunt."

He terminates the call before I can reply.

Meeting Terri Flynn

I look up from my phone and find the woman sitting across from me staring into my eyes. She's also chewing gum and snapping it loudly. Normally gum chewing, or any type of chewing for that matter, is a pet peeve, but I let it slide because she's a redhead and in my experience, they're an 11 on the 10 point crazy scale and the last thing I want to do is start an argument with a ginger in an airport lounge.

"Did you just get fired?" she asks bluntly.

"Excuse me?"

"You have a look on your face like you just got fired. I've seen that look before. Up and coming actors always have that same look after they bomb auditions."

So she's a redhead and an actor -- that's twice the crazy, and I'm not in the mood for crazy.

"Why didn't you stand up for yourself?" She has no intention of letting this conversation die.

"I'd rather not talk about it."

"That's your problem. You're the type of guy who would rather not deal with conflict. It's no wonder your former boss doesn't respect you."

Who the fuck does this woman think she is pretending to have insight into my life?

"Is that so?"

"Yeah. I mean look at you. You're a good-looking guy who is obviously successful based on the way you dress and that thousand dollar laptop bag, but you don't have an ounce of fight in you."

I mentioned before that I ate well last year so yes, it's true that I've done well for myself but what I don't need now is some ginger actress psychoanalyzing me in the middle of the LAX Delta Sky Club.

"Do you know why I asked you to watch my bags?"

"Enlighten me."

"Because you look safe. I knew you wouldn't rifle through them like some of these other people."

She motioned around to the other lounge guests, who all stared at her, and then me, with mouths agape.

"You think I need Julie fucking Andrews over there to find the pocket rocket I keep in my purse? Hell no."

The woman she was referring to did resemble Julie Andrews, but Mary Poppins Julie Andrews, not Sound of Music Julie Andrews.

"I think I'd rather be left alone right now."

"Of course you'd rather be left alone, but I'm not going to leave you alone because you need me."

"All I want to do is go back to New York in peace."

"How funny, I'm going to New York too. Where are you seated?"

The nice thing about flying so much is that I often get upgraded to first class and today, being fired over the telephone notwithstanding, I got the nod from the Delta powers that be that I was worthy of a loyalty upgrade.

"3A," I reply.

She then shows me her boarding pass and points to her seat assignment; 3B. I also notice her name at the bottom of the pass -- Terri Flynn.

"Seat buddy!" She cheers with her arms in the air. "This calls for a celebration. Do you want some champagne?"

"Champagne? It's 8am."

"Have them put some cassis in mine. I'll watch your bags."

I walk over to the bar, order a glass of champagne with cassis for her and an OJ for me. When I come back, I see her rifling through my bag. By the time I'm at my seat, she's going through my travel wallet.

"Is Kelly your wife? Why do you have her frequent flyer cards?"

My Kelly sense is tingling and I can foresee what is about to happen so I don't respond. When she opens my passport to evaluate my picture, she puts two and two together.

"Fuck me in the ass and call me Charlie," she exclaims, much to the chagrin of the family sitting nearby. "Your parents named you Kelly?"

Reluctantly, I explain the circumstances of my birth.

"So what you're telling me is you have a small dick?"

For the record, I have an average-sized penis. While it's certainly not going to cause a woman any massive degree of pain upon penetration, it's also not going to feel like a stick in a cave. But the story of how my parents were expecting twin girls due to the inability to spot my dick on an ultrasound has been told so many times by my parents that I can't help but get defensive about it.

"I was a fctus!" I arguc.

"Relax there, Kel, I'm just giving you a hard time. But I can't, in good conscience, call you Kelly and I'm not a last name kind of girl because that's too military and my dad was in the military and I've spent the better part of my adult life trying to undo all the rigidity of my upbringing. So I'm gonna give you a nickname."

Her blue eyes shoot up and to the left while she taps her pointer finger on her lips.

"Clark!" She exclaims.

"That's the best you could do?"

"You remind me of Clark Kent -- quiet and reserved but something about you gives me the impression that Superman's hiding inside. And you know what, Clark, call me 'Lois' because I'm going to help you find your inner superhero."

By this point I realize I don't know anything about her aside from her name and my assumption that she's an actress. My thoughts are interrupted by a voice over the loudspeaker.

"For those of you traveling on Delta Flight 3827 to New York's Kennedy Airport, I am sorry to inform you that due to bad weather in New York, your flight has been cancelled. Please see us at the full-service counter and we will do our best to accommodate you."

"Fuck," I say, much to the ire of the family matriarch beside us.

I stand and grab my bag, intending to walk to the counter solo but Terri follows me. Once we get to there, I ask the representative, a woman named Beverly, why the flight was cancelled and not simply delayed until the weather improves.

"The northeast is getting slammed," she responds. For

whatever reason, Beverly's counter is adorned by pictures of hand drawn ninjas. While I'm certainly curious about that, I focus on the travel situation.

"How bad is it?" I ask.

"All airports from New Jersey up to Maine are closed. We can book you on the first flight out tomorrow and offer you a free night in a hotel."

Terri pipes up, "Could you send us anywhere else?"

"Oh, hi, Ms. Flynn, my husband and I are such big fans," Beverly says while blushing. "Of course we could send you anywhere in the US you'd like to go, so long as the airport is open."

"Terri..."

She corrects me, "I told you, Clark, call me 'Lois.'"

"Lois," I say through my teeth, "What are you doing? I need to get back to New York."

"For what? It's not like your boss is going to fire you if you don't show up at work tomorrow."

That stings a little, but I can see her logic.

"What, do you have a wife at home who needs you to knock on Heaven's door and fulfill every sexual desire?"

If only she knew the truth.

"No, but..."

"Then no buts. What you need is an adventure and I'm going to give it to you."

I hear Beverly tapping away incessantly at her keyboard.

"I can get you both on a flight to Maui. It leaves in 40 minutes."

"Lodging?" Terri asks, flashing a Hollywood smile if I ever saw one.

"That's against the rules in this situation, but let me see

what I can do."

Beverly taps no fewer than 100 keystrokes then looks up and smiles.

"Ritz Carlton okay? That's where we put our flight attendants and I can get you in there for two nights"

"Deal," Terri says.

Before I can object, Beverly starts tapping again and the dot matrix printer behind her comes to life. A second later she hands us two boarding passes to Hawaii.

"Come on, Clark, it will be fun."

She walks ahead of me and exits the lounge. I shake my head and against my better judgement, follow her out.

At the Gate

While Terri only has a small head start, she's already navigated to a Starbucks kiosk two gates away. There are five people ahead of her in line and they all look like the types who order complicated drinks.

"I don't think we have time for this," I say.

"Relax, Clark, the flight leaves in 40 minutes, plenty of time."

I'm pretty anal about getting on planes early for two reasons; one, it helps me relax and two, it insures my carry-on makes it to an overhead bin near my seat. I get very anxious when my bags are rows behind where I'm sitting, as it means I'll be getting off the plane later or, worse, inconveniencing the passengers behind me. I never want to be that guy.

"But the flight is likely boarding."

She responds to my protest with a roll of her eyes.

Finally, it's her time to order.

The barista is a blond-haired boy of about sixteen whose nametag reads Squeaker; if the lead singer of Flock of Seagulls had sex with Bea Arthur and they had a baby, I'm pretty sure it would look like Squeaker.

"Oh my god, Terri, how are you?" Squeaker says in a voice pitched so high I thought the lenses of his glasses would shatter.

"Doing okay, Squeaker. How's your mother?"

"One day at a time. Are you done shooting? I thought the production schedule had you at Universal through the Spring."

"I don't want to talk about work, but what I would like is an iced caramel macchiato."

Squeaker took a plastic cup and wrote the order down.

"Will that be all?"

Terri motions to me using the classic hitchhiker's thumb.

"And what kind of drink can I get for you, sir?"

"I'll just take a small coffee?"

Squeaker rolls his eyes and shouts "tall blonde roast" in a tone that scolds me for not ordering in proper Starbucks vernacular.

"That will be $7.69."

Terri turns around and bats her eyes and smiles at me. "How would you feel about buying my coffee?"

I reach into my wallet, take out a ten, and hand it to Squeaker who immediately puts my change into the tip jar.

"Can I get a name for the order."

Without thinking, I give him my first name.

"Kelly is your name? Is that some kind of joke? You think this is funny? Am I fucking here for your amusement?"

I am perplexed by his response and wonder if other customers give fake names as a way of being rude and dismissive toward the barista class. Then again, if they are, it's probably in reaction to baristas intentionally misspelling customer names; all's fair in love and war -- even when buying overpriced, burnt coffee.

"Excellent Joe Pesci impersonation, Squeaker," Terri proclaims. "But tone it down a bit. You went a little overboard on the Jersey accent."

"Thanks, Terri, just wait over there, honey. Your drinks will be up shortly."

Terri and I walk over to the area designated for pickups.

"Squeaker wants to be an actor."

"You don't say."

"Why are you so grumpy, Clark? We're going to Hawaii, savor the moment!"

A thousand other men in my circumstance would be excited as hell to be taking a free trip to Hawaii with an attractive red headed actress whom they just met, but all I feel is anxiety. I've just lost my job and need to make a plan for my future; I'm eager to talk this through with my sister who I rely on for her expert guidance, but she's five thousand miles away from Maui and the time difference will make it difficult for us to talk.

"I just want to get on the plane."

"Kelsy, your order is up," comes a deep voice from behind the counter.

I don't move because my name isn't Kelsy.

"Kelsy," the deep voice says again. "Iced Carmel Macchiato and a tall blonde roast."

I begrudgingly retrieve our order. When I look on the red cup containing my drink, I see that Squeaker added some artwork.

"What's that on your cup?" Terri asks.

"Nothing," I reply curtly.

"It's not nothing, it looks like something. Come on, show it to me."

And that's the first time I show Terri my penis. Well, not MY penis, but the one drawn on my cup. She responds by laughing so hard I think she's going to lose her breakfast.

"I'm glad you find this funny, but what the fuck am I supposed to do with this monstrous cock on my cup?"

"At least you didn't order a Venti. It would have been even bigger!"

I take a sip and she loses it again.

"Oh my god, when you drink, the tip looks like it's going into your mouth."

We pass by ten gates and finally get to ours, where I find they're already boarding Zone 2; my anxiety rises ten notches and here's why -- this means they've boarded the elderly, families traveling with small children, first class, business class, active military, passengers with premium status, passengers with missing limbs, left handed people, clergy, atheists, airline union members, people with service animals, and Zone 1. And worst of all, it means our carry-on bags will be checked at the gate.

"Fuck," I say.

"What's the matter, Clark, they didn't leave without us."

"They are going to make us check our bags. I hate checking my bags."

"So what, we check our bags, big fucking deal."

"My bags never make it when I check them."

"Clark, listen to me, they're going to check them right here. The plane is right there. They are going to personally put them on, and because they're getting on so late, they'll be LIFO."

I look at her with a raised eyebrow.

"Last in, first out."

"Isn't that accounting speak?"

"When I moved to LA to pursue acting full time, I took some classes at a community college to appease my parents. I loved accounting."

There's a tall, skinny blond woman who has joined us at the gate. She's talking onto the phone and I overhear the strangest conversation I've ever been privy to.

"Gentle domination is $400 an hour. If you want water sports, that's an extra hundred."

"Did you hear that by any chance?" I whisper to Terri.

"Sure did," she whispers back.

"I wonder what her father did to her?"

"That's the difference between you and me Clark," Terri says. "I'm wondering if the guy she's talking to is going to spring an extra Benjamin so that she can spring a leak on him. It's only a hundred bucks fella, get peed on why don't ya?"

I try to put that out of my mind and approach the gate agent. Just as I suspect, after the three of us hand over our boarding passes, we're told we have to check our carry-on. I'd rather be peed on. I watch as she prints out labels and straps them to our bags.

"Just leave these at the end of the jet bridge and enjoy your flight to Hawaii."

We do as we were told and then board the plane. Thankfully, Beverly transferred our first-class seats to the new flight so we settle into seats 3A and 3B. As we sit down, the flight attendant, another tall blond -- this one would look at home on a fashion show runway -- asks if we want a cocktail before takeoff. My traveling companion orders a vodka-tonic and I opt for a cranberry juice.

"Are you in recovery or something?"

"What? No, I just have a rule about not drinking before 6pm."

"Why would you have such a rule?"

"I don't know, I guess I have control issues."

The flight attendant comes back with our drinks and offers to take our Starbucks cups. When I hand her mine, she gives me a dirty look, having assumed I drew the colossal cock on my cup. As such, irreparable damage is done to the passenger/flight attendant relationship.

As a piece of advice, you never want to upset a flight attendant. They can make your flying experience a pleasure or a living hell. For example, say you're on a plane with your own TV screen -- if you were rude to a flight attendant when you boarded, don't be surprised if it doesn't work. Conversely, an ounce of kindness will get you an extra snack or maybe even a free drink.

"I didn't draw that," I protest in an attempt to defend myself. She just huffs and walks away.

My phone starts to vibrate, and I awkwardly shift around until I can extricate it from my pocket. I don't recognize the 212 number, but because it's a New York area code, I pick up.

"This is Kelly," I say.

"Please hold for Pam Hart," an effeminate voice says.

I wait a few seconds and the voice that comes on the line sounds like it belongs to Mel Blanc if Mel Blanc smoked no fewer than two thousand cigarettes a day.

"Kelly, this is Pam Hart from the Hart Literary Agency. Is now a good time to tawlk?"

Six months ago, I sent out a number of query letters for a manuscript I was shopping around. Writing has always been a passion of mine and I know how important getting an agent is -- the big publishers won't take you seriously if you don't have one. The problem is, it's harder to find an agent who will take a chance on a first-time author than it is to find a virgin in a sorority. I had sent queries to a few hundred agencies and received a few hundred rejection letters -- the only one I hadn't heard back from was Hart Literary and now the founder was on the phone.

"I just boarded a flight, but I have a few minutes before they close the door."

My statement is interrupted by the flight attendant coming across the PA system.

"Ladies and gentlemen, we have just closed the airplane door, please turn off and stow all electronic devices and make sure your phones are in airplane mode."

I know from my extensive travels that nothing upsets flight attendants more than people who don't follow this instruction, as if a cellphone will take down an airliner. Nevertheless, I always comply with it for fear of rocking the boat, which I've already done here with that cock-art. However, now was different -- I finally have an agent interested in my book so I don't hang up.

"This will only take a New Yawk minute," Pam says.

I feel a tap on my shoulder and it's the tall blond stewardess motioning for me to turn off my phone; to say she looks agitated is putting it mildly.

"I'm sorry, it's my agent. Just one minute," I whisper and hold up my index finger to underscore one minute.

I fully realize I sound like every Hollywood asshole she sees on the LA to Hawaii flight and this wins me no points.

"We are interested in representing you, Mr. Carson.

Could you make it to Manhattan for a meeting next Monday morning, say 11?"

I do some quick math; today is Friday and I'm on the way to Hawaii. I would have to leave Hawaii first thing Sunday morning to make a Monday morning meeting. It seems reasonable and since I've just been shitcanned by Pete Jackson, I have nothing else to do Monday. "Absolutely," I reply.

At this point, Eva Braun -- the obvious nickname for the Germanic looking stewardess -- is standing to my right with her arms folded and her face red with anger.

"Wonderful. I'll email you a confirmation. See ya then, g'bye."

I hang up and make a grand display of turning off my phone for Eva, who mimes the directions coming over the PA system. While she's showing us how to put on our oxygen masks in the event of a loss of cabin pressure, Terri starts playing twenty questions about my call.

"Agent?"

I tell her about my writing, in the sparest detail, and that Hart is the first agent to call back.

"That's incredible, Clark, but I got bad news for you."

I had a feeling she would attempt to take the wind out of my sails.

"What's that?"

"You failed the first test."

"What do you mean?"

"She asked you to come to a meeting, right?"

"Yes, Monday morning."

"And you didn't propose an alternate time?"

"I did't want to risk her changing her mind."

"Clark, Clark, Clark," she said, exhaling. "She's already

interested in you. You're her ticket to money and you need to be in control of the conversation. By not pushing back, you just hurt your negotiating position."

This is all new territory for me, the conflict-averse.

"It's not in my nature to push back," I argue.

"You aren't going to last long in the entertainment business if you let people walk all over you."

She says it in a way that indicates there's more story there, but I don't want to probe too deeply; we've only just met, after all.

"I'll put it on the long list of things I have to work on."

"What's it about anyway?"

"What's what about?"

She looks at me as if I have three heads and raises her hands in the air. "Your book."

"It's about a guy who gets fired three weeks before Christmas and goes on an adventure with a Hollywood starlet." I say it deadpan; it's my first attempt at humor since meeting Terri, and I don't know if it's the vodka or if my comment was actually funny, but she begins to laugh.

"If you want to read it, I have a copy on my tablet."

"Good. I'll read it on the flight because I hate watching movies on the plane."

I pull my tablet from my thousand-dollar laptop bag and hand it to her as the pilot's voice comes over the PA.

"We are number one for departure. Flight attendants, please prepare the cabin for takeoff."

Terri immediately grabs my hand and squeezes it hard as we begin our roll down the runway.

"I'm scared to death of flying, Clark, just wanted you to know."

The truth is, I don't mind her choking my hand – it's

been a long time.

320